Amish
Christmas
Kinner

More from Lenora Worth

The Memory Quilt
The Forgiving Quilt
The Christmas Quilt

More from Rachel J. Good

His Unexpected Amish Twins
His Pretend Amish Bride
His Accidental Amish Family
An Unexpected Amish Proposal
An Unexpected Amish Courtship
An Unexpected Amish Christmas
An Amish Marriage of Convenience
Her Pretend Amish Boyfriend

More from Kelly Long

The Amish Bride of Ice Mountain
An Amish Man of Ice Mountain
The Amish Heart of Ice Mountain
An Amish Courtship on Ice Mountain
An Amish Match on Ice Mountain
An Amish Wedding Feast on Ice Mountain
Marrying Matthew
Courting Caleb

Amish
Christmas
Kinner

LENORA WORTH • RACHEL J. GOOD
KELLY LONG

KENSINGTON
PUBLISHING CORP.
www.kensingtonbooks.com

KENSINGTON BOOKS are published by

Kensington Publishing Corp.
119 West 40th Street
New York, NY 10018

Special book excerpts or customized printings can also be created to fit specific needs. For details, write or phone the office of the Kensington Sales Manager: Kensington Publishing Corp., 119 West 40th Street, New York, NY 10018. Attn. Sales Department. Phone: 1-800-221-2647.

ISBN: 978-1-4967-4702-0 (ebook)
ISBN: 978-1-4967-4544-6

First Kensington Trade Paperback Printing: October 2023

10 9 8 7 6 5 4 3 2 1

Printed in the United States of America

Contents

Christmas Eve Baby

Lenora Worth

1

Best Christmas Program Ever

Rachel J. Good

121

Loving Luke

Kelly Long

205

Christmas Eve Baby

LENORA WORTH

I'd like to thank Kensington Books and especially Alicia Condon for allowing me to write the Shadow Lake series and this novella. I found so much joy in writing these stories.

Chapter 1

Christmas Eve
Shadow Lake Inn
Pennsylvania

The winter wind howled and moaned, causing Colette King Mueller to pull her shawl closer as she stared out the front windows of Shadow Lake Inn. Lake Erie crashed and crested out over the far horizon, making her shiver with cold as she remembered the night a year ago when she'd been out in the snow with a dangerous man.

But that was over now, even if she did still have the occasional nightmare. She'd just become a married woman in October, but already she dreamed of having *kinner*. Maybe two or three little ones. Christmas made her heart tug toward motherhood. So she focused on her dreams instead of the brutal weather. Her sister Abigail now had two children. A boy they called Jon and a *bobbeli* named after their *mamm*—Sarah Rebecca, with the nickname of Becca. Tonight during their supper with the inn's staff, they'd learned the middle King sister, Eliza, was with child. Colette smiled, thinking of the joy on Eliza's and Levi's faces. Another little one in the family.

"Maybe you'll be next," Mamm had told her in private after the staff members had left to get home before the looming snowstorm. "I know it's hard to wait, but the Lord knows our plans."

"I've just married," Colette had responded with a laugh, her cheeks blushing. "I have time." She couldn't tell her *mamm* that the idea of having a *bobbeli* was a bit unnerving. Her midwife *mamm* had delivered many babies, so Colette knew she'd be well taken care of. *Neh*, she worried about what came after the birth. "What if I'm a bad mother?"

"How could you be a bad mother?" Mamm had replied, touching a hand to Colette's cheek. "You are strong. You proved that when you were put to the test. Now you and Matthew are married and enjoying your new home. You will do just fine when you have your first child."

"I will do my best."

Colette watched the heavy snow falling now, thinking this Christmas would be special to all of them. The King sisters had managed to find love with three strong, capable men. But it hadn't been easy. Thinking that story was for another time, she took one last look out the window.

And saw a shadow moving through the snow.

"Matthew," she called, "*kumm* quickly."

Her husband of two months rushed to the window. "What's wrong?"

"Someone is out there." She pointed to the figure moving slowly up the snow-covered drive. "I . . . I see someone."

Matthew held her close. "You know you're safe now. The man who tried to harm you is not here, Colette. He's dead."

She nodded, touched that he always wanted to protect her

when she had nightmares or thought she'd heard or seen something. After being kidnapped last Christmas, she'd tried to get her life back on track, to forget the horrible memories.

But she wasn't scared for herself. The storm was growing worse. Maybe one of the staff members had been forced to turn around.

"I'm not worried about my nightmares," she said. "Look, that's a woman. And she's out there alone in this freezing weather."

"I'll go check," her husband said after glancing out the window, his dark eyes filled with worry, his face filled with concern.

"I'm going with you," she replied. "Let me get my cloak."

Before he could argue, she hurried to the employee room and fetched her cloak and her heavy bonnet.

"Where are you headed?" Mamm asked, her hands on her hips, surprise in her voice.

"I saw a woman on the drive," Colette said over her shoulder. "Mattie is going to check on her."

Mamm hurried after her. It seemed the whole group had heard and decided to tag along. Soon, her entire family and the staff members who were spending the night at the inn stood by the window, watching as she and Matthew moved through the deepening snow to the woman.

"Help," the stranger called out when she looked up. "Please help me."

Colette saw the fear in the woman's eyes. Fear and pain. A shiver danced down Colette's spine. What had happened to this young woman?

"I've got you," Matthew called to the frightened woman, reaching out his hand to help her up the slope of the hillside. The sound of the lake crashing in angry waves and the snow howling all around made it hard to hear anything.

Colette met them at the bottom of the white stone steps, trying not to slip. "We'll get you inside. It's warm and safe here."

They guided her up onto the porch, where the gaslights showed her fatigue and exhaustion, her dark blue eyes bright with apprehension and fluffs of golden blond hair lifting from her dark bonnet. "I . . . I'm about to have a baby."

Then she screamed and doubled over, her hands on her stomach. "It's too early. This can't be happening now."

Mamm appeared on the porch at that moment and went into action. "Abigail, get a bed ready on the lower level—one of the private rooms. Find my liners and bring one to protect the mattress. Jonah, get boiling water ready. Levi, build a fire in the fireplace in that room." She glanced around while she and Colette led the woman inside the big lobby. "I don't have my medical bag."

"I'll go get it," Matthew said. "In the cottage?"

"*Ja*, in the mudroom." She described the blue canvas bag and two smaller equipment bags. "Please bring me all three."

Henry, the *Englischer* who worked the front desk, called out, "I'll get extra blankets and I'll keep watch for any others who get caught out there."

Mamm nodded as she rushed up the hallway to the rooms off to the left of the big kitchen. "*Denke*, Henry."

Colette held the woman's hand while she and Eliza took her to the nearest room. They only had two rooms on the first floor, and both were available.

Eliza motioned to the nearest one at the back of the house with a slight view of the lake from one window. "I just cleaned it and put fresh linens on today, in case we needed more room."

At times such as this, people could get stranded. The Kings never turned down a stranger in need even if they did have a *Closed* sign on the door.

Abigail returned from the large linen closet with a plastic mattress protector. "Here we go," she said to the woman. "Let's sit you in the chair while we prepare the bed."

"*Gut,*" Colette said to Abigail. "I'll go help Mattie with Mamm's bag."

"*Neh,*" the woman screamed, her fingers digging into Colette's arm. "Stay with me. I'm so scared. It's not time for the baby to come."

"I won't leave," Colette told her, indicating to Abigail she'd stay. "Let me get these wet clothes off you, *ja?*"

The woman shivered and shook. Her teeth seemed to rattle, but she tried to get her heavy cloak open. "Okay."

Colette helped the woman lift the cloak away. She was Amish, no doubt about that. Her hair was still mostly tidy in spite of the wind howling outside. Her black bonnet and heavy wool cloak were both soaked with melting snow. She shivered as they helped her onto the bed, her deep blue dress damp up to her knees, her boots and socks soaked. If she'd been out much longer like this, hypothermia would have set in.

"She's cold, Mamm." Colette grabbed extra blankets and covered the woman as they undressed her.

"Here you go," Mamm said as she helped them get the woman's boots off. "You're safe now." Mamm's serenity always amazed Colette.

The woman nodded, her voice husky. "*Denke.*"

"I'm Sarah King. What's your name?" Mamm asked after they'd managed to get the woman into a nightgown and in the bed under the blankets and quilts.

"Leah, Leah Kauffman. My husband is Simon."

"Leah, we are going to take care of you, ain't so?"

"*Denke,*" the young woman said again. "I was supposed to meet Simon here, but my buggy got stuck up on the main road, and I had to leave the horse and buggy there. I tried to walk the rest of the way and I got lost. He's coming home on a bus from Ohio, which was to make a stop in town. We'd hoped to find a nice place for a quiet supper, and a friend had suggested your inn. But then my water broke and here I am. I'm afraid he won't make it in time."

Mamm nodded and patted her hand. "Listen to me. I'm a midwife. We will do our best to help you. And I'll see what I can find out about the bus."

"A midwife?" Leah's expression changed from panic to relief. "I am thankful. *Gott* led me here."

Mamm lifted her chin. "I'm sure He did just that."

The woman nodded, and then she moaned and her face turned into a tight, twisted frown of agony. Mamm checked her stomach, then looked at the woman as she fell against the pillows.

"You are having contractions, for certain sure. I'll need to examine you," Mamm explained. "Do you live in Pennsylvania? Here in our community?"

"I used to live in Lancaster, but we recently got married and moved to a house not far from here. A few miles out from the township proper. Simon works all over Pennsylvania and Ohio. He had gone home to Ohio to visit his sick sister. The doctor told me to stay behind."

"And you came here instead of the bus stop in town to meet him?" Mamm asked as she checked Leah's vitals and prepared her equipment. "You must have started out just before the weather got worse."

"*Ja*," the woman said. "We decided to meet halfway and this is about halfway. We'd planned on spending the night here. I was concerned about the weather, but when I called earlier, a nice man said the inn is normally closed to the public over Christmas, but he saved us a room anyway."

Mamm smiled, her expression giving away nothing. "That would be Henry. He works at the check-in counter and books most of our guests. He's been told to save a room every year just in case."

Leah's eyes filled with tears. "In case of emergency?"

"Exactly," Mamm said. "Or in case of a miracle."

Chapter 2

Colette and her sisters stayed close to see if Mamm needed anything. They were on standby with the things she'd want to help Leah. Hot water simmered on the stove, clean towels and sheets were on the dresser, even an extra nightgown and robe for the frightened woman. Mamm had her birth bags ready. The heavy bags contained her sterilized birthing instruments and equipment, a blood pressure monitor for Leah, and a Doppler monitor for the baby, a baby scale, and an oxygen bag. It sure took a lot to birth a baby.

Colette stood in the corner as Mamm used the blood pressure cuff to make sure Leah was steady. Then Mamm checked Leah's heartbeat with a stethoscope.

"You're doing *gut*," Mamm assured Leah. "Pressure is a bit high, but that's normal since you're in labor. I'm going to use what we call a Doppler on your stomach so we can also hear the baby's heartbeat. Is this your first?"

Leah nodded, her gaze moving from Mamm to Colette. "Do you have children?"

"Not yet," Colette said as she moved closer. "I just got married two months ago."

"We've been married a year," Leah said. "Had our ups and downs, but we love each other. This was a special treat, meeting here for a nice supper. We thought we had time. This one wasn't due until the first of the new year."

Mamm smiled. "Little ones are on their own time. You do look like you're near your due date."

"Another week I thought," Leah replied through a grimace of pain. "I'm worried this is happening now."

"That's also normal. Sometimes they *kumm* early and sometimes they *kumm* late."

Colette swallowed her fears while she watched Leah's expression change from worry to pain. Why did childbirth have to hurt so much? Love and marriage sure brought many different complications. But it had to be worth it, she figured. Jonah and Abigail beamed with joy over their two children. Eliza was flushed with happiness expecting her first child, and Levi walked around all puffed up like a rooster.

She thought of Matthew and knew in her heart she'd love to give him a *bobbeli*. But being here, seeing Leah so concerned and in such agony gave her pause. She'd have to think this through, but *bobbelis* did come into the world all the time.

Mamm must have sensed her discomfort. Her gaze bounced from the woman in labor to Colette. "These pains will come and go. Contractions only mean the baby is working to enter the world. It's not pleasant at times, but it will be over soon."

Leah nodded. "I know but I wanted Simon here."

Colette took her hand. "My brothers-in-law and my husband have gone to see if they can find Simon. They took horses because the roads are so bad. But the bus might have stopped somewhere else for the night."

"What if there was an accident?" Leah asked, her eyes wide

and misty. "What if Simon doesn't make it? Or he can't make it because he's hurt?"

"We won't focus on that," Mamm said in a firm tone. "You must calm down and focus on birthing this child. *Gott* will take care of the rest."

Leah nodded. "I will try. I'm relieved the men are checking on my Simon. Even if the bus makes it to the township, I fear he'll wind up spending the night in the bus terminal."

Eliza came in and heard Leah. Then she glanced out the window. "They planned to get your horse and buggy off the road, too. They know what they're doing, and if anyone can find your husband, it will be those three."

Giving her mother a nod, Eliza said, "I'll go and check with Henry. Maybe he's heard another weather report on that fancy radio of his."

Colette stayed with Leah while Mamm went about her work. "I know how you feel," she told Leah. "Matthew and I have known each other all our lives, but I almost lost him to another woman."

Leah's eyebrows slanted up with interest. "You must tell me about that."

Colette explained how Matthew had inherited a vast Amish estate in Missouri. "She came with it. But she had another boyfriend—a very bad person—who wanted her to go after what he thought should be his."

"So he wanted his woman to marry your man in order to get the inheritance?" Leah asked, her voice rising as pain hit.

"He did, but it didn't turn out the way he'd expected, because the woman couldn't go through with the plan. We found out the truth and . . . unfortunately he died trying to harm us."

"That's awful," Leah said, her agony deepening as pain hit her again.

Colette shivered, dark memories coming to mind. "That's the gist of it. You don't need details right now."

Leah nodded as another contraction began. Mamm coached her on her breathing and offered her some ice chips. "We need the baby to appear before you start to push. Otherwise, you will use your energy too soon."

"How much longer?" Colette asked, the wonder of it all making her feel small and unsure. Birth was such a *wunderbar gut* thing. But scary, too. On the other hand, women all over the world seemed to keep birthing children. She giggled at that thought.

Mamm gave her a curious frown and checked her watch. "The contractions are getting closer together now. Not much longer."

"But Simon is not here," Leah said. "I want my husband."

"I'll go and see if there is any news," Colette offered, needing to escape the birthing room. She certainly hadn't anticipated something like this happening tonight.

Eliza met her in the hallway. "I haven't heard any news, nor any screams of pain from our patient. Is she okay?"

"Leah is scared but holding her own," Colette said. "I, on the other hand, feel faint."

"Are you afraid?" Eliza asked, clutching her stomach. "It is a strange but miraculous thing, birthing a child."

"I was thinking that, exactly," Colette admitted. "Both frightening and exciting."

Eliza held her stomach. "All women go through it."

Colette did not feel confident. "I did remind myself of that, too. I suppose if Mary went through this in a stable, we should be able to survive it with Mamm's help," she replied. "I believe a little miracle happens with the birth of each child."

Eliza twisted her lips. "I think you could be correct, sister. We worry and fear, but it is a natural occurrence. You might as well be prepared."

"Are you?" Colette asked, curious.

"I have to be," Eliza said. "Abigail has been sweetly coaching me, of course."

Colette huffed a laugh. "You mean, nagging you and bossing you, don't you, sister?"

"Well, *ja*, that too." Eliza laughed with her. "I can be bossy myself. My children will fear me and always be proper."

"*Ja*, I do believe that." Colette didn't believe those words for a minute, but she humored her pregnant sister anyway.

Abigail had been on bed rest for a time while pregnant with little Jon. But she'd done much better with Becca. Colette prayed Eliza would have a smooth birth. Her sisters were strong and determined, so she must be the same. Or they'd never let her forget it.

"We'll all be okay," she said, trying to sound confident. "We have Mamm."

Eliza grabbed Colette's hand. "Really, I'm terrified, but we must remember Mamm is the best at what she does. She will take care of us in the same way she takes care of any woman in need."

"We are blessed to have her," Colette said. "I'm surprised one of us hasn't followed in her footsteps."

Eliza grinned. "We aren't that brave."

Colette laughed at her sister's words, but she knew they were all brave in their own way. And they would all provide grandchildren for Mamm and Daed. She had to admit that witnessing this birth had opened her eyes to what her Mamm really did to bring *kinner* into the world.

When she thought of Daed's heart condition and how he'd almost died last year, she closed her eyes and thanked *Gott* for her blessings—for giving her *daed* a few more years on earth and for allowing her and Matthew to overcome all that stood between them. She was thankful for her *mamm*, too, for being so understanding and giving the best advice to her daughters.

Again, she remembered how each of her sisters had struggled to find true love. So many obstacles had been in their paths. But they'd pushed through each challenge, they'd survived, and now they were strong and secure.

Leah would be the same. She might be a stranger, but Colette felt she knew her well, knew her fears and knew the fierce kind of love she felt for her husband, for her unborn child. It was the way of their world. *Gott*, faith, family, *kinner*.

I want a child, she thought. *I want that kind of legacy to show my love for my husband.*

Then she smiled. She wouldn't fear having a *bobbeli*, a *kinner* of her own—Matthew's child. Now she knew she'd welcome being a mother.

Had Mary been scared? Had she doubted herself on that cold night in the stable? *Ja*, but Mary had been brave and strong, too. And she'd had a beautiful boy.

Was there anything more sacred?

Chapter 3

Eliza took over with Leah while Colette went to help put away the food from their earlier supper. Mamm moved about, laying out her supplies and making sure everything was ready to go.

Leah was dozing between contractions but she woke with a scream of pain. "Where is the other one? Colette?"

Eliza took her hand and smiled. "She is the kitchen supervisor, so she had to help put away the food from our Christmas supper tonight."

Checking the blankets, Eliza studied the frightened woman's face. "I'm the middle sister, Eliza King Lapp. I've only been married a year myself." Touching her stomach, she said, "I just discovered I'm pregnant. Levi and I officially announced it at our Christmas gathering tonight." Then she leaned close. "My *mamm* already knew and asked me about it three weeks ago. She has an uncanny way of knowing these things, due to her work."

"Not uncanny," Leah replied, still unsure. "Instinct, I'd think."

"*Ja*, and she is *gut* at her job so you need not worry about anything. She knows all the local doctors, too."

"I can hear you, you know," Mamm called from the bathroom.

Leah's fear subsided as her eyes grew wide with curiosity. "You have the same golden-red hair color as your sisters, but your eyes are more hazel than theirs. Colette's eyes are more blue-green. And Abigail's are all green."

"We are a bit different," Eliza said, impressed that Leah had noticed. "Colette is feisty and stubborn, and Abigail is bossy."

"And this one is all sweetness and light," Mamm said in a sarcastic tone as she came back into the room. "Although I have to admit marriage and pregnancy have changed her a bit."

"Changed all of us," Eliza replied with a smile. "I think we had to grow up, after all."

Mamm gave a soft huff of approval. "I need some more gauze," she said. "I'll be right back."

"I also had to learn to forgive," Eliza said after Mamm left. "It's true that I used to be a tad skeptical about love, but now I'm very happily married." She touched her growing tummy. "And curious about birth, of course."

"That's *wunderbar gut*." Leah grimaced. "Although right now, I don't feel so *gut* about the whole idea." She took a long breath. "You mentioned you had a big Christmas meal? Tell me all about it since I won't be able to have the meal I'd hoped for. This little one and I will both be hungry tonight."

"We had a feast," Eliza replied, remembering how she used to take such things for granted. "We always have the whole staff for this special meal. We shut the inn down for three days—Christmas Eve, Christmas Day, and Second Christmas."

"Second Christmas is fun," Leah said, gritting her teeth as a wave of pain hit her. "So fun—"

Eliza helped her with her breathing as Mamm had taught her to do. "In and out, in and out. You'll be able to push soon. If you push now, the baby will only go back in when you stop. So try hard to wait until the child is ready to greet the world."

The contraction ended just as Mamm returned to check on their patient. "You're doing so great, Leah. The contractions are coming closer and lasting longer now. You will soon have a Christmas baby."

"And Simon?" Leah asked, her voice hoarse. "I have to hold on until he can be here."

"We haven't heard anything about the bus station," Eliza replied, her own concern hidden behind a smile. Mamm had taught them over the years that a serene smile often calmed everyone down. Eliza prayed she'd pulled it off. "But my husband and Jonah and Matthew are very familiar with the roads around here, and they took Samson."

"Who is Samson?" Leah asked, her curiosity taking over again.

"Oh, he's my baby—I mean he's a big Percheron. He's spoiled and lovable. He does most of the heavy work around here."

Leah almost snorted. "A draft horse?"

She nodded. "I love horses. I run the stables along with Jonah—my brother-in-law who came to us from the lake, and my husband, Levi, who was my first sweetheart. He went away after we broke up but then came back when I broke my leg."

"You must have worked that out," Leah said in a pragmatic tone. "Let me guess—that's another long story?"

"*Ja*, but we won't got into details. We were talking about Second Christmas. I hope you'll be able to get home for that."

"We weren't really planning anything," Leah said, her tone

bleak. "We have very little money and a small home, but it's a start. We are invited to our neighbor's house, but I don't know if we'll be able to visit them now."

"Where is your family?" Eliza asked, thinking how sad it was that Leah was all alone at Christmas and having a child with strangers all about.

"They won't be around," Leah explained. "They did not approve of my marriage to Simon. I haven't talked to them since we got married."

"Oh, my." Eliza held her hand and helped her through another, stronger contraction. After the contraction had passed, she said, "I'd be lost without my family."

"I did get lost," Leah said, her gaze misty with tears. "I wish my *mamm* could be here. I've lost my family and even though I wrote the directions down today, I still got all twisted around. If anything happens to my baby—"

"Nothing is going to happen," Mamm said as she took over and held Leah's hand tight. "You just stay focused on doing your best. I've checked and the baby is in place and headed in the right direction." She shot a glance at Eliza. "Your contractions are steady at five minutes apart. Your cervix is dilated but not quite enough right now. You're about halfway there. Things will pick up in a bit, so try to sleep. I might have to get you up to walk around later."

Leah glanced out the window. "If only I'd gone the right way."

"Listen," Mamm said in her calm, certain tone. "Even if you'd made it here earlier, Simon is still stranded on that bus or on the road. We are thankful you found us, or you might be all alone in a buggy." Touching Leah's arm, she added, "I can't imagine how horrible that would have been."

"You're right," Leah said, her tone quiet now. "I'll stop complaining. I'm just so tired."

"Rest," Mamm said. "You're tired and afraid, but we are here and we will get you through this. You'll need your strength later."

Eliza glanced at Mamm. "I'll go check with Henry again. Maybe he's heard something by now. Jonah did take his phone."

"You have phones?" Leah looked surprised.

"For our business," Mamm explained. "I need one for midwifing and the girls and their husbands need them for the inn and stables. It comes with being open to tourists. We had to modernize just a bit."

"I don't mind," Leah replied. "But my family took my secret phone when they found out I'd been using it to talk to Simon."

"That's terrible," Eliza said. When she saw Mamm's frown, she quickly amended her tone. "We all got in trouble when we'd use our business phones to call our boyfriends."

"That is a fact," Mamm said. "My girls got in trouble for a lot of things—hiding an *Englischer* in the carriage house. That's our Jonah, who is Amish now. They kept secrets from me and snuck out to talk with men they were forbidden to be with, that would be Abigail and Colette. This one just had to keep a secret because she'd made a promise. Complicated. All that aside, we still adhere to the old ways in most things."

Leah giggled. "I really need to hear all these stories."

"Later," Eliza said. "We will fix a feast for you and Simon, and we'll tell you our stories, along with all the drama."

"Drama," Leah said, shaking her head. "I've prayed about that in my own life. I want *Gott* to forgive me now that I'm responsible for another human being. I want my *kinner* to know *Gott*'s love."

Eliza turned Leah's care over to Mamm, but she had to stop before leaving the room. She had to think about what Leah had just said. *Responsible for someone else.*

She had not thought of that when she'd found out she was expecting. She and Levi were thrilled, of course. But it would mean a whole new world after a year of being on their own. Could she deal with a new *bobbeli* and her horses, too?

Ach, vell, the menfolk did most of the stable work now even if she still liked to believe she was in charge. But she could bounce a baby and talk to a horse all at the same time, couldn't she?

Worry crested like a rogue wave in her mind. "I hope I'll be a proper *mamm* to my child."

Leah frowned in pain and then smiled. "If you can handle big ole Samson, I'm thinking you'll be a great mother."

Eliza giggled at that. "You have a point. I think you'll be a great mother, too."

Leah lifted her head and let out a yelp. "I don't know about that right now." Rubbing her tummy, she whispered, "Okay, little one. Stop making me scream and come out into the world." Then she put a hand to her mouth. "I mean, wait for your *daed*."

Eliza held her hand again while Mamm went to work, coaching and talking to Leah. "This one is taking its dear sweet time," Mamm said, her smile solid and firm. "But we've got time here."

"I'm ruining your holiday," Leah said. "And I'm so tired."

Mamm patted her moist forehead with a cool rag. "You haven't ruined anything. Birthing a baby is a *wunderbar gut* thing, a precious gift. Tell us about you and Simon," she said. "In between your contractions."

"It was love at first sight," Leah said, her blue eyes widening. "He came to do some work for my *daed*. I first saw him up on a ladder, fixing some shingles after a fierce storm. Daed hired him for several tasks. But that first glance, the way he smiled at me, his sweet hazel eyes, his kindness." She stopped, a tear falling down her face. "I don't have brothers or sisters. I'm my *mamm* and *daed*'s baby. I believe my parents wanted to keep me nearby because they are aging."

"That happens," Mamm said. "Abe and I just moved into a smaller *grossdaddi haus* behind what we call the cottage—a walk up the hill from here. We are definitely aging."

"And Levi and I took the cottage because his *mamm* is sick and we help with her medical bills," Eliza added. "I love being there near my parents and we're saving money on not building yet, if ever."

Mamm laughed at that. "We have Jonah and Abigail farther up the hill in their own home. Colette and Matthew, who have known each other since birth, live on the other side near the main road and the waterfall. They have a small house with room to add on as needed."

"A waterfall." Leah blinked. "That would lull me to sleep. You all have such romantic stories."

Mamm and Eliza both laughed, knowing there was more to every story than it seemed at first.

"We left out some important details such as the quilts each of us made," Eliza said. "But now we want to hear about your romantic story."

Leah nodded and dozed a bit. "Love at first sight." She yawned and closed her eyes. "Can you make a quilt based on that?"

Eliza glanced at her mother. Mamm smiled. "I know how that feels. And I think I know the perfect quilt."

Leah sank into slumber, a soft smile on her face.

"Let her rest," Mamm said to Eliza. "I'm concerned the contractions aren't growing closer."

"What does that mean?" Eliza asked as they moved away from the bed.

"It could mean several things," Mamm replied. "If they are

slowing down, her labor will be longer. If they don't get moving soon, we'll need to get her to the hospital for a C-section."

"How can we do that?" Eliza asked, shocked when she glanced out the nearby window. "It's a whiteout. I don't know how we'd manage to get her to the hospital."

Mamm checked the sleeping woman, then pulled Eliza aside. "We find a way, Eliza. Like we always do. We find a way through."

Chapter 4

Eliza watched as Leah slept fitfully, then woke with another contraction. She didn't want to leave the room, but she also didn't know if she should stay when the birth happened.

Thinking about Levi, she prayed he and the others would find Simon. This was not the best night to be out on the roads.

The storm had hovered for days before roaring to life late this afternoon. Although the yard and trees looked lovely covered in the fluffy white powder, the storm could be dangerous. But she knew Levi was strong and he knew the roads around here. As did her two brothers-in-law. She marveled that her sisters and she had found such wonderful husbands. Soulmates, helpmates, lovers. But with that love came worry. They'd all three come so close to losing the men they'd fallen in love with. With love, she'd discovered, came responsibility and maturity, along with a full heart and new hopes.

Touching her stomach, she said a silent prayer. *Lord, help us now. Help Leah and her little one, help Simon as he tries to get to her in time, and please keep our family strong so we may be of help to them. Bless us all and protect our growing family.*

Feeling better, she picked up a book placed on the dresser. She and her sisters always left a few books in each room of the inn. They'd learn all about books from the now-deceased *Englisch* couple who'd left them the Shadow Lake Inn. Even when they were scholars, they always had a lot of books placed around the inn and the cottage. She loved the little sitting room and library just off the front lobby. Some had frowned on the sisters always carrying around books, but Mamm and Daed had allowed their daughters to read as much as they wanted, starting with the Bible, of course.

They'd all learned about real life, and how books could have happy endings but sometimes life did not. Still, love would always win over evil. That much they knew. Christmas was certainly a testament to the power of love.

Leah wouldn't have time to read, but Eliza could skim the book and read to Leah while they waited for this birth. It was a love story, of course.

Much later, after Eliza had read aloud the first chapter of the historical novel she'd found, Abigail tiptoed in and smiled, her apron crisp and fresh, her dark green dress matching her eyes. "How's the patient?"

Leah was sleeping again, but she continued to be restless.

"Mamm says her contractions need to come faster."

Abby's brow furrowed in concern. "I hope we can get through this birth without needing a doctor. Mamm's had to call the ER at times, but surely not tonight."

Leah woke as a contraction hit. Abigail took her hand on one side and Eliza held her other hand.

Mamm came in and helped her through. "Don't push yet. Just do your breathing and hold on. This *bobbeli* has slowed down a bit, just like the snow outside."

Leah nodded and gritted her teeth between huffs. Then tears rolled down her cheeks. "I want my husband and I need my *mamm*."

"You have us," Abigail said, her voice cracking. "You have us for now. We won't leave you."

Leah nodded. "I'm sorry. You've all been so *gut* to me."

"What are you so sorry about?" Mamm asked, holding a · cool wet cloth to Leah's head.

"I've done everything wrong. I shouldn't have been so stubborn about driving all the way across the township to get here. I don't know if I can be a *gut* mother after all."

"Nonsense," Mamm said, shaking her head. "You have to think of this little one. You can't send this *bobbeli* back now."

That made Leah laugh. "Ain't so. That would be awful."

Abigail laughed with her. "We all feel that way when the baby starts to come. But trust me, when you see that little face and hold your child in your arms, you will be glad you went through it."

Leah's face, damp with sweat, twisted in pain again, but with their help she managed to get through the contractions. Then she nodded and lifted her face, her eyes clear. "I'm ready. No matter what, I do want my baby to be healthy and safe. And I have all of you to thank for that."

"Tell us more about Simon," Abigail said. "You know, my Jonah had no memories when I found him on the shore, wounded and nearly drowned."

"She didn't even know his name," Eliza explained. "So she called him Jonah."

"Like Jonah in the whale?" Leah asked as she rested.

"*Ja*," Abigail said. "I threatened to throw him back a few times, but soon, I knew I loved him."

Leah's expression turned from surprised to awestruck. "And he loved you enough to come back here to be with you?"

"He did," Abigail said. "He gave up the world out there to be here with me."

"That is true love." Leah dozed a bit, then opened her eyes.

"Simon told me he'd do anything for me," she whispered. "Even run away together, if need be."

"Colette and Matthew almost did that," Eliza told her. "But they knew running wouldn't solve their problems. They had to wait for the Lord to show them the way."

Mamm checked Leah's vitals, and seeming satisfied, gave a gentle sigh. "And the man who tried to harm them isn't here anymore, thankfully." She sat back. "I know we are to forgive, and we did forgive Shelah—the woman who was part of his plan. But I've had trouble forgiving that man."

"How . . . how did he die?"

"Samson," Eliza said. "My horse does not like evil people."

Leah gave Eliza a measured stare. "I see. I hope he likes Simon," she murmured as another wave of pain hit her.

"I think he will love Simon," Eliza assured her. "He'll see the best in the man you love, same as you."

Eliza and Abigail stood by while Leah huffed breaths in and out, sweat on her brow despite the cold wind outside. Mamm timed the contraction, then gave a slight shake of her head.

"Tell us more," she said, her expression still serene even though her gaze held concern.

"Simon is the best," Leah said, once she could speak again. "He's cute. Golden-brown eyes, shaggy light brown hair. Steals pie and cookies. Makes me laugh. Loves to climb up onto roofs and fix them. He'll take a barn-raising any day."

"A hard worker," Mamm said with admiration. Then she looked at her patient. "Leah, the birth has slowed down. I don't want to alarm you, but we might need to consider getting you to a hospital if your contractions don't come any faster."

Leah's eyes widened. "But the weather—"

"We will find a way," Mamm assured her. "Let's hope it doesn't come to that. Do you think you might be able to get up and walk a bit?"

Leah took in a breath. "Will that help?"

"It could. And I'll be with you. We'll all assist you."

Abby nodded. "I had to walk with my two. We'll give it a try if you're up to it."

Leah looked confused. "On the one hand, I want this to be over. On the other, I want Simon here. But I have to think of the baby first right now."

Eliza started giggling. They all looked at her, Mamm with a frown. "What's so funny?"

"The baby has to come first, because first the baby has to come."

Abby smiled and shook her head. "My sister and her humor. But literally the baby has to come first—in all ways. Because *kinner* always come first in our lives."

"Good logic," Mamm finally said as she helped Leah turn around on the bed and sit up. "Take it slow. If it's too much, we'll get you back to bed."

"The window," Leah said, motioning, her eyes burning with pain. "I want to see the snow. Or maybe I'll see Simon."

They draped a robe over her and slowly made their way to the big bay windows that gave a partial view of the lake. Eliza pulled back the heavy curtains. The outside lights lit up the garden, showing the world all white and pure.

"Christmas Eve," Leah said. "I never dreamed I'd be here in such a beautiful place having my child on such a holy day."

"As you said," Mamm told her as Leah stood and held on to the windowsill, "*Gott* brought you here."

"He did." Leah's eyes watered again. "Do women always get so emotional when it's time?"

"Women stay emotional," Mamm said with a laugh. "But *ja*, your hormones are making you weepy and happy at the same time."

Leah nodded and stared out at the night, then turned to walk back and forth across the wide room.

"Ready to get back in bed?" Mamm asked after they'd had a few turns and two contractions.

Leah nodded, holding a hand on her stomach. "But one more look out the window."

Abigail and Eliza guided her to the window again. Leah stood quietly, her gaze moving over the silent night. Then she lifted one hand and pointed her finger toward the portico drive as she let out a yelp of joy. "I see them! I see three men on horses, and one of them has an extra man with him. The big horse—that must be Samson." She turned to Eliza and Abigail. "That has to be Simon on there with the other man, right?"

Colette came running into the room. "Simon's here. He's with Jonah, riding Samson. They're home."

"We see and we are thankful for that," Mamm said, guiding Leah back to the bed to get her tucked in. "I'm thinking now will be the time for this little one to make up his mind about coming into the world."

"And not a moment too soon," Abigail said, relief in her voice.

Eliza wiped at her eyes. "They're home." She couldn't wait to hug Levi. And she felt sure her sisters would do the same with their men. Simon had to be so exhausted and worried, but he was here. He'd be so glad of that.

Now he could be with his wife and his newborn baby.

"Where is Daed?" Eliza asked, out of the blue, needing to see her own father. He'd stayed out of the way the whole night.

Mamm gave her a soft glance. "He's been at the front windows, watching and praying."

That made perfect sense, Eliza thought. Daed could pray with the best of them. He'd get an extra hug, too.

Chapter 5

Abigail ran into Jonah's arms as soon as he dismounted. "We were so worried. It's terrible weather out here."

The young man who'd already jumped down grabbed her arm. "Where is Leah?"

Daed nodded to Simon. "In one of our guest rooms. My daughter will take you there. Mother and child have been waiting for you to arrive."

Simon looked up at the inn. "Born? My child is already born?"

"*Neh*," Eliza said. "They are waiting for you so he can be born. Her contractions have slowed, but maybe your arrival will help."

Daed chuckled and sat back down by the fire. He tired so easily these days. "What an exciting Christmas Eve," he said, smiling softly. "A *bobbeli* on the way and people to share our blessings with."

Abigail's husband held her close, then stood back. "It was rough going for a while. But we made it to town. The bus was late, but we waited, hoping."

"When did it arrive?" she asked as Colette talked to Matthew. Eliza and Levi had hurried Simon into the inn to be with Leah.

Jonah glanced back at the lane to the highway. "It didn't. We had to go across town to the main road. That's where we found the bus, bogged down in mud and snow."

"So you got Simon off and brought him home with you, as we can see."

Matthew grinned. "Not only that. We flagged down a tow truck and helped the driver pull it back onto the road."

"That's even better," Abigail said. "I'm sure the passengers appreciated that."

Jonah glanced at the others and then back to her with his *please understand* gaze. "Uh . . . there's more."

"What?" Abigail said, knowing that look. "What happened?"

Then she heard the roar of an engine near the side portico.

"What's going on, Jonah?"

Daed cackled. "They invited everyone on the bus to come here," he said, nodding his approval. "The roads are only going to get worse. Henry checked the weather, and we can expect at least two to three feet of snow tonight. It was come now or spend the night parked on the road. Too dangerous, of course."

Jonah gave her a moment to let this news soak in. "So we offered them a place to stay."

"Here?" Abigail let out a whoosh of air. "How many people were on that bus?"

"Over twenty," Jonah replied, grinning along with her *daed*. "It was a small load."

"A small load." Abigail whirled like a drill sergeant. "We only have eight rooms, and some of them are small."

"We'll make do," Daed said. "It's Christmas."

Abigail bit back her complaints. "You're right, Daed. We can't let them sleep in that cold bus."

Jonah kissed her forehead. "I told them you'd say that, and . . . that they might need sleeping bags but some actually have them."

"We have cots," Matthew added. "And we have the carriage *haus*. It can hold a whole family."

Jonah nodded, his gaze on his wife. "I sure loved my time there."

Abigail giggled at that. "*Ech, vell*, we will make this work. I'll bring out the hot chocolate and turkey. We'll make sandwiches for everyone. They must be starving."

Jonah tugged her close. "This is why I love you so much."

Abigail's heart did what it always did when her husband was around. It pitter-pattered with love and contentment. These men had been so thoughtful to bring the stranded passengers here.

"It's so late," Jonah said. "Just give them cookies and hot chocolate. Tomorrow, I'll take some of the turkey meat we have left and make a big pot of soup. We have plenty of vegetables to add."

"Why not make the soup now?" she replied. "I'll give them cookies and snacks, but they need proper nourishment."

"Okay." Jonah looked at his watch. "It's almost eight. I can get the soup together and let it simmer for a while."

"We can help," Matthew offered after hearing their discussion. "I know my way around this kitchen."

Abigail gave in. "Okay, but Colette will want to supervise."

"*Gut* thing Edith is visiting Aenti Miriam and Levi's mom tonight," Matthew said. "Our cook would not be happy we're messing in her kitchen."

"She's retired," Levi reminded them. "Okay, semi-retired. They all planned to be here tomorrow, however."

"I'll talk to Colette," Abigail told them. "Leah has taken a liking to her and doesn't want her to leave the birth room."

Matthew smiled. "That's my lady. Everyone falls for Colette."

Abigail rolled her eyes. "*Ja*, she is the best sister ever."

They all chuckled at that, even Daed. Then he said, "I wonder how the birth is going."

"I'll check on that, too," Abigail replied. "I think now that Simon is here, the baby will be born."

Daed stood and tugged her close. "I believe you are correct. Now Henry and I will get all our visitors inside and settled. I still know a thing or two about running this place."

Abigail chuckled as she headed down the hallway to check on Leah. "Don't overdo," she called over her shoulder.

Colette looked up when Abigail came to the door. Abigail admired how Colette had stayed with Leah. They were about the same age; no doubt they'd be friends for life now.

Simon looked both terrified and excited as he held his wife's hand.

Colette motioned Abigail in. "She's almost there. The contractions are coming fast now. Mamm says it might be a Christmas baby. Or at least a Christmas Eve baby."

"Born on Christmas Eve," Abigail said with a sigh, her eyes misting. "That would be so *wunderbar gut*. The best present ever."

Colette bobbed her head. "Or possibly Christmas Day. Now I know how Mother Mary felt. I think we all do."

Abigail wiped at her eyes. Eliza came into the room. "What's wrong?"

"Nothing," Abigail said. "Everything is right. The baby is coming now."

"Oh." Eliza's eyes grew wide and then they got all misty. "Oh, this is happening."

Mamm glanced up. "It is, indeed. I don't think we need an audience for this part of the show. I hear we are to have a crowd of visitors. You all should go to the kitchen and get as many rooms ready as possible and find all the extra rollaway beds we have. We've got this birth under control now."

Colette hurried to Leah's side. "Will you be okay if I go to the kitchen?"

Leah nodded and smiled at her husband. "I will now. *Denke*, Colette. I'll never forget you."

"You won't be able to," Colette said. "You're family now."

Leah bobbed her head as a contraction hit. Mamm shooed them out and Simon held on for dear life, his eyes full of awe.

"Will she be okay?" Abigail heard him ask Mamm.

"She will be just fine," Mamm replied. "This is where the real work begins."

The three sisters closed the bedroom door and huddled for a hug. "A *bobbeli* on Christmas," Abigail said. "So amazing."

Then they scurried to the kitchen and found their men chopping vegetables and stirring the soup pot.

"Adorable," Colette said, smiling.

"Lovable," Eliza replied.

"Ours," Abigail said. Then in her pragmatic way, she whispered, "We should get a picture of this. It won't happen again for a very long time."

"Save it in your mind and sketch it for us," Eliza said.

Her sisters laughed as they hurried to help with supper. Abigail saw Daed and Henry in the vast lobby, serving hot chocolate and almond crescent cookies to a half-dozen children by the fire. The adults were laughing and smiling, and the children were in awe of Daed. Abigail noticed two Amish families in the crowd. They both had children with them who were now laughing and chattering with the *Englisch* children.

"Are you Santa?" one cute little blond *Englisch* girl asked Daed, her question eager.

"*Neh*," Daed said. "Here, we celebrate the birth of Christ, so while we might not see Santa, we will have presents under the tree. Small tokens of our love for each other and this special day."

"Will I have a present?" the persistent little girl asked. "Mommy said Santa might leave our presents at Grandmamma's house even if we're late."

Daed touched the girl's head. "I believe you'll find presents when you arrive to see your grandmamma, for certain sure. And I do believe there will be something special from us for you to take with you."

The child smiled and took a long sip of her cocoa.

"He does kind of look like Santa Claus," Jonah said as he passed Abigail.

She scoffed and then she laughed. "He is our Santa, but if I know Daed, he will keep telling them about Christ instead of Santa."

Sending her *daed* a big smile, she went about getting linens out of the closet and issuing orders to the staff members who were staying the night and had offered to help.

"No room at the inn is not happening here," she told Matthew and Colette. "Find everyone somewhere to sleep. Use the couches if need be."

Henry lifted a sniffling toddler and calmed the little fellow down. "You're okay. It's all going to be just fine. You're safe now, little one."

Two Amish women who didn't have family with them came up to her. "We're sisters traveling together to see a friend in Harrisburg," one of them explained. "What can we do to help?"

"You're our guest," Abigail replied, touched. "No need for you to do anything."

The sisters looked like twins, both with brown hair and stern features. But one was much younger than the other, and their eyes were different. The older one's eyes were a deep brown, while the young one had green eyes.

"But we want to help," the older one said. "I'm Gayle and this is my sister, Gloria. We know our way around a kitchen. Our parents ran a café back in Ohio. They got too old to work, so they passed it on to our brothers—and us. Please let us help."

Abagail let out a sigh of gratitude. "*Denke.*"

Then she took them into the kitchen and introduced them to the staff. Soon, they were laughing and chopping vegetables.

Abigail started heating a big tray of rolls they'd made days ago. She had to admit, she felt the truth of what Henry had said earlier. Here she felt safe and loved.

Chapter 6

Midnight.

Abigail sighed and stretched, exhaustion taking over. They'd fed soup and rolls to two dozen people and served brownies for dessert. Now everyone had a bed, even if some of the *kinner* would be sleeping between their tired parents or in roll-out beds and sleeping bags. At least Jon and Becca had slept through most of the chaos. They were safe in the crib she now kept in the quilting room. She'd be sleeping with them tonight. The old floral couch they kept in there wasn't so bad. Not if she'd be snuggled against her husband.

Jonah walked up behind her and tugged her close, reminding her of the days she'd kept him hidden in the carriage *haus*. He'd held her this way back then, tempting her mightily. But he'd also been kind and considerate of her beliefs. And he'd returned to her, even after learning he was *Englisch*. She thanked *Gott* for that every day.

"What are you thinking?" he asked, his breath warm against her neck.

"That I'm happy and safe and I love my life."

Jonah whirled her around and touched a hand to her cheek. "I feel the same."

"Do you ever miss the life you had out there?" All this time and yet she had to ask.

"*Neh*, I do not. I have everything I need here. I have you. You make my life peaceful. You've healed me."

"*Gott* healed you, Jonah."

"Maybe so, but He put you on that beach the day I washed up and then you took over, as you're accustomed to doing."

She slapped at his arm. "Are you implying I'm bossy?"

"I love bossy women." Then he held up his index finger. "Make that, I love one bossy woman."

"That's better," she said as they stood in the dark kitchen, the security lights outside casting a soft glow over them. "All is quiet now," she whispered. "Levi and Eliza will get Daed to his *haus*, and Colette and Matthew are staying in the cottage, too, so they can get here easily in the morning. Mamm won't get much sleep, but she has a cot in Leah's room if needed."

"I suppose we're having Christmas at the inn then."

"We are," she said. "But we'll have a bigger gathering than usual this year."

"And one newborn," he replied, his eyes bright. "It's been a long day."

"And yet, the little one is still not here."

They went to check on their children and to get some sleep, but Colette came around the corner from the birth room before they made it to the quilting room.

"He's here," she said. "A healthy baby boy! Born two minutes before midnight."

Abigail's eyes misted over. "Oh, I'm so thankful. How is Leah?"

"She's tired, of course, but she is so happy. And Simon is beaming with joy." She glanced back. "Mamm told me to give them some privacy before we clean up. Birthing babies is messy."

"Don't I know it," Abigail said. "Do you still want children then?"

"I do," Colette replied. "Even more so."

"I'm glad to hear that," Matthew said as he walked up to them. Hugging Colette close, he smiled. "I had fun with the *kinner* tonight. Children are just children, no matter their faith. They bring all of us together on a night like this."

Colette sighed. "This is why I love you."

Jonah chuckled. "Everyone is sappy tonight."

"It is Christmas," Abigail reminded him. "I want to see the *bobbeli*. What did they name him?"

They were headed to the birth room when Mamm blocked their way. "I thought I told you they needed some privacy."

Eliza and Levi returned with clean sheets and gowns and some baby clothes Abigail had passed to Eliza. "What did we miss?"

Mamm did an eye roll. "They can't have all of you gawking at them in the middle of the night."

"What did they name him?" Eliza asked, repeating the earlier question.

"Liam John," Mamm replied, her calm expression back in place.

"What a nice name, after their *grossdaddis*?" Abigail asked.

Mamm shook her head. "*Neh*, after Levi, Matthew, and Jonah. They wanted all of your initials in there."

All three men burst out laughing.

Jonah's expression brightened as he spelled out the name. "I guess we're all three in there somewhere."

Matthew squinted. "At least they didn't name him Lima John."

"Well, now Lima *Bean* is in my head," Colette said on a giggle.

"Or Lemon John," Levi added.

Matthew made a face. "But the M isn't in caps. Not sure how I feel about that."

"You can pronounce it with emphasis on the M," Mamm said. "Le-M John."

"Ah, I like that better," Matthew agreed, puffing up with importance.

"I think we are too tired," Eliza replied. "We are giddy with baby love and lack of sleep."

Mamm gave them her famous stare and then added a grateful smile. "You helped to get Simon home, and they told me they'd never forget that."

"*Ach, vell*, now we must see them," Colette said. "I mean, I saw them briefly when Mamm came to grab me, but I think I'd like to see them again." When everyone gave her questioning looks, she added, "Born on Christmas Eve in our inn. Liam John is a special *bobbeli*."

Mamm, weary and knowing, said, "Let me get Leah cleaned up and proper for visitors. A quick visit from just the girls. Tomorrow, we will all check on them. We don't want to give the baby any unnecessary germs."

"We're all very clean," Levi teased.

"Right." Mamm wagged a finger. "Get some rest. We'll all need it."

A little while later, Colette, Eliza, and Abigail slipped into the room to see the baby. Simon was snoozing in a chair pulled up by the bed, holding his sleeping wife's hand.

Little Liam John was bundled and cocooned between two pillows beside his *mamm*. A nice little bed.

Simon lifted his head as the women entered the room.

"Hi."

They all waved in silence. Then Abigail bent over to look at little Liam John. Whispering, she said, "Oh, he's so perfect. So sweet. I can't wait to hold him."

"We'll all get that chance, I'm sure," Eliza replied, her gaze dancing between mother and child. "I need to practice more."

Colette stood back in awe. "I can't believe how tiny he is."

Simon came over to smile down on his son. "Don't say that to my wife. She kept saying he must weigh a ton." Then he whispered, "He's a little over six pounds."

After admiring the newborn, they all left and went to find places to sleep. Jonah took Mamm home, but she would be just up the hill in case the couple needed her, and Abigail would be right down the hall in the quilting room, tucked in with Jonah and their children.

After they'd stoked the fires, checked on the kitchen again, and made sure everyone had a bed, Abigail finally settled down on the comfortable old couch, but Jonah took up most of the space.

"Are you cold?" he asked as he tugged the blanket over them.

"Not anymore," she whispered, content.

Jonah gave her a kiss on the cheek and then threw an arm over her. Abigail drifted off, thinking of little Liam John, and thinking of Baby Jesus. What would tomorrow bring?

More snow. Colette got up and quickly dressed in her burgundy wool winter dress and tied a black apron over it. After tidying her hair and putting on her *kapp*, she hurried from the bedroom, and left Matthew sleeping away.

Christmas!

She stopped to look at the world outside, all white and crisp and beautiful. The inn stood as stately and pristine as ever, red brick mixing with stark white so the place looked like a Christmas card.

That would be a *gut* idea. She'd keep the *kinner* busy with making Christmas cards for their parents and friends. And they could hold a singing. Those things were a tradition around here each year.

But first, she had to get to the inn kitchen and warm up the cinnamon rolls and cook a pot of scrambled eggs. And bacon. Everyone loved bacon, didn't they?

She'd just made a cup of tea when Eliza came into the kitchen, yawning.

"I'm always so tired now," her sister said. "And Mamm said I need to drink decaf tea or *kaffe*."

"That explains why you're also grumpy a lot lately," Colette replied. "I'll find you some herbal tea."

Eliza nodded. "And crackers. I need crackers."

"Morning sickness?"

"*Ja*, but not too bad."

"Why do women have to do all the work to get babies?" Colette asked, still sleepy.

Eliza started giggling. "Well, men do play a part in things."

Colette blushed and laughed. "*Ja*, I suppose that is correct. Yet, we carry the *bobbeli*, feel sick most of that time, then have the labor of bringing them into the world. Then they are attached to our hips until they become mostly self-sufficient."

"That's why we are to be as Proverbs thirty-one says. We are more precious than jewels because we work with willing hands."

"And we rise while it's still dark," Eliza added, nodding toward the darkness past the windows. "Our lamps do not go out at night."

"You two," Levi said as he entered and walked to the coffeepot.

When they both made faces at him, he hastily added, "She opens her mouth—I mean she is so wise. Her husband calls her blessed."

"*Gut* answer," Eliza said, reaching for his hand.

"It's Christmas," he replied. "And we have a big day ahead of us. We're going to get a bonfire going out by the pavilion and take the *Englischers* on buggy rides. Since they're missing their Christmas with loved ones, we want to make up for that."

Chapter 7

"A great idea," Colette said. "We'd better get started."

They put on coats and boots, scarves around their necks, and headed down the path to the inn. The sun seemed to rise out of the lake, shimmering like a Christmas tree ornament as it lifted over the water.

"Beautiful," Matthew said, catching up with Colette. She looked over at him, but he wasn't staring at the sunrise. He was smiling at her. "Next year, we might have a *bobbeli*, *ja*?"

She blushed again. "*Ja*."

"Do you want that?"

"I do. He'll look like you."

"Or she will be pretty like you."

They'd made it halfway when a snowball landed near their feet. Colette let out a yelp and saw Jonah ducking behind the front of the barn.

"Oh, you will pay for that," she said, grabbing her own clump of snow and shaping a ball.

Jonah hid so she waited until he peeked out, then aimed at

him. The snowball hit just over his head, bursting and falling onto his hat.

She hurried the rest of the way to the inn while he and Matthew tried to see who could throw the most snowballs.

When she entered the warm kitchen and saw her *mamm* at the stove, she rushed up to her.

"Is everything okay with Liam John?" she asked Mamm.

"He's doing fine, but Leah is not feeling well."

"What's wrong then?"

Mamm gave her a worried glance. "She has a slight fever. I'm going to make her some herbal tea and have her try to eat. Heat up some bone broth for me, please. I'm afraid she might have caught a cold being out in that chilly wind last night. She's exhausted, the poor thing."

"Has she been able to feed the *bobbeli*?"

"Yes, but only briefly. I'm going to help her with that, too."

Colette told Mamm to go back to Leah's room. "I'll bring the soup, tea, and crackers. And I can help with the baby, changing him and holding him at least."

Mamm warmed a towel and hurried up the hallway. "I'll send Simon out to eat a bite, too."

Colette worked on Leah's meal while Abigail and Eliza got busy making breakfast. Henry entertained the hungry people in the café and made *kaffe* in the big industrial pot, while the sisters got the food ready.

Abigail made sure the dinnerware was set up. "We'll do this buffet style to keep things moving," she said, checking at the pass-through. "Let's set the food on the big Queen Anne sideboard, near the *kaffe* and juice."

They heard the back door opening and Jonah came in, his deep blue eyes shining. He greeted everyone, the scents of winter wafting in with him.

"As soon as breakfast is over, we'll check the roads," he said.

"But it's a whiteout, so I think we'll have our visitors for most of the day. We will clear one of the lanes toward the apple orchard and give them rides. We'll need hot chocolate."

"Don't worry, we'll get that going," Colette said. "I have the makings for s'mores, too."

"That sounds *gut*," Levi added as he and Jonah took wood to the big fireplace in the lobby and got a nice roaring fire going.

Henry helped them build up the fire, and then he cleaned the rug in front of the fireplace and went to make a fresh pot of everything that could be served warm.

Colette took the tray she'd promised and went toward Leah's room, her prayers with the sweet family that had a newborn to care for. What a joy and a challenge. At least they were safe and warm here in the inn.

She prayed Leah wouldn't be too sick to enjoy her baby boy.

Mamm stood over Leah, taking her temperature.

"It's at a hundred and one," Mamm told Leah. "I'm going to give you an over-the-counter fever reducer. It's light but it might help."

"Can you sit up?" Colette asked after setting the round tray on a nearby table. "I've brought the tea and some crackers that have protein. Mamm's recipe."

Leah lifted her chin as Mamm placed cushions behind her. She kept her eyes on her baby. "As long as he's all right, I'll be fine."

"Right now, he is *gut*," Mamm said. "I'll check him, too. He might be as tired as you are."

Simon went over and studied Liam John. "He looks strong. He has *gut* lungs, *ja*?"

"He's a fine boy," Mamm replied. "Leah, does your throat hurt?"

Leah took a sip of the lemon-mint tea. "A bit, but I figured that's from hollering so much all night."

Simon grinned and kissed her forehead. "You were so brave."

"Not that brave," she said, eyeing one of Mamm's homemade crackers. "I wanted to send him back."

Simon made a face. "I'm glad you didn't do that."

"I explained how that was not possible," Mamm said, her eyes bright with mirth. "Although at times, I've wanted to send mine back."

"Mamm!" Colette tried to look shocked. "You must be referring to my older sisters."

"Of course." Mamm continued checking Leah over. "Does your stomach hurt?"

"*Neh*. But it is empty," Leah said. She nibbled on her cracker, then sipped the soup from a cup. "This does taste *gut*."

Simon glanced at Mamm. "Will her fever go away?"

"I hope so," Mamm said. "We try to avoid infection, and I did everything to keep the surroundings as sterile as possible, but sometimes we miss things."

Colette patted Leah's forehead with a cold compress. "This should help."

Mamm gave Colette a worried glance, then pasted her calm face back on. "Let's hope the fever subsides. If not, we'll find a way to get you to a doctor."

"I won't leave Liam John," Leah said with a stern glare.

"You won't have to leave him unless you are a danger to him," Mamm said. "We will not let that happen."

Simon gave Liam John a long stare. "He's so little and so helpless. He depends on us."

"He does," Leah replied, lifting up to see her baby. "I can't be too sick to care for my child. I won't let that happen."

Mamm patted her arm. "Let's give it an hour or so and see if your fever goes away. It could just be from all the exertion, and nothing more."

Leah nodded. "I think I'll rest now."

Simon went back to his comfortable chair. "What if he needs feeding?"

Mamm's eyebrows went up. "Well, Leah will need to take care of that if she's feeling better. If not, we have goat's milk. It's much better for little ones than cow's milk."

"It might be frozen," Colette deadpanned, "but still it will work."

Simon looked unsure and then laughed. "Okay."

Leah fell asleep. Liam John yawned and let out a yelp, then settled again.

Colette stood in awe of this couple and their love. She felt the same for Matthew. When she thought about how close she had come to dying, she thanked *Gott* all over again for giving her so many reasons to fight for her life.

As she left the happy couple, she prayed Leah's fever would go away. Now Colette had to slice turkey and heat up stuffing and make biscuits and gravy. They had at least ten pies of various flavors, from chocolate to coconut cream, along with apple and pecan. And cakes—Italian cream, cream cheese pound cake, red velvet, and a ten-layer chocolate with marshmallow icing. Not to mention side dishes of sweet potato casserole, mashed potatoes, green beans with bacon, corn pudding, squash casserole, and lots of stuffing and cranberry sauce made fresh. They'd been preparing for days, and all the food would come in handy now.

She stood in the kitchen and gazed out the window as the men gave their visitors buggy rides in the snow, Samson doing his part with a red bow in his braided mane. Eliza spoiled that big horse.

Abigail kept the hot chocolate flowing, along with cookies and popcorn, and s'mores. The firepit was warm and made a nice place to stop after a long ride. Sandwiches and chips made a fine midday meal, and then as the day wore on, she gathered their guests around the fire.

"You're all invited to a Christmas supper. I know you've missed getting to your loved ones, but the snow has stopped and the main roads are being cleared. You should be able to leave in the morning. While you are here, and it is Christmas, we want you to feel at home. So we're preparing a big feast."

Everyone clapped at that.

Eliza stepped up. "And for the women, we have quilting lessons before or after supper. You can make a panel as a reminder of your stay with us. We'll show you how."

Abigail spoke next. "As you all might have heard, we have a newborn with us, too. A Christmas baby named Liam John. We are putting together a baby basket for the Kauffmans. We are also using some panels we've been working on to make them a baby quilt, if anyone would like to help."

"I'm a quilter," one woman called out. "I'd be glad to help."

"My grandmother made quilts and I helped her," another one said. "What a thoughtful thing to do."

The other Amish sisters immediately agreed to the quilting frolic. "This will be so much fun," Gloria said to her sister.

"And what about the men?" an older gentleman asked.

Jonah stepped up. "We can take you out to hunt this afternoon, or just to hike. You'll see deer and other forest animals."

"And we have the lake," Levi added. "Not much fishing, but we can tell you what kind of fish you'd find there."

"That might be interesting," another man said.

Levi laughed. "The barn always needs cleaning."

They all groaned at that, but some raised their hands.

The King sisters smiled at each other. "We need to remember we haven't shared our Christmas gifts," Abigail said. "Maybe after supper and once the quilting is done?"

"It's going to be another long day," Colette said. "But a

nice Christmas. Different, but nice. We still have Second Christmas."

"We'll always have room at the inn," Eliza said. "And we will always remember this Christmas." She touched her tummy. "Next year, I'll be the one with a wee *bobbeli*."

"I could be right behind you," Colette said. "One day."

Chapter 8

The sisters stood in the quilting room, ready for the first of the lessons. Eliza nodded as women entered and found spots. So far they had five who were interested enough to come to the session. But three extras showed up to observe. Supper was ready and warming in the kitchen, where Matthew was taking over until the quilting was finished.

They'd tried to keep their visitors entertained all day with food, books, history, buggy rides, and walking tours. Most of the guests had walked through a foot of snow down to Lake Erie to take photos of the frigid water. There was something so peaceful about snow and water.

When she looked up to see Henry hovering at the door, she figured he had a question regarding his domain—the lobby.

"Henry, is everything all right?"

"I have two things to tell you," Henry said, his suit and bow tie as tidy as always even though he'd had to wear them for two days. "One, we have a young doctor in the house. He heard us talking about Leah having a fever and realized the baby had actually been delivered here. He's willing to check

Leah over if she feels comfortable with that. His name is Jack Hinson. He's an ER doctor in Ohio and has helped deliver a lot of babies."

Eliza motioned to Mamm and told her what Henry had said. Mamm nodded, relief washing over her. "I'll go talk to Leah. Her fever is low-grade but he might be able to prescribe her some medicine. I can call my friend to meet one of us at the drugstore in town, and we'll send someone on horseback to get what she needs."

Mamm left, but Eliza grabbed Henry. "What else?"

"Oh, Simon came out and asked to use the desk phone to call Leah's parents. He wanted to let them know about the baby."

"That's thoughtful of him. What did they say?"

"He left a message at the phone booth near their home, hoping they will hear about it." Henry shrugged. "I hope they'll at least call back."

"And what about Simon's family?"

"They all live in Ohio. He's been traveling with a construction company, but now he's trying to find work closer to home. He and Leah will visit Ohio when the baby is older."

"We haven't had much of a chance to get to know them," Eliza said. "They are the sweetest couple."

Henry nodded in agreement. "And to think we had a room available."

"Something usually happens over the holiday every year," Eliza said. "But never have we had a baby born here near Christmas."

"A perfect time for a birthday."

Eliza gave him a pat on the arm. "*Denke* for letting me know. Did Simon tell Leah about calling her parents?"

"Not yet. He didn't want to get her hopes up."

"Probably for the best. I can't understand why they didn't want her to marry Simon."

"I think they expected her to marry a local boy," Henry said. "A local boy she didn't really like."

"Ah." Henry always found out things about people. He didn't snoop or ask questions. He just listened and people poured out their hearts to him. Levi and Jonah had both done that when they were confused and so had Matthew, all the time, since he'd practically grown up in this inn.

"I'll go and see what the doctor says," she told Henry. "You've been such a help."

Henry smiled. "I've gotten to know a nice lady from the bus. She's traveling to see her grandchildren in Philadelphia, but she has fallen in love with the inn and the township here."

"Really now." Eliza had always wondered why the dignified *Englisch* front desk manager had never remarried after his wife had died. "Are you saying you're sweet on this woman?"

Henry chuckled and nodded toward a petite woman with a beautiful head of white hair cut in an attractive bob. "She knows all about quilting. Her name is Marcy Bennett. I'm sitting with her at supper." Then he shrugged. "Who knows? But there is something about her. She's easy to talk to."

Eliza gave him a playful slap. "Henry, you're blushing."

"It's Christmas," Henry said, straightening his red bow tie. "I might give her that ride to Philadelphia. I think my pickup could get us there despite the snow."

Eliza's heart lifted. "You deserve someone special in your life, ain't so?"

"I might not deserve her but I sure do like her." He waved at Marcy. She giggled like a schoolgirl and waved back.

Eliza couldn't wait to tell her sisters about this new development. But right now, they had some quilting to do.

* * *

They taught the ladies all about panels, designs, batting, measuring, and using colorful scraps to make a quilt. Then they started the quilt for Liam John, each person adding a scrap of fabric they'd picked from the remnant basket.

Sisters Gayle and Gloria Deardorff did know what to do, so they measured the panels and showed the others how to cut them and stitch them, even if they themselves couldn't agree on anything. They also started preparing the batting material that would be put between the back cover of the quilt and the paneled front.

Eliza beamed with pride. "This quilt will tell little Liam John's story. He will grow up knowing the story of how and when he was born."

"Colorful," Abigail said. "As this child will surely be."

Eliza showed the women how to make faceless Amish people and how to cut materials to form animals and bouncy balls and toys. "We'll add puffs of snow everywhere, along with things all boys love."

They soon had sewn enough together to let Mamm and the others complete the quilt in time to give it to Leah before she left. "We'll finish batting and stitching this," Abigail assured the women. "Remember, you each had a hand in this one."

Mamm came in and listened, then added, "And also remember a fabric remnant is useful and can be made into something beautiful if it's stitched with love."

Gayle nodded. "Like humans. We need to be stitched with love." Her sister nodded in agreement, but her stoic expression didn't exactly shout love and peace.

"Who made those exquisite quilts displayed in the lobby?" one woman with long, dark hair asked.

"We did," Abigail replied. "My sisters and I."

"They each tell a story," Eliza explained. "Of how we fell in love with our husbands."

"Who did which?" an older woman asked.

Abigail grinned. "I did the one with the predominantly brown and red colors. It's a memory quilt. Eliza did the one with the fall colors—a forgiving quilt. And Colette did the Christmas quilt."

Henry's new friend said, "Now I understand. They certainly tell a story, and that means you all must have very romantic stories."

"We do," Colette said. "But it would take more time than we have here to tell them."

"Obviously, it all worked out," the woman added, hope in her words. She and Henry would make the cutest couple.

Colette glanced around, sheepish. "*Ja*, we are thankful that we each found our happy ending."

Mamm worked her way around the table to help or admire the panels. "Keepsakes," she said. "Of your time spent with us."

"I might come back next Christmas," a young woman said. "I don't have family nearby but I grew up near Dallas, Texas, on a farm. My mama made quilts all the time. I still have one of hers. I was on my way to visit a friend in New York, but this has been nice."

"We'll be here," Mamm said. "You are welcome anytime."

After the women had finished up their personal panels, Mamm turned to the girls. "Dr. Hinson checked Leah over. He thinks it's just a mild cold, but he's afraid to give her certain drugs while she's nursing. So we will watch and see for the rest of today, and hopefully tomorrow her fever will continue to drop. If not, then we will have to get her to a hospital."

"How is she now?" Eliza asked while she put away the remnants, scissors, and batting material.

"She's up and walking some, and she did feed Liam John. The doctor examined him, too. Says he's fine. No fever there. Just a hungry baby."

They finished up and gathered before they went out to supper. "Let's pray for Leah and Simon and the little one," Mamm suggested.

They held hands and silently lifted up their prayers.

Then they walked out to greet their guests.

"Christmas," Mamm said. "Always a special time."

"Let's eat," Matthew called out.

Everyone cheered and asked about the newborn.

After explaining how the birth came about, Mamm and Daed stood by their places at the main table. "We Amish pray in silence," Daed explained. "You may pray as you see fit."

The others bowed their heads and did the same out of respect. After Abigail explained the buffet line, everyone got in place to fill their plates.

"We have tables everywhere," Matthew called out. "So find a spot and make new friends."

Henry managed to sit by Marcy, and she told him all about the baby quilt. The handsome doctor sat by the single woman traveling to New York. They kept exchanging big smiles.

Eliza couldn't stop her own smile. She'd never had so many thank-yous and compliments about the café's cooking.

"Like home."

"The best sweet potato pie ever."

"I'm definitely coming back next year."

"We did it," she told her sisters after they'd all feasted. The family went to each table to chat with their guests, and Henry entertained the whole crowd with "front-desk" stories.

Then one little boy raised his hand.

Daed nodded at him. "Would you like to say something?"

"I got presents from Santa in my room, but my favorite thing was riding the buggy with Samson."

Everyone laughed at that. Then the boy added, "But I haven't heard the Christmas story yet. My grandpa always reads that story. You know, the one from the Bible, about Jesus. Can I hear that now?"

Chapter 9

Daed laughed in surprise, then rubbed his hand down his gray beard. "That is an excellent suggestion, young man. Who wants to read for us?"

"You," the little boy said. " 'Cause you kinda look like Santa."

Daed nodded and touched the boy on his nose. He'd heard the same thing so many times today. "I'm not Santa, but I would be honored to read about the night Jesus was born. Matthew, please fetch me a Bible."

Matthew hurried to the small library where he and Colette had both fought and made up and grabbed one of several Bibles placed there.

When he came back, he glanced at Colette with such sweetness, she blushed down to her feet. Eliza knew her sister loved her new husband. Matthew was so kind and loving, and finally Colette had seen that.

Jonah suggested they move toward the fireplace. Soon a row of little children made a circle by Daed's chair, waiting while he opened the Bible.

The whole inn went quiet, the only sounds the crackle of the fire hissing and the wind howling outside. Then Daed began.

"In those days . . ."

Colette and Matthew held each other as her father read in his firm but kind voice, a voice that had never been raised in anger to anyone. Mamm sat nearby, wiping at her eyes.

Jonah held little Jon while Abigail stood swaying with a sleepy Becca. The doctor and the pretty traveler sat cross-legged on the floor by all the children.

Henry and Marcy stood nearby.

Eliza and Levi stared at each other, her hand on her tummy, his hand on her arm. She watched the *kinner*, saw the fascination in their eyes. Her baby would be here next year—tiny but here.

"I wish Leah and Simon could be here," she whispered to Levi. "But it's best to keep them isolated. Liam John is so tiny and new, and germs are everywhere with so many people at the inn."

Levi touched her stomach. "I've thought about us becoming parents. Next year, our baby will be the tiny one. Did you ever believe we'd see this day?"

"I daydreamed about it and told no one," she admitted. She'd been mighty stubborn about ignoring Levi when he'd returned. But he'd won her over. "Now my dreams have *kumm* true."

"Mine, too." He hugged her tight. "I just wish my *mamm* could be here with us."

"I'm sorry she's having a hard time," Eliza said. "The weather is just too brutal for her. But she has Aenti Miriam and Edith to take care of her. They won't be lonely."

Eliza wished everyone could be here. But she said a little prayer for those who were not and thought about the amazing thing she'd witnessed here in a place she loved so much.

Levi smiled at her, and her heart filled with love as they listened to the story of the birth of Christ.

When Daed had finished, the same little boy clapped and said, "Hey, my daddy told me a baby was born here. Is that true?"

His mother looked mortified. "Christopher!"

Daed only chuckled. "Liam John was born here, and he is sleeping while his *mamm* and *daed* watch over him."

"Just like Jesus," Christopher replied, without missing a beat. "Good thing you had room at the inn!"

Daed let out a big laugh. "Out of the mouths of babes."

Christopher grinned and ran to his mother for a hug.

"That was *wunderbar gut*," Eliza told Daed as he stood and moved to talk to some of their guests.

"It for certain sure was," he replied, giving her a quick hug. "Now I think I'm ready for a long night's sleep."

Eliza walked with him to find Mamm. "Tomorrow we must have our family gathering."

Daed glanced around. "Tonight, we had a big family gathering. I did enjoy it, but *ja*, we'll gather once more to rejoice and count our blessings. The temperatures should be warmer and the roads should be clear."

"And if not, we have plenty to keep sharing, ain't so."

"That is so, *dochder*, it is for sure."

The next morning, the bus driver came in to announce that most of the main roads were clear. Those traveling on to Pittsburgh and beyond should be able to make it through.

A few of the remaining people lived nearby, so Henry helped them arrange for either taxis or buggies.

After their guests thanked them, Dr. Hinson came up to Daed with a white envelope in his hand. "Abe, we all agreed we can't thank you enough for letting us spend Christmas here. We took up an offering for you and your family. The G-sisters told us you'd be insulted and refuse, but will you please accept this on behalf of all of us? It's a rare day when an inn owner doesn't charge people for a stay. You could have profited off of all of us, but you were kind and didn't. This is a gift, not a donation or charity."

Daed glanced around, clearly touched. Abigail came up beside him. "You are very considerate, all of you. We will take this money and put it with the funds we raise each fall during our festival here. The money goes back into the community to help both Amish and *Englisch* who are in need."

Daed cleared his throat. "I believe that is a *gut* idea. *Denke*." Then he nodded at the two sisters, Gayle and Gloria. "They were correct, but it would be rude in this case to turn away money that can help others."

The family and staff all stood on the long wide front porch of the inn, waving goodbye to those who would be traveling on.

"Be safe," Abigail called out.

Their departing guests waved out the bus windows until they were out of sight.

Then she turned to find the G-sisters waiting for her.

"We like it here," Gayle said. "We might stay."

"You mean here at the inn?" Abigail asked, wondering how to handle that. They'd planned to shut down for at least one day, and these two, while helpful, would be alone in the inn. She could only imagine them arguing over the food, the rooms, and anything else they wanted to tackle.

"In Shadow Lake," Gloria explained. "Gayle is a widow now and her four children are married and scattered here and there. And I—I've never married. We would need a place to stay and jobs, of course."

"Of course," Abigail said, surprised. "Since this is a bit sudden, let me discuss it with my staff. We are short a few people. As it's the off-season, we'd have to start you part-time, but you two do know your way around a kitchen and a quilting table. What about your own café back in Ohio?"

"We don't work there a lot these days," Gayle explained. "We own it and work as needed, but for the most part, our brothers run the place and their bossy wives have taken over." She placed her hands together over her apron. "We have different opinions about things."

"I see," Abigail said, wondering how many opinions they had regarding the inn. "Let's sit down and have some *kaffe* while we talk about this a bit more."

"*Gut*," Gayle said. "If you don't mind, we'd like to stay here for a couple of days. Our friend is sick, so she told us it'd be better if we didn't visit. We can catch the next bus out in two days."

Wondering if the friend was truly sick, Abigail could only nod, several different thoughts passing through her mind.

"And we won't bother any of you," Gloria replied. "We can take care of Leah and Simon's needs and help with little Liam John."

"All right," Abigail said. "We're planning to rest and visit today, and your help would be a comfort to all of us. We'll only be right up the hill at the cottage."

In the end, after hastily calling a meeting with her sisters and their husbands, she agreed to let the sisters rent the carriage *haus* apartment at a low rate until they could find a proper house, but they couldn't move in and start working part-time until late January. They agreed to the offer because they had things to take care of back home, such as explaining their big move to their brothers and Gayle's children.

Abigail feared the carriage *haus* apartment might become their permanent dwelling, and that they'd fuss with each other day and night. But maybe that was all part of *Gott's* plan for these two.

"You'll be expected to help with laundry and cleaning, but

mostly you'll help in the kitchen. We might let you take over some of the ongoing quilting lessons we give once or twice a week." Then she added, "And ladies, we have our own way of doing things around here. You can make suggestions but my sisters and I run things together and we have a system that works. Am I making myself clear?"

"Clear as a bell," Gloria said, her eyes zooming in on Gayle. "Did you understand that? You can't be bossing everyone around. You'll just be the hired help."

"I have ears," Gayle replied. "I know my place." She leaned in. "That would be perfect. I'm a mite tired of being the boss, anyway. And maybe Gloria will find a *gut* man."

"Sister, I've told you over and over I don't need a man. I like my independence."

"Hmm," Gayle replied. "That's why you don't *have* a man."

Abigail soon learned this was how they communicated, by constantly fussing at each other. Would she and her sisters be the same? Mamm and Aenti Miriam had this same kind of loving fussiness about them when they talked.

And maybe she and her sisters already did the same without really noticing.

After she'd negotiated with the two sisters, she went up to the cottage, where the family was meeting to finally enjoy their own quiet celebration and pass out homemade gifts to each other. Because they'd been cooking and cleaning nonstop, they'd made simple sandwiches for the midday meal, and they'd have cookies and cake for dessert.

Later, they'd pull out the last of the Christmas supper and enjoy what was left.

"I was too tired to go visiting today," Mamm said after they all sat down at the table. "I left the G-sisters at the inn with Leah and Simon. I'm so glad her fever went away."

"Me too." Abigail passed the sandwiches and handed everyone a bag of potato chips. "I hope the sisters don't scare that poor sweet couple."

"They are a bit frightening," Jonah replied. "They came to the stables and made some pointed comments."

"I can't believe you hired them," Colette told Abigail. "I could hear them fussing all day long yesterday."

"They are hardworking and they need something new," Mamm said. "They remind me of Aenti Miriam and me."

Daed nodded and chuckled. "And we've all heard how you two go on and on."

Mamm gave him a glare.

"I mean how Miriam goes on and on," Daed said, a twinkle in his eyes. "You're so kind and considerate, always."

"That's better." Mamm burst out laughing. "I have my ways."

Jonah winked at Abigail, making her blush. "You know, Dr. Hinson and that single woman with the long brown hair seemed mighty chummy getting on the bus today."

"Her name is Bridget McCullough," Colette said. "I talked to her a lot at supper last night. She just broke up with her boyfriend about six months ago. Now I think I know why."

"Why?" Eliza asked, always loving a good story.

"Because *Gott* wanted her to meet Dr. Handsome—I mean—Hinson."

They all laughed at that, then Eliza asked, "Did you notice Henry talking to Marcy? Those two hit it off, for certain sure."

"I noticed," Mamm said. "He did offer to give her a ride to Philadelphia, but she declined. Then she told him she'd like to book a room here at the inn, for New Year's Eve."

"Ah." Daed shook his head. "We might be losing Henry soon."

"Or she might want a job like the two sisters," Eliza replied.

Abigail let out a sigh, but she wanted to hear about Leah.

"So how are our patients? Will they be able to make it back home soon?"

Mamm put down her sandwich and wiped her hands on a napkin. "I advised them to stay with us a couple more days. Leah's fever is better but going back out in this weather is not a *gut* idea for her or the baby."

Jonah lowered his head and then glanced back up. "We need to stall them. I wanted to let you all know, Simon had Henry get in touch with Leah's family in Lancaster. I'm waiting to hear if they're coming here or not."

"Oh, that would be such a blessing for Leah," Mamm said. "What a thoughtful gesture."

"If they'll actually come," Eliza added. "Leah made it sound as if they really haven't spoken since she left to get married."

"I have a feeling it will all turn out," Daed said.

"So we'll have them a while longer." Eliza clapped her hands. "I love holding little Liam John."

"Your hormones are showing," Colette said. Then she patted her sister's arm. "But I like holding him, too."

"A Christmas baby," Jonah said as he passed the mustard. "I don't think any of us will ever forget this Christmas."

"Of course we won't," Mamm said. "We're making Liam John a quilt that has a lot of references to his birth."

"It's so sweet and cute," Colette told them. "But we'll need to get it done soon. We can put the finishing touches on it before they go."

They all agreed on that. Then they started fighting over the cookies. Abigail watched them all and laughed.

She'd never been so content. But tomorrow, it would be back to work on a full-time basis. Never a dull moment around Shadow Lake.

Chapter 10

Leah couldn't take her eyes off her baby boy. The *bobbeli* was the prettiest, or rather the most handsome, child she'd ever seen. "Liam John, you are a special little boy."

Simon came over and touched Liam John's fuzzy fawn-colored hair. "Could you be a little biased there, *mei lich*?"

"I might be a tad proud of him, but you have to admit he's handsome. Like his *daed*."

"I think he looks like you," Simon replied. "I think his eyes will be blue like yours."

"And he has your hair, thick and maybe light brown."

"We will find out when he grows," Simon told her. "I believe he's grown overnight."

Leah looked out the window, wishing they were home but thankful for this beautiful place they'd landed in. "How is the weather? I can see it's not snowing now."

"From what Henry told me before he left to go home, the roads are clear. The bus loaded up early this morning and went on its way."

"Then we should be able to get home, too," she said, lifting up to hand her sleeping baby to Simon. "He's full and content for now."

Simon gently put their son back in the little basket Abigail had made for him. It had a soft, clean pillow and padding all around it. "He likes to eat."

"Don't we all," Leah said. "I'm starving."

"I'll go find you something in the kitchen."

"*Neh*, I need to walk a bit. You watch over him and I'll find the kitchen. But first I need to make myself presentable."

She slowly made her way to the bathroom, admiring how pretty it was. "Fancy," she mumbled with a smile. But no complaints from her. She'd been pampered by everyone here and she was taking advantage of that.

Soon she had on her best dark blue dress and a black apron. They'd both been washed and smelled like a winter day, all fresh and full of sunshine. This place was like falling into Christmas, but the old-fashioned kind the Amish loved to celebrate. Not too many decorations, just handmade ornaments, with fresh greenery and locally made candles everywhere.

She gave Simon a kiss and promised him a cinnamon roll, then she walked slowly up the long hallway to the café centered behind the big lobby. The smell of fresh *kaffe* and bacon tickled her nostrils.

That's when she found the G-sisters, as everyone called them. "*Gut daag*," she said, suddenly shy. "Where is everyone?"

"*Ach*, there's the new *mamm* everyone's been talking about," the older of the two said as she guided Leah into the kitchen. "I'm Gayle and this is my sister, Gloria. We're watching over things while everyone else takes a break for Second Christmas."

"Oh, that is today, ain't so?" Leah wished she and Simon

could have contributed and helped out, but that had not been possible. "I believe they all deserve a rest, for certain sure."

"We told them the same thing," Gloria said as she bustled over to help Leah into a chair. "Now, what would you like to eat, *liebling*? We made a late breakfast for our meal. Or we can prepare you some soup and crackers."

Leah wasn't sure if she should even be here, but she was ever so hungry. "That bacon smells *gut*. And maybe a little *kaffe*. I don't want to mess up *mei melke*."

"One cup won't hurt, but how about a nice apple cinnamon tea after the first cup?" Gayle suggested.

"I suppose that would do better," Leah said, nodding.

Soon she had a plate of bacon, eggs, and toast, along with some thawed blueberries and strawberries from the big freezer in the back. After taking a sip of her *kaffe*, she let out a contented sigh. "This is nice," she told the sisters. "Why are you two still here anyway?"

"That's a long story," Gloria said. "But if all works out, we'll be back at the inn in January to live and work."

Leah wanted to hear that story. So she sat and listened while the G-sisters told her all about what she'd missed while giving birth to Liam John. That included the stories of how each of the King sisters had found love and happiness here in their own home.

After the G-sisters finished with what they'd learned and pieced together regarding the Kings and their epic romance stories, she laughed and clapped her hands together. "They all mentioned they'd made quilts. So those quilts you're describing are on display here in the inn?"

Gloria bobbed her head "*Ja*, you want to see them?"

She did. The two interesting, talkative sisters walked with her to the lobby, one holding her arm on each side. The King quilts, as they were called, were hanging on display in the library room, its pocket doors open so everyone could see.

"Amazing," Leah said after she'd studied each quilt. "I can see the stories, based on what you've told me. These quilts hold so much love."

"They do," Gloria said, her tone wistful. "I'd love to have a story like that one day."

Her older sister let out a long-suffering sigh. "You need to flirt a little more."

Gloria frowned and then she smiled. "I'm going to learn how to flirt. I've watched all the women around me these last few days, so I think I've got the hang of it."

Leah smiled and nodded. "I'll help. I sure flirted with Simon. Got in a lot of trouble, but it was fun."

"I need some fun," Gloria said on a firm note. "You'll show me."

"I will, a bit." Leah glanced back toward her room. "But Simon and I will need to get back home and take care of things, especially our son."

"But you don't live too far away, do you?" Gloria said. "I heard your home is right over the next hill."

"It's a bit farther than that, but not too far," Leah said. "We can certainly visit back and forth."

"Everyone here will love that," a voice called out.

They turned to find Sarah King smiling at them. "Here I was coming to see my patient and she's up and talking to you two."

"Did I do something wrong?" Leah asked. She might have overeaten.

"Of course not," Sarah replied. "I'm glad to see you up and about because Dr. Hinson has left the building. He won't be able to help us now."

"Oh, I wanted to thank him for his kindness," Leah said. "He is such a nice doctor."

"You're right, he is very kind," Sarah replied. "I'm glad we had him for a second opinion. Midwives get bad publicity sometimes, so we need to brag when doctors agree with our opinions."

"You delivered a *bobbeli* during Christmas," Gayle said. "I'd say that is something to brag about."

"It's my work," Sarah explained. "Now Leah, I did come to check on you but also to see if you and Simon and our little Liam John want to come and visit with us later today. We're having leftovers for supper and we will share small gifts." She gazed at the G-sisters. "You two are invited, if you'd like to join us."

"I'm in," Gloria said, grinning. "You people have more fun than anyone I've ever seen."

"Do you think they've had fun taking care of all of us?" her sister asked.

"I thought so," Gloria said. "They certainly don't gripe the way you do."

Sarah narrowed her eyes. "Ladies?"

"We'd love to *kumm*," Gayle replied, all sweetness and light. "But how do we get *mamm* and *bobbeli* to the cottage?"

"I'll work on that," Sarah said. "They will be provided with a winter buggy to ride up the hill."

"That's not necessary," Leah said. Then she thought about that high hill. "On second thought, I'd appreciate the ride."

"Just bundle that boy," Gayle cautioned. "He's barely two days old."

"She has a point," Sarah replied. "But I believe if you and Liam John are bundled up and inside the buggy with a blanket warmer, we can smuggle you inside the cottage and then get you back down here before dusk."

"*Ach, vell*, the snow has stopped," Gayle said, looking unsure and ready to make another point.

But two other women came in, both puffing and huffing. "Miriam," Sarah said, moving toward the women. "I see you and Edith made it here safely."

"We did," Miriam said. "And just in time from what I hear. Is it true that a baby was born here on Christmas Eve night and you delivered it?"

Sarah's calm amazed Leah. "Leah, Gayle, and Gloria, meet my sister, Miriam, and our retired cook, Edith. They've been staying with Levi's ill mother and her two teens while the weather was so bad."

"And we're back here now," Miriam said, scanning the lobby and then the quilts. "My, these are as pretty as ever. Have you heard the story—"

"We have," Gayle replied. "So romantic and sweet."

Leah had to hide a giggle. Miriam looked disappointed that she'd not been the one to give them the scoop. The other one— Edith—went straight to the kitchen, then turned and came back.

"I commend whoever cleaned the kitchen. It is spotless, with just a tad of leftover bacon scent."

Gayle and Gloria beamed. "We were left in charge while everyone else got caught up on resting."

Edith gave them a once-over. "I see. So things have changed over the last few days."

Sarah shook her head. "Nothing has changed. We had a big crowd of people who needed shelter and food, so we provided it, but they were able to move on this morning. I'm sorry you both missed it." Then she turned to Leah. "Let's get you back to your room to rest and feed little Liam John before we get you ready to go up to the cottage."

Leah thanked the ladies for brunch and nodded toward Miriam and Edith. "I hope to see you all there."

That began a choppy conversation between the G-sisters

and Miriam and Edith. It reminded Leah of hens cackling, and she almost giggled.

But when she and Sarah were out of earshot, she whispered, "Are you really sorry your sister and the cook missed out?"

Sarah gave her an admonishing glance and then chuckled. "Not sorry one bit. Not one tiny bit."

Chapter 11

A few hours later, Leah looked at herself in the mirror and laughed. Most Amish frowned on vanity, but she wasn't being vain right now. "I look like a big snow-woman," she told Simon.

"So do I," her husband replied.

She turned to find Simon all bundled in a big black wool coat, his hat, and gloves. "You're adorable," she said, thinking her husband would always look handsome to her.

"You are perfect," he replied with a soft smile. Then he gave her a solemn stare. "I should have been here with you. I travel too much."

Leah rushed to him and hugged him tight. "You are doing your best to take care of us, Simon. I love you for that. It's not your fault our son came into the world early. You had to visit your sister. I'm glad she's better now."

"But I should have been here. Almost missing our child's birth made me think I need to find a different kind of work."

Leah gave him a soft kiss. "Let's discuss this later. I want to hear you out, but we're going to be late."

Simon nodded. "You're right. I'm fretting when I should be rejoicing. You are both safe and healthy. Nothing else matters right now."

"You matter, too, and I love you." She hurried to get Liam John. "Our little snow-baby is sleeping like a sweet lamb—that's our blessing."

Sarah and the G-sisters had helped her swaddle the baby in a blue wool blanket. He had on a cute onesie Abigail had passed on to them, and a warm beanie to match. Lifting him up, she turned as Simon wrapped another soft wool blanket around him until the only thing showing was his nose and mouth.

"That ought to do it," Simon said, giving her a quick kiss. "I love you both."

"And we love you." She went quiet as Simon touched a gloved hand to her cheek.

"I know you miss your folks. I wish they could be here. If they ever get one glance at our son, they will come around."

Leah didn't want to cry. "I hope so. I've prayed for that."

"One day," Simon said, sadness in his own eyes. "We have each other, remember. And now we have new friends we can visit as often as possible."

"I'm happy about that," she said. "Let's go. Our first outing with our *bobbeli.*"

He escorted her to the front door and out onto the porch. The sun shined across the snow, the drip of melting mush falling softly from the porch roof to hit the wet shrubbery. Then they looked over to the covered portico.

"Oh, my," Leah said, smiling. "What a thoughtful thing to do."

The black-topped winter buggy had a red bow tied on its side and Samson, the big horse that had helped bring Simon here, wore a red bow in his mane. The magnificent grayish-white animal shot them a solemn stare, his dark eyes wide, then shook his mane and neighed a greeting.

"I think he remembers me," Simon said with a smile.

Jonah hopped down from the seat. "Ready?"

"We are," Leah called. "This is so nice."

They hurried into the buggy and found it warm and cozy, just as Sarah had promised.

The G-sisters and others had walked back to the cottage.

"You two need this time alone with your *bobbeli*," Sarah had told them. "It's his first buggy ride."

"Finally, it's our Christmas," Leah said, her eyes on the tiny baby in her husband's arms. "But I need nothing else. I am content."

"This is our best Christmas," Simon told her in a cracked voice. "I know I don't have much to offer, but right now my heart is full."

"You have everything to offer," she said, emotion filling her soul. "And I love you even more now."

They huddled together and glanced back and forth from their son to the beautiful landscape. Jonah said he was taking them the long way around. Snow covered the trees, making them look like frosted Christmas trees. The land was white, glistening in the sunshine that would eventually melt the snow to mush.

The outbuildings and the three houses perched on each hill behind the inn looked like something out of a holiday card.

"This is beautiful, Jonah," Leah said. "I love the fresh air and the scenery. It's truly very festive."

"Fewer bumps and bounces this way around," he said. "And a little more time to enjoy the beauty of the countryside."

"Another thoughtful gift," Simon whispered in her ear. "I'll do something nice for them when we are back home. Maybe make a bench they can put somewhere on the property."

"You do have a gift with your woodwork," Leah replied. "That's a *gut* idea. And I'll make one of my pound cakes."

"Ah, your pound cake. Wish I had a piece right now."

"You're about to be fed," she said, laughing.

"Oh, so I am."

The buggy rolled up to the quaint white cottage with the big front porch and soon, they were inside, surrounded by all the people who'd seen them through the birth of their child.

Leah had to wonder if Mary and Joseph had felt this way when they'd taken Baby Jesus for his first excursion. Parents had a lifetime of surprises. She prayed she'd handle the good and the bad as her son grew up.

"The food was so *gut*," Leah told Abigail after they'd eaten warmed-up stuffing and gravy, along with slices of turkey and prime rib. "I need that cranberry salad recipe."

"I'll write you up a copy," Abigail promised. Her son ran by giggling, but she took the interruption in stride.

"I need to take parenting lessons from you," Leah said, laughing. She admired the sleeping babe in her arms. "I'm sure this one will be like that too soon."

"They do grow rather fast," Abigail said. "But you will love each new thing he learns, even the naughty things at times."

They watched as Jonah scooped up his son and made Jon giggle and squeal. Jonah shot Abigail an endearing glance, then kissed his son on the cheek.

"I was just thinking about that on the way here," Leah admitted. "I hope I'll handle all of it."

"You will." Abigail laughed at her husband and son; then Jonah took Jon by the hand to put him to bed in one of the downstairs rooms.

Soon the men had moved to the big living area to enjoy the fireplace while the women gathered around the kitchen table.

"So are you ready to return home?" Colette asked Leah while they shard hot tea and pecan pie.

"We are, but we don't want to get caught in any more bad weather. Your *mamm* suggested one more day here."

Sarah nodded. "Our little pumpkin seems healthy and happy, and Leah is free of any fever, but it's a ways to their place, even in a cab. Staying here a while longer won't hurt."

"I'm still sore, of course. But I'm feeling better," Leah added. "I was dizzy for a while but now that's gone."

"You went through a lot," Sarah replied. "Dizziness is expected. But you've had plenty of liquids and your appetite is back."

"*Ja*, I could devour that whole pie," Leah admitted, staring at the few slices of sweet potato pie sitting on the counter.

On the other side of the long kitchen, the G-sisters, Miriam, and Edith tried to outdo each other cleaning up.

"We will send you home with plenty of pie and other food," Eliza said, grabbing a big cookie as she settled down. "I seem to be ravished all the time these days."

"You'll have a new baby next year around this time," Leah said to Eliza. "I know you're excited."

Eliza nibbled her cookie. "Even more so now than ever. We've all seen Mamm leaving the house for births, and we had one employee, Maggie, who almost had her baby at the inn, but we've never had a guest give birth here. You'll go into the Hall of Fame." She shrugged. "First, we need to establish a Hall of Fame."

Leah couldn't stop her smile. "I'm so glad I found this place. Now we have new friends and great memories."

The sisters and Sarah smiled at her. Then Miriam, Edith, and the G-sisters scraped chairs and made a fuss of sitting down at the big table.

"We've cleaned the kitchen," Miriam said with pride, as if no one had noticed. "And all the extra food is being distributed to each household, including Leah and Simon. I'll take some back to Connie tomorrow when I return to duty there."

"How is Levi's *mamm*?" Sarah asked.

Miriam explained Connie's illness to the others. "She has *gut* and bad days, of course. She couldn't come out in this weather, but we made sure she and the youngies had a nice Christmas. She had neighbors calling on her, too. Levi and Eliza are going to visit her and spend some time with her later in the week."

"That's correct," Eliza said. "We'll stay with Connie through the weekend. I have gifts for Jamie and Laura."

Leah didn't understand Parkinson's disease, but she did understand how important a caring family could be.

"I wish I could go visit my folks," she blurted before she could catch herself. "I miss them so much and I'd like them to see their new grandson." She touched Liam John's cheek. "I'd like them to accept my marriage and my husband."

Sarah glanced at Jonah, then back to Leah. "I wish that were so, too. I will pray on it."

"I'd appreciate that," Leah said, still worried she'd never see her parents again. That prospect was unimaginable.

The next morning, Leah woke to sunshine and clear skies. Liam had woken them twice last night for diaper changes and feedings, so she must have slept late.

"*Gut* morning, sleepyhead," Simon whispered as he leaned down to kiss her. "I brought you a tray from the kitchen."

She sat up and took the hot tea and biscuit full of ham and a fried egg. "*Denke*." After chewing awhile, she asked, "Can we go home today?"

"Not yet," Simon said too fast. "I mean, remember that Sarah wants you to stay another day at least. We're in no hurry. I have the rest of the week off."

"I know," she replied after she'd nibbled more biscuit. "I just miss our house, and Liam John's room is ready and waiting for him. I thought we could leave early if we're careful."

"Tomorrow, *liebling*." Simon's eyes held a bright concern she assumed was from either lack of sleep or being a new *daed*.

"Is everything all right?" she asked, suddenly in a panic. "Is there something wrong with our baby that no one wants me to know?"

"Our baby is fine, other than being hungry and needing a diaper change every few hours. But that's what *bobbelis* do."

"Is it me, then? My fever is gone and I feel fine."

Simon tugged her into his arms. "We are all okay. Now why don't you go freshen up before LJ wakes."

"Did you just call our son LJ?"

"I did, but Matthew wants an M in there, too."

She had to laugh at that. "We can't call him LMJ, that's just too long."

"I think Matthew will be fine with knowing we did add him into the name. Liam John can be LJ or he can be Liam for short." He held up his finger. "Matthew teased me and told me they'd all decided if we say Lee-M John, with emphasis on the M, we'll be okay. Frankly, I think he's the only one requesting that."

"We'll worry about that later, but I think it's cute," she remarked before she finished her tea and went to get dressed. "If it's warmer, maybe you and I can take a short walk. We have several willing nannies to help out."

"We do, indeed," he replied. "I'd love a walk with my beautiful wife."

"That's a date."

She finished dressing, still humming to herself when they heard a knock on the door.

Simon was holding Liam John, but he opened the door while she quickly covered her bun with her *kapp*.

"Hello," Simon said, letting out a sigh. Then he turned from the open door to where Leah stood unable to see who'd knocked, his face gone white with shock and caution. "Leah, we have visitors."

Startled, Leah came around to see who had surprised her husband; then she let out her own gasp. "Mamm? Daed?" Putting her hand to her throat, she couldn't speak. Finally she said, "You came. You came."

Chapter 12

Her petite mother rushed to her and hugged her tight, her gray eyes shining with tears. "We are here now, *dochder*. We are here. I'm so sorry we stayed away for so long."

Leah looked over her mother's warm shoulder and saw Daed. Then she let go of Mamm and rushed to him. "Daed?"

"Leah." Her father took her into his arms and held her tight, then said in a wobbly voice. "I'd like to see my *kinskind* now, if that's okay?"

"It's more than okay," Simon replied, tears in his eyes. "Here is our little Liam John."

Mamm and Daed looked at the baby and smiled, their cheeks damp, their anger vanished. Leah only saw raw love and astonishment in their gazes.

"This is the best present I could ever receive," she told them as Simon handed Liam John over to Leah's *mamm*.

"I feel the same," Mamm said. "I'm so glad your friends here reached out to us."

Leah could only bob her head in a reply. So many blessings. How could she ever be worthy of so many blessings?

"*Kumm* and sit," she offered, motioning to the small sofa in the sitting area of the room. "I had been saying I was eager to go home, but now I don't want to leave. Can you stay awhile?"

Her parents took the sofa and she sank onto a chair, her joy warring with jangled nerves. How long would they be able to visit?

"*Ach*," her mother said, keeping her eyes on the *bobbeli*. "We can, but we'd thought we could follow you home and stay a few days with you, to help with Liam John?"

"That would be so amazing." Leah glanced at Simon, afraid she'd overstepped. Her *daed* had not been kind to her husband. "Simon?"

"We'd like that," her husband said, nothing but joy in his words and his voice. "Very much. You can see Liam John's room and, well, the whole house. We have a spare bedroom on the first floor."

Leah silently gave him a thankful nod and smile. Her husband was a kind, forgiving man. Maybe her parents would see that now.

"That will suffice," Mamm said, clearly relieved.

"*Denke*," Daed said. "We have wronged you, young Simon. I hope you can forgive us."

"Already done," Simon replied. "We will speak of it no more. You have given your daughter her best wish for Christmas."

"I wouldn't have missed this for anything," Mamm replied, tears in her eyes. "And this place is so beautiful. I'm glad you found it in time."

"We will leave tomorrow," Simon told them. "I was delaying here, waiting and hoping, but I didn't tell Leah that."

Leah looked at her husband in shock. "You were in on this secret?"

"I was. I'd hoped—"

"—that we'd do the right thing?" Daed asked.

"I had just hoped it could all work out," Simon admitted.

"It has worked fine," her mother replied. "We have much to talk about, but right now I want to keep holding my grandson while I visit with you two."

Leah wiped at her eyes and began to tell her *mamm* the whole story. Her very own Christmas story.

The rest of the day was a whirlwind for Leah and Simon. Mamm and Daed wanted to meet and thank the entire King family, and then Gloria came to sit with Liam John, so Leah and Simon could have midday dinner with her parents.

Now they were in the café eating. Abigail and her sisters came over to greet them.

"Hello," Abigail said to Leah. "So these are your parents?"

Leah bobbed her head and stood. "*Ja*, my *mamm*, Elizabeth, and my *daed*, Isaac. The Myers." She smiled at her parents and motioned to the sisters. "This is Abigail, Eliza, and Colette. They run this place."

"With a lot of help," Abigail admitted. "We've been busy this morning getting back to our regular hours. We had a lovely holiday, though."

"You had a full house from what I hear," Isaac replied. "And still managed to cook this great beef stew and corn-bread."

"We're used to cooking," Colette said. "Every day."

"We don't have much of a choice unless we shut down," Eliza added. "But business is slow today. Just you all and the G-sisters for now, and they are doing half the work."

"We could help," Elizbeth offered. "I'd love to get this recipe anyway."

"We have recipe cards," Colette told her. "You don't need to help. You're our guests. And we are so glad you came to visit your new grandson."

"We are, too." Elizabeth gave Leah a soft smile. "We're happy to be following them home tomorrow."

"Then we will pack you a basket of goodies," Abigail said. "Now we have some quilting to finish."

"Oh, I love to quilt," Elizabeth replied. "Could I at least help with that?"

"You can," Abigail said. "In fact, you can help, too, Leah, and Gloria can watch little Liam John."

"Really?" Leah clapped her hands. "I don't have to go back to bed?"

"*Neh*," Eliza said. "We'll hide you from Mamm."

"Mamm is right here," their mother said from behind them. After introducing herself, she turned to her daughters. "You will not hide a recovering mother from her midwife."

They all turned pink and lowered their heads in shame.

"But you will allow her to sit on the softest cushion we have in the quilting room, understood?"

"You mean she can help us finish the quilt for little Liam John?" Colette blurted out.

"Wait, you're making a quilt for us?" Leah wouldn't cry again, but her emotions were so wild these days. She took a breath. "I'd love to help with that."

Abigail and Eliza glared at Colette. "You can't keep a secret, ever."

"I kept a lot of them before," she said in defense. "I didn't tell Matthew I loved him until I was forced to do so."

"Well, we all knew that already," Sarah said in a teasing voice. "I'm amazed you held things so close to your heart when you finally realized you loved him."

"It's okay," Leah said to stop them from continuing. She was glad Colette had spilled the beans. "I want to help with the quilt. I had no idea there was a quilt."

"It was a secret," Eliza explained. "We wanted to surprise you. But we do need all hands on this so we can finish it. Liam John needs his own special quilt."

"A baby quilt," Colette replied, her tone tart but cheerful. "Fitting that his *mamm* might want a hand in it."

"Fitting," her sister chanted. "No surprise, but fitting."

Soon they cleared the table and sent all the men except Isaac off to the stables to see to the animals and check out buggies and equipment. While Isaac chose to read in the small sitting room, the women gathered cookies, hot spicy tea, and *kaffe*, then went into the quilting room.

"After hearing all your stories, I've wondered what this room would be like. So many memories, ain't so?" Leah asked in awe. She missed having her baby in her arms, but Gloria was watching him while he slept.

She'd never seen such a big sewing and quilting room. Everything was neatly organized either on high counters or the shelves that lined one wall. She saw panels and patterns, scissors, all kinds of colored threads, a small basket of marking pins and seam rippers, and just about anything else one would need for mending, sewing, and quilting. The big, long quilt table beckoned her.

"A lot of memories woven with each stitch," Sarah said. "From quilts passed down and reworked, to brand-new ones that should last a long time."

"And none of them perfect," Abigail said as she gathered scraps and found the batting basket. "But we make them anyway."

"Those in the room near the lobby are gorgeous," Elizabeth said. "Leah mentioned they'd been made by you three." She glanced from Abigail to Eliza and Colette. "What an amazing thing—to make a quilt that tells how you each fell in love."

"It's been an interesting few years," Abigail said. "But that's a long story."

"So they keep telling me," Leah replied. "But I know enough of it to believe them. And I've seen all of you with your husbands. You are all in love."

"And bearing fruit," Sarah said with a laugh. "But I'm not complaining."

"Me either," Elizabeth replied, grabbing Leah's hand. "Where is our little Liam John, anyway?"

"Gloria is with him," Leah replied. "But she and Gayle are going to help with the quilting, too, and they'll bring him with them." She leaned close. "I think they are lonely and don't get along well with their own family."

"I believe you are correct," Sarah said. "They will work out great here with us and they can visit back and forth with their kinfolk."

"Like us," Elizabeth said. "Leah, your *daed* and I are so sorry about how we treated you and Simon. After you moved away, we had several people vouching for him. About how hard he worked, and how kind he was to people."

"I tried to tell you that," Leah said with gentle admonishment. "I could not marry Peter Schultz, Mamm. He was mean and self-centered and thought everyone should bow down to him."

"We figured that out after you left," Elizabeth said. "He . . . he spread rumors, saying he'd dropped you because you were flirting with another man. Then he belittled Simon to some people who work for Peter's *daed*, Michael. Michael heard him and took him to task, telling him he could learn how to do a *gut* day's work if he followed Simon around. Apparently, Simon had done some renovations on their barn and silo. If he impressed Michael Schultz, then he will do fine."

Leah perked up. "Really? I can't believe that. I thought everyone loved Peter. Except me."

"The bishop is now talking to Peter a lot," Elizabeth replied. "Peter wants everyone to think that he's the best, but he suffers from the sin of pride. We do not want that kind of man for you."

Leah shook her head. "So that's what it took for you and *daed* to give Simon a chance?"

All the women around them gave her *mamm* a curious glance. Elizabeth took Leah's hand. "*Neh*, we talked to the bishop, and asked for forgiveness before we ever learned about Peter. We regretted letting you leave without our blessings and we missed you terribly. So that is why we're here. That and . . . how could we stay away from you after you'd given birth?"

Leah nodded and hugged her *mamm*. She had to forgive, too. She wouldn't ruin this wonderful week doubting her parents' intentions. *Gott* had made all of this possible.

She'd leave it at that and once she got home, she'd make her little boy a grand quilt from his parents to go with the one the King sisters were putting together. Even if her stitches weren't perfect.

Chapter 13

They laughed and cried together.

Leah had never had close friends, but these women made it so easy to relax. She'd always been shy and standoffish. That was why she'd been so surprised when Peter Schultz started paying attention to her. It didn't take long to figure it out, however.

He wanted to use her and then move on. She didn't fall for his act and that made him mad.

But she didn't care. The moment she'd seen Simon up on that ladder, smiling down at her, she knew he was the one.

Now she was helping to make a quilt for their son. She was so happy she wanted to shout it to the world.

"Life is so unpredictable, isn't it?" she said after hearing the whole story of Abigail and Jonah. She looked at Abigail, her needle in midair. "Did you ever dream you'd marry Jonah?"

"Never, well not until I got to know him. And fell in love with him."

"*Gut* thing he liked us enough to come back," Colette said.

"Would you have left with him?" Leah asked Abigail, needing to know. "The way I left with Simon?"

Abigail glanced at her *mamm* and sisters. "I never had to make that choice, but I can say it now. *Ja*, I would have gone with him. I loved him and I still love him." She lowered her head. "I'm sorry, Mamm."

Sarah let out a grunt. "Do you not know that I saw that in you, knew what you'd do?"

Abigail put down her scissors and tied off a knot. "You did?"

"Of course I believed you'd run away with him. You snuck out almost every night to see him."

"That I did," Abigail replied. "Are you disappointed in me?"

Sarah gave Abigail a soft smile. "I could never be disappointed in you. I would have missed you, prayed for you, and forgiven you. And I'd always love you, no matter what."

Leah glance at her *mamm*. "Did you feel that way?"

"I will always love you," Elizabeth said. "I did much the same—I prayed, I mourned, I worried. But in the end, I had to let *Gott* guide me as I'm sure He guided you."

Leah held the bright red and blue panel she'd been working on to her heart. "Every day. I prayed every day that somehow *Gott* would show me the way. The right way. I knew I loved Simon, but I missed you and *daed*. I'm an only child. I've only ever had you two." She swiped at her eyes. "Then a few months after we married, I discovered I was expecting."

"And that was your answer?" Elizabeth asked, her words husky.

"I believed it was."

"When we got word," her mother said in a near whisper, "I went to your father and told him. I said we must *kumm* and find you and see the baby. I wish I could have been with you."

"I had plenty of help," Leah replied, wishing the same. She'd always regret not having her *mamm* here during the birth.

"You're here now and that is the best gift." Then she asked the next question on her mind. "But Mamm, if you found out about Peter's bad ways after I left, why didn't you reach out to me sooner?"

Elizabeth stopped stitching and put her hands in her lap. "We wanted to let you know, but we were afraid you wouldn't listen, that you wouldn't even hear our account of things. Many times, we decided we'd visit and many times, we backed out. We were heartbroken and so miserable. I finally told your dad I had to get rid of the misery. The only way would be to see you again and tell you we were wrong."

"It's been well over a year," Leah replied, her own heart battered. "If you hadn't got word about the *bobbeli*, would you even be here now?"

Out in the stables, Simon watched Levi care for the horse that Leah had abandoned during the storm. The poor horse had spent a cold night underneath some trees surrounded by hills and rocks. Levi pampered the big Morgan by cleaning his frogs and trimming his hooves.

"Eliza is a stickler for a properly shoed horse," he'd explained earlier.

"Ralph here is a tough one. He was Leah's growing up," Simon replied, wondering why Isaac had made an excuse not to join the men at the stables. Maybe he still felt awkward about the way he'd treated Simon. "I can't believe she drove that buggy from our house feeling the way she did."

"She told us she was fine until she got a few miles from here," Jonah said, his tone reassuring. "Then she got the pains and that flustered her."

"And she got stuck and realized she was lost," Abe said as he threw another twig into the roaring fire they had built just outside the open doors of the barn. "Women can be determined at times."

"Oh, you mean stubborn," Levi retorted with a big grin. The Morgan gave him an eye roll on that one.

"Nobody mentioned that word," Matthew said, stomping his boots to stay warm. "But we did get run out of the inn earlier when they started gathering for their quilting frolic."

"We have homes we could gather in," Levi pointed out. "I'll be finished here soon. The buggy is not damaged and fortunately gave Ralph a bit of protection from the wind. We could go up to the cottage."

"I should be leaving soon," Simon reminded them. "*Denke* for all your help. I wish you'd let me pay, Abe."

Abe chuckled. "I tell you what—you *kumm* back in the spring and we'll have you mending barns and climbing on roofs. There is enough work here and on several of the farms around here, to keep you busy for a long time."

"I'll be glad to do that," Simon replied, feeling hope in his heart. "I've been thinking of how I can make ends meet without traveling so much."

Jonah dusted off his hands and lifted his fingers to the fire. "You could start your own business. We have a strong Amish community here. You'd be busy all the time."

Simon sat down on a hay bale. "I don't think I'd be ready for that yet. A steady job makes more sense than taking off on my own."

"Not if you know people who know people," Jonah said. "We know people."

Simon nodded his head. "I'll need to discuss this with my *determined* wife."

They all laughed at that. Finally, after they'd talked about where he should start and how they could help, Abe looked at Simon and patted him on the shoulder. "I know of one investor who'd be willing to help you, Simon."

"Really, who would that be?"

"Me," Abe said.

"And me," Jonah added. "I have a little extra from way back when."

"And me," Levi added. "I can squeeze out a few dollars here and there."

Matthew looked sheepish. "Colette and I have a house but we're looking to add more rooms soon. I could hire you as the construction supervisor when we do that." Then he added, "And I also own property in Missouri. You won't need to travel there, but I have a little money set aside from that property. I can invest in your company, too."

Simon grinned from ear to ear. "*Denke.*"

They shook on it.

Simon left them at the stables and took his time walking back to the inn. The big pavilion behind the inn stood solid and pretty with its slanted roof and shining beams. No wonder so many people booked rooms here. With the lake down below and the cove and waterfall nearby, Shadow Lake had a lot to offer. He'd never forget his time here.

Now if he could just pry his wife and his new in-laws away.

Leah heard someone calling her name.

When she looked up, her *daed* was coming toward her with a worried look on his face. The quilting frolic was over and Leah had been in her room feeding Liam John. She was about to go find Simon and let him know Henry could call them a taxi van to take them home safely.

"Daed, what's wrong?"

"Your *mamm* isn't feeling well," he said. "She doesn't think she'll be able to travel on to your place."

"What? But I want you both to visit us. I'll go see about her."

"She might be resting," Daed said. "Sarah is in with her now. She doesn't want to give any sickness to Liam John."

"Is she upset with me?" Leah asked. "I badgered her while we were making the quilt."

Her *daed* stopped and whirled around. "About what?"

"About why you waited so long to get in touch and if you came only because of Liam John."

"We wanted to see the *bobbeli*, *ja*," Daed said, his dark eyes sincere. "But we really wanted to see you and tell you we were sorry. She took it real hard when you left. She . . . she hasn't been filling *gut*."

Leah walked with him down the hallway toward her parents' room. "How long has this been happening?"

"A few months now. It comes and goes."

"I want to see her."

Sarah stepped out of the room.

"What's wrong?" Leah asked. "Can I see my *mamm*?"

Sarah took her hand. "She's sleeping now." She turned to Isaac. "I believe Elizabeth is having heart problems. I'm not a doctor, but you should get her to a specialist soon."

"Heart problems?" Leah held a hand to her face. "I wish I wasn't so persistent with her earlier."

Sarah shook her head. "That might have upset her some, but she told me she's had these spells before. It reminds me of when Abe started feeling weak and had to lie down."

"I shouldn't have gotten her worked up," Leah replied. "I should have just enjoyed seeing you both."

"It wouldn't have changed what happened," Daed said. "She's been fighting it. I've tried to get her to a doctor."

"This is why you were afraid to go to the stables with the others, right? Do you watch over her a lot?"

"When I can," he admitted. "And honestly, this is one of the reasons we didn't try to visit you sooner. Traveling tires her out so much. But she wanted to be here with you."

Sarah nodded. "She kept telling me that." Then Sarah looked from Leah to Isaac. "I've called a local doctor. He doesn't live far from here and he just got home from a trip early this morning. He'll be here in a few minutes. You can trust him. He helped Eliza when she broke her leg a couple years ago."

"What can he do?" Leah asked. "Shouldn't she go to the hospital?"

Sarah turned to face Leah. "He can examine her and he has more knowledge than I do, but I'm pretty sure from the symptoms she described it's similar to Abe's heart problems. I sure know all the signs, but I can't make the diagnosis."

Simon came walking toward them. "What's wrong? Is it the baby?"

"*Neh*, it's my *mamm*," Leah replied. "She's been sick and I just found out. While we were quilting, I had a serious discussion with her about . . . things. I think I made her feel worse."

She burst into tears and ran to Simon. "It's my fault."

He held her close. "I'm sure it wasn't your fault. Even good surprises can bring some stress. Maybe she just needs to rest."

Leah prayed her husband was right, but in her heart she wished she'd just stayed quiet. Her parents were here now, and that should be the only thing that mattered.

Chapter 14

Dr. Merrill came into the lobby where Leah and Simon sat with Eliza and Levi. Everyone else joined them in prayer, then went about their business doing what needed to be done. But a pall hung over the inn.

Leah didn't understand how she could be so happy one day, and so sad the next. Why had she questioned her sweet mother? Did it really matter at all why her parents had come to see her now that they'd apologized for being so angry toward Simon?

She stood and faced the doctor. Her *daed* was in with Mamm. "Doc?"

Dr. Merrill nodded to Levi and Eliza, then glanced back at Leah and Simon. "It's not her heart yet. But she does have high blood pressure and that could lead to a heart attack or a stroke. With proper medication and a healthy diet, I believe she will be able to get back to normal." He held up a hand. "Having said that, I've given her the name of a specialist in Lancaster County. I set up the appointment so she won't miss it."

"*Denke*," Leah said, relief washing over her. "Can she travel?"

"I think so. She just needs to rest. I called in a prescription that will help until she can get to the specialist. I went over her symptoms with him and he agrees this is the best plan for now."

"So she and my father need to go back home?"

"That would be for the best, given her need to see a specialist." Dr. Merrill gave Leah a stern look. "Had they planned to stay here with you?"

"They'd planned to go with us back to our home," Simon explained. "It's about twenty miles south of here."

"That should be okay," the doctor said. "If you take a cab instead of a buggy. Neither of you need to bounce very much right now."

"We'd planned to do that," Simon said. "We're trying to think of our *bobbeli*, too."

"Finding a good ride would work for both," Dr. Merrill replied. "And speaking of that baby, Sarah told me I had to check in on the little fellow since I'm passing through. And I never disregard anything Sarah tells me."

They laughed at that. Simon nodded. "We'd be glad to let you see our *sohn*. He's growing already."

"I like hearing that," Dr. Merrill said. "And Eliza, I'll want a full report from you when I come back. Along with a strong cup of coffee and a big piece of apple pie."

Eliza giggled. "I'll get on that, Doc. You might as well stay for supper. We've had a busy day, but few visitors. We have a big pot of beef vegetable soup."

"I'll stay for that," he added, smiling at Leah and Simon. "Nobody ever wants to leave this place."

"We know," they both chanted as they took him to see Liam John.

Leah's relief that her mother was okay caught up with her. After the doctor had pronounced their boy as just about perfect, she hurried to her parents' room.

"Mamm," she said, rushing to her mother's bed, "I'm so sorry for being rude to you and asking so many questions. All that matters is you came and we can be a family again."

Mamm patted her hand. "*Dochder*, don't you see? If we hadn't *kumm* here, I might not have ever seen a doctor. You actually helped me accept that something was wrong."

Leah shook her head. "I caused you to get upset."

"*Neh*, you needed the truth. My frailness was one of the main reasons we couldn't come, but the baby made me ignore the risk, and here we are. Now I can get the medicine I need and visit you as often as possible."

"But—"

"But nothing. You did not cause my illness. I should have been checked a long time ago but I keep ignoring the symptoms." Mamm patted the bed so Leah sat down beside her. "Now we will start over, and I am going to go with you to your home and help with Liam John for a few days. I can rest there easily. We will have our own special Christmas. All is forgiven on my side. How about you?"

Leah wiped at her eyes. "All is forgiven. I did say we'd not mention this again, and so we won't."

"Glad that's settled," Simon said to Isaac. "I think we can find some food if you're hungry."

"Starving," Isaac said. "This had been a wild week, ain't so?"

Simon laughed. "And I have more news. I need your advice on something."

They walked out of the room together, acting like old friends.

"See," Mamm said. "We're all happy now, and I will be fine. I'm going to take care of myself so I can come often to help you."

"I'd liked that," Leah said, hugging her *mamm*. "You rest and I'll bring us a tray. We can eat here together."

Mamm nodded. "*Denke*."

Leah went into the café and headed to the long table the family used. Everyone was gathered there. "Am I too late?"

"Never too late around here," Jonah told her as he stood to help her with her chair. "We're all glad your *mamm* is going to be all right."

"So am I," she replied. "I only came to get a tray for my *mamm* and me. We'll eat in her room. But aren't you all about ready to get rid of your last lingering guests?"

"You're no longer guests," Abigail told her. "You're family."

"And so are we," the G-sisters both shouted from the kitchen.

"We'll see how that goes when Edith comes back part-time after the New Year," Colette whispered.

"I heard that," Gayle called out.

Daed chuckled and lowered his head. "Now we have even more determined women around here."

Mamm smiled and leaned over to give him a quick kiss. "You love it and you know it."

"I'm blessed to have you," Abe said. "I have always known that."

Sarah took his hand in hers. "I feel the same, *liebling*."

They finished up and Colette took Leah into the kitchen. "Let's get you two some soup and a biscuit or two." She found the soup ladle. "Want me to add a brownie or some red velvet fudge?"

Leah let out a sigh and nodded, then helped her with the bowls and the food. "You've all been so kind to us. How can we ever repay you?"

Colette put two linen napkins on the big wooden tray. "I think you'll be able to help us a lot, especially since I heard the men talking about hiring Simon for several projects."

"Really?" Leah asked, so proud of her husband. "Then I could visit and offer my help for certain sure."

"Of course. You're new here but this community is very

tight-knit and caring. We hold a lot of events, and if you wanted to work part-time at the inn on those days, you'd be able to bring little Liam John with you. Abigail is thinking of making a storage room in the back into a nursery. Gayle and Gloria said they'd love to help run it."

"That's amazing," Leah replied. "The Lord always provides, one way or another."

"As long as we provide for Him with grace and kindness and our belief that He will hear our pleas," Colette added. "Let's take this to your *mamm*."

Leah nodded and held her hands together as Colette carried the tray. "I could get used to working here," she said, her smile wide. "After all, my son was born here."

Now that Leah had explored several rooms in the inn, she could feel herself falling in love with the place. She stood just outside the little library she'd heard so much about, with Liam John swaddled in a sling shawl against her chest. Her baby smelled so clean and fresh. She still couldn't believe how tiny he was or that he truly belonged to her.

When she entered the room, she laughed. Colette stood there studying the three quilts. Leah's gaze moved over the beautiful artwork the three sisters had created, marveling at how clearly each story was told in the panels. Colette turned in surprise when she saw Leah and the baby.

"Hi," she said, putting an arm around Leah while she admired the sweet, sleeping child. "We hate to see you leave tomorrow."

"We aren't that far away," Leah said. "To think just days ago, I was so lonely and struggling to cope with becoming a mother. It took me getting lost in a snowstorm to find a friend who was willing to hold my hand and stay with me even though I was a stranger."

"That's how things work sometimes," Colette said. "It took Matthew going to help his *onkel* to show me how much I loved him. I almost lost him forever. But Mamm kept telling me to wait for *Gott*'s will."

"He always shows us the way," Leah said. "I love it here, and I'm so glad I found all of you during one of the scariest nights of my life. And now the happiest night of my life. I promise to always be your friend, Colette."

"And I promise you the same, Leah. We can visit back and forth and you can come and stay with us when Simon is working here, ain't so?"

"I'll be here," Leah promised. Then she turned to Colette. "I never got Liam John's quilt. Is it finished?"

Colette held up her hand. "We'd planned to give it to you tomorrow. Abigail is putting the finishing touches on it tonight."

"I can't wait to see it finished," Leah replied. "Mamm told me she even helped with it a little this afternoon. That's the other thing I need to say *denke* for. I have my parents back, and I owe that miracle to everyone here who helped Simon make it happen. So things turned out the way they should have, even Mamm's getting sick here."

They walked out of the library to go to bed and Colette looped her arm around Leah's waist. "I don't think I'll ever forget this Christmas."

"I won't, either," Leah replied. "And Liam John will hear the story of his birth, just as he will hear all about the birth of Christ. He will know where his quilt came from."

"I can't wait to watch him grow," Colette said, smiling at her new friend. "He's already so adorable. He will make a fine little toddler."

Leah gave her new friend a quick hug before they parted for the night. "And who knows, maybe this time next year, you'll have your own *bobbeli*. Or one on the way."

"I might," Colette said, holding a hand over her tummy. "I just might."

Leah waved good night, then went to find her husband. They'd be home soon, and while she was ready for that to happen, she'd miss her time at the Shadow Lake Inn.

She planned to return very soon.

Chapter 15

The next morning, the whole family lined up by the inn's front doors and waited for Leah, Simon, and baby Liam John to come out of their room. Her parents were with them, smiling and laughing. Isaac held his wife close, making sure she was feeling better. Elizabeth had reassured all of them she felt much better today and she'd take the medicine to get her blood pressure under control.

"We are so thankful for all of you," she said now while they waited. "You took our *dochder* and Simon in when you could have turned them away. We appreciate all you've done."

Abigail watched as Mamm hugged Elizabeth. "We would never turn away someone in need, especially a woman lost and afraid. We were able to witness a birth on Christmas Eve. That was a true blessing for all of us."

"It was for Elizabeth and me, too," Isaac said. "We needed something to nudge us back into our daughter's life. This sure did it. A *kinner* born and you all as friends we can count on."

"Amen to that," Abe said.

Abigail stood silent, remembering the last few years. Four

years ago, she'd been walking on the beach, fretting that she'd be an *alte maidal* the rest of her life.

Now she was married to an amazing man who loved her and their two *kinner*. Jonah also loved her entire family and they had grown to love him as well.

As if he could read her thoughts, Jonah came up to her and held her close, their gazes meeting in a silent communication that wove their hearts and minds together like a tapestry.

"I love you," he whispered in her ear.

"I love you," she whispered back.

She smiled over at Colette and Matthew, watching as they whispered sweet nothings to each other. Eliza and Levi were doing the same. She loved how he kept touching Eliza's growing tummy.

"More *kinner*," she said to Jonah.

"What's that? You want more?" Jonah acted shocked.

Abigail slapped his muscular arm. "Maybe one day, but right now I was referring to my sisters. Eliza is all starry-eyed and happy and Colette is bursting at the seams to have her own baby. We have competition in that department now."

Jonah growled in her ear. "They can't compete with us."

When they heard a door opening down the hallway, Henry summoned the whole staff to the lobby.

Abigail, Eliza, and Colette grabbed the baby quilt and spread it out, Colette in the middle holding it up while her sisters held the corners of the little covering.

Leah and Simon were talking about which road to take when they looked up and saw everyone waiting for them.

"What's all this?" Simon asked, glancing from one person to the next. Then he saw the sisters with the quilt.

"Leah," he said, nodding toward the fireplace.

She turned and let out a joyful squeal that stirred the little one in her arms. "The quilt, Simon. Liam John's quilt. I haven't seen it finished."

Abigail beamed as they stepped forward.

Simon took Liam John into his arms. "Look, *sohn.* That's for you, and it's all about you."

The couple stood, their eyes moving over the panels.

"A woman in the snow, walking up the hill," Leah said. "And I see the abandoned buggy and horse off in the distance."

"It was hard to make those tiny figures out of denim," Gayle said with a smile. "But Gloria and I worked on that part."

"It's beautiful," Leah replied. "I love the snow and the tiny birds and the faceless woman. That's me. I had on those colors."

Simon pointed to another panel. "A bus! And then three Amish men in hats and coats."

"And a fourth man walking from the bus," Leah said. "Look, Liam John, that's your *daed.*"

They moved on to the next panel, a room in the inn, where all the furnishings were shown in vibrantly colored primitive shapes. In the center was an Amish figure with a black bag representing Sarah, the midwife.

Then they came to the panel with an Amish figure sitting in a rocking chair holding a swaddled *bobbeli.*

"That's you and your *mamm,*" Simon said to Liam John. The baby was awake and listening, his dark eyes bright. "We love you so much, little one."

The panels then showed a gathering of Amish people sharing a Christmas meal, the colors green, red, and white.

Then the quilters had added ponies, bright-colored balls and lunch pails, tree swings, a dog, and a red barn with a silo.

"Our life," Leah whispered.

In the very middle was the faceless image of a young Amish boy standing sturdy and strong in the night with the guiding star—the Christmas Star—sparkling up in the sky behind him.

"Your birth," Leah said, giving her son a kiss, tears on her cheeks.

She looked up at the people standing around her, most of them with their own tears of happiness. "I'll never forget any of you or the way you took us in without question and helped us bring our *sohn* into the world. You brought my whole family back together, and you did it in the midst of a fierce snowstorm. We are forever grateful."

Mamm walked to Leah and hugged her. "We consider you as part of our family now, Leah. You are all *welkom* here anytime."

"I think we should meet here each year around Christmas," Elizabeth said. "We will let you all celebrate with your families first. But we will definitely pass this way again during the holidays."

"That is a great idea," Mamm agreed. "A true celebration of friendship and kinship."

"And Simon, we aim to hire you next year," Jonah said. "We will stay in touch and give you a list of things that need to be done. I think you'll make a great independent contractor."

"*Ach, vell,*" Abe said. "We always need work around this old place."

The G-sisters came up with a basketful of food and jars of jam and vegetables. "This ought to last you a few days," Gayle said, patting Simon's arm.

"And either of us can ride over and babysit if you need help," Gloria replied. "We'd be happy to do so."

Edith and Aenti Miriam had arrived earlier to say goodbye. Edith handed Elizabeth a fresh pound cake and Miriam gave the couple a basket of baby clothes she'd bought in town.

They visited a few more moments, then Abigail and Eliza folded the quilt and handed it to Simon.

Everyone watched from the porch as the little family got in

a van and headed for home. Simon would be back next week to get the horse and buggy Leah had abandoned a few nights ago.

After waving them on, everyone went back inside the inn and went about their business with smiles on their faces. Soon, the noon crowd came in and the café and inn bustled with customers once again. All in a day's work.

Chapter 16

Colette walked through the front lobby and saw Henry talking to the woman from the bus. The woman he'd taken a liking to during Christmas.

"Marcy, you made it back," she said, greeting the *Englisch* woman with a quick hug. "Will you stay overnight?"

Marcy's shy smile widened. "I've booked a room for two nights, and Henry says now that the roads are passable, he'll give me a tour of the whole area."

"She might be interested in moving here," Henry replied, his brown eyes bright with hope.

"*Ach, vell*, I think you will like the landscapes and the vistas we provide." She shot Henry a meaningful glance. "Henry is a great tour guide."

Marcy giggled like a schoolgirl. These two would make a great couple. Happy that Henry had found someone after living alone as a retired veteran for twenty years, Colette enjoyed watching them watch each other.

"We have a special dinner on New Year's Day," she told Marcy. "Pork roast with sauerkraut, mashed potatoes and gravy, and desserts, of course."

Marcy patted her blue jeans. "I'll gain five pounds."

Henry laughed. "You'll still be cute as a button."

"Cute as a button." Colette grinned. "I think he likes you, Marcy."

Henry blushed. "I'm just glad she was passing back through."

"I am, too," Colette replied. "I'll leave you two to your tour planning. Remember, midday dinner will be a feast tomorrow."

Excited for them, and happy about friends and family planning to come over for a singing and some supper tomorrow, Colette went about her work in the kitchen, making sure the few people in the café were being fed.

A couple hours later, she heard the bells tinkling as the front doors opened. Then she had to laugh again. The traveling doctor who'd first checked on little Liam John stood inside the lobby, smiling as he glanced around.

"Dr. Hinson, welcome back. Henry stepped away but can I help you?"

The handsome doctor with the thick dark hair looked embarrassed. "I booked two rooms for tonight," he said. "One for me and one for—"

"—the pretty woman with the long brown hair?" Colette asked, thinking the inn had become a matchmaking place.

Surprised, Dr. Hinson looked around. "Did she really come back?"

"She's not here yet," Colette said. "Are you supposed to meet her here?"

"I asked her to meet me here," he explained. "We had a good time on the bus ride, and we've been calling and texting and . . . since we were both going to be alone tonight, I asked if she'd meet me here. I didn't want to be at a big New Year's Eve party. I wanted a quiet, pretty spot to get to know Bridget better."

"And you picked our inn," Colette said as she went behind the check-in desk. "This place does seem to have that kind of effect on people."

"It sure does," he said as he followed her. "But I don't know if she's going to show up or not."

"I see your reservations here," Colette said. "Jack Hinson and Bridget McCullough. Two rooms."

The cute doc looked as nervous as a wild horse caught in a corral. Colette leaned forward. "You like her, ain't so?"

"Is so," he said, his hand brushing through his hair. "Like I've been struck by lightning."

"I know that feeling," Colette said. "Hurts so *gut*."

"Yes, that." He poked a finger against the counter. "Exactly like that. What if she doesn't come?"

"I have a feeling she will be here," Colette replied. "I'm going to fix a special table for you two in the smaller sitting room. The library."

"Where all those pretty quilts are?"

"That's the one."

"She'll love that. And she prefers coconut pie—with all that fluffy browned icing."

"We have a fresh one sitting on the counter."

"And flowers. Lots of flowers."

"We have poinsettias and tabletop baby spruce trees."

"That could work."

"Anything else?"

"Candles. She bought a few of those when we went shopping."

"Candles. We have many."

He bobbed his head, then glanced at the doors. "I thought she would have been here by now."

"I'll get it all set up," Colette replied, smiling. "We have a couple of filet steaks we can cook for you two. And fingerling potatoes?"

"That'd be great. She eats a lot of salad."

"I think we have fresh greens in the big refrigerator."

"Did I forget anything?" he asked, his expression so comically sweet.

"Just to breathe," she replied. "Doc, you've got it bad."

He laughed and took the key she gave him. "I hope she can make it here to meet me. She was taking the train out of the city and then planning to use a cab or Uber to get here."

Then he took off upstairs to his room.

Colette stood there, smiling. Two new matches right here in the inn. "Let's see," she said to herself. "A baby born, a family reunited, and love in the air everywhere. Who would imagine such blessings?"

But even those blessings didn't stop the steady work this place took each day. She got busy again, but later, she had something very important to discuss with her two opinionated sisters.

Chapter 17

She had a bistro table that normally sat in the corner of the library moved to the bay window, so Doc Hinson and his Bridget could see the lights along the curve of the lake. Abigail and Eliza found a pretty white poinsettia and tied a lacy bow around the clay pot, then placed candles everywhere. Along with a crackling fire, they gave the small room a cozy feeling.

"I'd like to have dinner here," Eliza said. "It might even beat eating on my bench in the stables."

"It sure beats the quick meals Jonah and I used to share in the carriage *haus*," Abigail replied. "I sure like my home much better, especially because Jonah is there with me."

"Out in the open," Eliza replied with a grin.

"Mattie and I always ate in the inn kitchen unless we ate at the cottage," Colette said. "I have to admit I like having intimate dinners with my husband. My husband—that has such a nice ring."

"You are still a newlywed," Abigail said. "But I must admit I like saying that, too. My husband."

Colette sighed. "Now, if only the mysterious Bridget actually arrives to enjoy this romantic dinner."

"Gloria has asked to be their waitress," Eliza said. "She loves a *gut* romance."

"Gloria needs a *gut* romance," Colette retorted. "We ought to fancy her up and take her to a frolic."

Abigail rolled her eyes. "Next year, sister. We've got much to do before the clock chimes the New Year."

They got busy preparing tomorrow's meal and making sure their few guests had a light supper for later.

Jack Hinson's romantic dinner was ready to go, the steaks marinating, the potatoes ready to serve, and the salad crisp and fresh. A whole coconut pie sat on the counter in the pantry.

Three hours later there was still no sign of Bridget McCullough. Everyone had orders to let the sisters know when she arrived. If she arrived.

"I haven't been this nervous since we hid Jonah in the carriage *haus*," Abigail admitted. "I hope she'll be here soon. We don't want the food to go to waste."

"Or that handsome doctor to have a broken heart," Gloria said with a note of forced sympathy. She had a bad crush on the *Englisch* doctor.

"She's standing by, if he needs her," Colette whispered as they cleaned rooms and checked the pantry inventory.

Where was Bridget?

Doc Hinson came downstairs and checked at the front desk. "She's still not here," he said to Eliza as she passed by. "This was a bad idea." Shrugging, he went on. "I thought we'd bonded. She's so smart and fun and, well, she's beautiful. Where did I go wrong?"

"You didn't go wrong," Eliza said. "You might have misread her or she might not be ready for such an intense courtship."

She gave him the brief version of her relationship with Levi. "I misunderstood my own feelings long ago. Now I understand completely. We fell in love when we were young, but we had to find our way back to each other as adults."

"I'm tired of adulting," the doctor said. "I guess I'll just pack up tomorrow and head back to work."

"Why does a doctor take a bus anyway?" Eliza asked. "Don't you make a lot of money?"

"I'm a country doctor and I work in a small regional hospital ER. I live near a big Amish community in Ohio. I'm thinking Bridget might not want to be saddled with a man who prefers the simple life."

"Has she told you that?"

"No, but she's a city girl. She grew up in New York, but she works in Idaho at a big law firm."

"Doctors and lawyers can move around," Eliza said. "Besides, aren't you getting ahead of yourself? First you have to continue getting to know each other. And I'm sorry, you still need to be an adult about this."

He laughed. "You're sure wise."

"I had to learn that lesson the hard way," Eliza admitted. "But then, the Amish tend to see simple solutions to problems. At least my *mamm* and *daed* are that way. I hope I can keep my little one safe and give him advice when he arrives in the world."

Dr. Hinson smiled at her. "You look healthy and happy. I think he's going to be just fine."

"Do you deliver babies at your ER?"

"All the time."

He kept glancing at the door. Finally, he said, "I'm sorry for all the fuss. I'll pay for everything. I guess I'm going back to my room."

Eliza felt so bad for the young doctor. "I'll send you a plate up. You still need to eat."

Just then, the front doors burst open, and there stood Bridget in a beautiful red dress and a heavy white coat, her dark brown boots shining with wet snow.

"Jack, I got delayed. An accident on the way to the train terminal." She shook out her long hair. "Then the taxi bringing me the rest of the way got lost."

"You found us," Eliza said. Her sisters came running, both of them smiling and wiping at their eyes.

Jack ran to Bridget and hugged her. "I . . . I thought you'd stood me up."

"Are you kidding?" Bridget said as she took his hands into hers, her leather gloves covering his fingers. "I wanted to be here with you tonight. Nowhere else."

Jack kissed his lady, good and proper.

The sisters busied themselves with bringing in the meal, Gloria volunteering to help with a dreamy smile. When they escorted the couple to their dinner, Bridget gasped and hugged Jack close. "It's beautiful."

"So are you," he said.

And then he motioned the sisters and starstruck Gloria out of the room.

"I feel a bit sad," Eliza told her sisters later when they'd gathered in the master bedroom back at the cottage. "We had a full house at the café again today and it was fun. But seeing Henry so happy with Marcy and that gorgeous doctor with his beautiful new love made me remember the days I dreamed of romance. Things at the inn will slow down now for a while. I kind of enjoyed the chaos and the romance, but my feet are tired."

"They get that way when you're expecting," Abigail reminded her. "How do you feel?"

Eliza rubbed her tummy. "I feel blessed and loved and also a bit terrified."

"That's natural, too," Abigail said. Then she looked at her sisters. "Things have changed around here, for certain sure."

Colette snorted. "Just a tad. This has been a busy Christmastime, no doubt about that." Then she gave them a somber stare. "I have been considering midwifery."

"What?" Eliza's eyes went wide. "Are you sure? You only just helped with one birth, sister."

"*Ja*, and that's why I'm certain sure I might want to train as a midwife," Colette replied. "It was so amazing."

"What about your dream of running the café and kitchen?" Abigail asked.

"I can still do that, same as Mamm has done for years. I'd get called away now and then, but you'll both be here, and we've got extra help now. Edith is only partly retired, so she's usually hanging around anyway."

"Have you discussed this with Matthew?" Eliza asked, sending Abigail a speaking look.

"I haven't. I wanted to see your reactions first, and now I know how you feel. You don't think I can do it, do you?"

"It's not that," Abigail said. "I believe you can do anything if you set your mind to it. But you just got married, and you're still working on your house. Maybe seeing Leah give birth inspired you to do what Mamm has done, but you need to be sure. It's a hard job that requires getting up in the middle of the night in storms or on hot summer days, leaving at a moment's notice. Are you prepared for that?"

"I'm well aware of what's required," Colette said. "And I'll take my time thinking it over. But it's in my head now and in my heart, too. I could be an apprentice to Mamm while I'm taking the courses to learn the skills I need. I think I want to do this."

"Does Mamm know?" Eliza kept rubbing her feet, but her voice was filled with concern.

Colette looked at her big sister. "*Neh*, not yet. I'm going to her next. I just needed to talk to both of you because that's what we do. I hope I can always come to both of you first."

"Always," Abigail said. "Just don't be annoying like you were when we were teens."

"I don't recall being annoying." Colette lifted her head high. "I have matured a bit since those days."

"Haven't we all?" Eliza stood and danced around the room. "I have a husband now."

"Uh, so do we," her sisters said, laughing. Then they all danced around the room.

"We are grown up." Eliza frowned. "I don't miss childhood. Well, maybe a bit."

Abigail stood and stared out the window, toward the carriage *haus*. "How can I miss anything now? I have everything a woman could want."

Eliza stood by her, glancing at the looming stable and barn off in the distance. "I thought my love for horses was strong. Turns out my love of my man is stronger still." She rubbed her tummy. "Add to that, a *kinner* on the way. My cup runneth over."

Colette joined them, her gaze shifting toward the inn. "And I have worked side by side with Mattie for so long, it's completely natural to have him with me now—always."

"Do you get tired of each other?" Eliza asked, a twinkle in her eyes.

"Do you get tired of Levi?" Colette retorted.

"*Neh*." Eliza hugged herself. "Never. He makes me laugh, and he makes me feel safe and content."

Abigail shook her head. "You two—still bickering. But that is the way of it, and yet we will always be sisters."

"Always."

They stood there at the window, looking down on the place they called home, and said their silent prayers, each thankful for the blessings of this past week, the blessings of Christmastime, and the hope that only *kinner* could bring on such a special day.

"How did we become so blessed?" Colette whispered while they watched the soft snow glisten in the moonlight. The world had gone silent and still, full of a gentle peace.

"*Gott's* will, sister," Abigail whispered into the night. "*Gott's* will."

Best Christmas Program Ever

RACHEL J. GOOD

Chapter 1

Tiny flecks of snow peppered the buggy windshield as Emily Flaud rushed toward the Green Valley Farmer's Market. The weather surprised her. Lancaster County rarely got snow in early November.

She flicked the reins. "Faster, Peach!"

If her horse didn't speed up, she'd be late for her first day of work. She'd gotten ready early enough, but with three of their foster children sick and the newest baby screaming for her bottle, Emily couldn't walk out the door and leave Mamm with all the work. Her younger sisters had already headed off for school, so Emily fed and changed the baby and tossed a load of sheets in the propane-powered washer. She wished she'd had time to do more, but she needed this job to help support the family.

The roads grew slippery, and Emily sighed in relief when she reached the market parking lot. After settling Peach in the shelter, she rushed for the employee entrance. Freezing wetness seeped through worn spots in her sneaker soles. Icy needles of snow stung her eyes as she fumbled for the door handle.

Suddenly, the door swung open, knocking her off-balance. She slid in the slush, flailing her arms to stay upright.

"Sorry," a gruff voice said. A man's strong hands reached out to steady her.

Emily blinked to clear the sleet from her eyes and the mush from her brain. Suspenders spanning a muscular chest came into focus first. Then she tilted her head up, up, up to a frowning face above a full reddish beard.

He let go so abruptly, her breathless *danke* ended in an *ach!*

Emily gathered her dignity and stepped over the threshold, her chin held high. But her drenched sneakers had other ideas. She skated past him on the smooth cement floor. To prevent a belly-flop, she clutched a nearby support pole and hugged it until her fluttering pulse slowed. Anyone's nerves would be frayed by two near falls. It had nothing to do with the sparks flowing up her arm ever since that giant grabbed her. Absolutely not. He hadn't even been pleasant. Even worse, he was married.

Although he wasn't looking directly at her, the grim lines in his face had deepened. Had he caught her clumsiness out of the corner of his eye? She'd made such a fool of herself, Emily intended to find out which stand he worked in and avoid him.

Hosea King never wanted to see anyone get hurt, so he couldn't have let her fall. But touching her had started a slow, deep ache in his stone-cold heart. Though he tried, Hosea couldn't shake off the memory of soft arms under his fingers. He could have almost wrapped his hand twice around her small wrists, so delicate and fragile.

As she slid along the aisle, he'd almost rushed after her to rescue her again. To his relief, she grabbed a pole. If he'd been less wary, he could have taken her arm and escorted her to the stand where she worked.

He shook himself to slough off the images and possibilities

his mind raised. Hosea had no time for relationships, no capability for love.

Despite the wind blowing wet flakes into his face and frosting his jacket with icy whiteness, he hesitated before closing the door. No sign of the new employee Daed had hired. With her being older, maybe she'd been afraid to drive in the snow.

Not that he blamed her. He'd learned firsthand the dangers of icy roads. Although horses were generally surefooted, *Englisch* drivers who raced too fast in this weather often slipped and slid across the road. And innocent families paid the price.

Slick roads meant fewer customers. Maybe he'd have enough time to prepare all the holiday cheese trays himself. Still, he could have used the extra help. He hoped this new employee would be dependable. They couldn't go into the holiday season without an assistant now that his brother had moved to Charm to live near his Ohio-born wife's family.

Daed had trained their new worker yesterday while the market was closed, and he'd assured Hosea she was experienced and dependable. She'd worked at Yoder's Restaurant for several years, and the owners recommended her highly. Daed insisted she'd been a quick study, picking up everything quickly.

She needed the work to support her large family. Hosea was happy to help someone in need. Plus, a former waitress and a mother who cared for many children should be able to handle the holiday rush over the next two months. He'd neglected to ask who'd be watching her children while she worked. What if she had to stay home whenever one of them was sick?

Hosea only wished Daed were here today. This morning, his father had complained his arthritis was bothering him. That worried Hosea. Daed never took time off work. Even when he limped with pain or struggled to slice cheese, he gritted his teeth, filled orders, and greeted every customer with a smile.

Well, no time for lollygagging. Hosea had a lot to do today—alone.

That word cut into him. He was alone, not only at work, but in life. Holding that young woman a few minutes ago reminded him of that.

This time of year only increased his pain. Hosea steeled himself before turning around. He'd rather stare out into a blinding snowstorm than face the onslaught of overdone holiday cheer.

All this foolishness grated on him. Not because the Amish didn't decorate for Christmas. Not because so many of the *Englisch* stands had dizzying arrays of Santas, elves, reindeer, lights, and trees. But because this time of year, his loss stabbed him. Little Daniel would have been nine next week . . . if a drunk driver hadn't plowed into his wife's buggy and killed them both.

Hosea smacked a fist into his open palm, but the sting did little to ease his pain. Why did life have to be so unfair? He'd lost the two people he'd loved most. Would this hole in his heart, this deep open wound ever disappear?

Hosea swallowed back his grief and hurried toward his stand. Although he regretted not having the extra help today, maybe he'd be better off alone when he was feeling so down.

Taking cautious baby steps, Emily headed toward Cheese Please. The overhead speakers squealed, then emitted sharp crackles and scritches before bursting into a tinny rendition of "Jingle Bells." Everywhere around her, Christmas decorations bristled from each shop. *Englischers* liked to go all out for Christmas. Emily still couldn't get over holiday décor weeks before Thanksgiving. And outside snow was falling, as if the sky were trying to match the holiday spirit inside.

Although she'd passed these decorations yesterday when she'd come in for training, the market had been closed and the lights had been turned off. This morning, the Amish stands stood out for their modest decorations. A few pine garlands, a Nativity set, or some verses from the Christmas story competed with *ho-ho*ing Santas, flying reindeer, tinselly trees, and blinking lights. A few stands had blue and white streamers, menorahs, or stars of David.

Craning her neck as she inched along carefully, Emily enjoyed the festive air. Her boss had told her yesterday that the market had a Christmas decorating contest every year starting in October. Other stand owners smiled and welcomed her as she passed by—unlike the grouch at the door.

Emily thanked God her boss, Freeman King, was a kind, jolly older man. She'd enjoyed training under him yesterday and couldn't wait to work with him. He seemed he'd be understanding about her being late.

When she reached Cheese Please, it stood empty. Maybe Freeman wouldn't realize she'd been late. She didn't want to enter the stand until he arrived, though, so she stood outside at the counter. To prevent any more mishaps, she propped one elbow on the ledge, hoping it would anchor her. Her toes stung from the slush inside her sneakers, which were leaking icy puddles.

"Sorry, but the market doesn't open for ten more minutes."

Emily turned toward the gruff baritone. Not again. She tried to keep her tone civil as she answered the frowning man who'd steadied her at the employee door. "I know. I'm waiting for Freeman."

"He won't be in today." Hosea averted his eyes from her sweet, cheerful face. A face that reminded him of all he'd lost.

"*Ach*, I thought he'd be training me."

It took a moment for her words to sink in. This was the new employee? Hosea had been expecting an older woman with multiple children. This girl standing before him appeared to be around eighteen or twenty. Hosea's fists knotted. He knew exactly why his *daed* hadn't told him. In fact, Hosea wouldn't have come in today if he'd known about his father's plot.

Both his parents had been hounding him about getting married again. Dodging their suggestions of nice, eligible girls took all of his strength and sorely taxed his self-control. He honored his parents and tried to follow their advice in all areas of his life but this one. His *daed* and *mamm* had been married for more than forty years. They couldn't possibly understand he'd never heal from his loss. Never again would he let another woman get that close.

Hosea shook his head.

The girl stared at him, wide-eyed and worried. "But I won't be able to handle everything by myself."

"Don't worry. You won't have to. I plan to do more than my share of work."

Her eyebrows drew together in a puzzled frown. A second later, light dawned in her eyes. "You work here too?"

"*Jah*, I do. I also own the stand." Hosea regretted his snotty tone. He'd not only sounded mean; he'd sounded prideful.

"But I thought I'd be working for Freeman."

She didn't say it, but Hosea read between the lines as clearly as if she'd spoken: *If I'd known I'd be working for a grouch like you, I never would have taken this job.*

Chapter 2

Although Hosea suspected she was too polite to say something like that aloud, he was pretty sure she'd been thinking it.

That made him ashamed of his impoliteness. He'd never treated anyone this unkindly before—even the women who'd chased him after his wife died. He'd thanked them for the meals and let them down gently. Now here he was . . . being nasty to a stranger. *Neh*, not a stranger. His new employee. It wasn't her fault she brought up all his old pain.

He dipped his head to show his remorse. "I'm sorry. Will you forgive me?"

She brightened. "Of course. And *danke* for helping me when I slipped." Then she held out her hand. "I'm Emily Flaud."

Reluctant to touch that softness again, Hosea hesitated, but only for an instant.

Hurt flared in her eyes, and she lifted her chin. "I take it you aren't happy with your *daed*'s choice. I can"—she swallowed hard—"try to find another job."

He thrust out his hand. "*Neh*, don't do that. I'm sorry. I was preoccupied thinking about something else." *My sudden and unexpected attraction to you. Which reminds me of the agony of losing someone you love.*

Her clipped "I see" as she shook his hand assured Hosea she'd have no interest in him after she discovered he was a widower. Why did that disappoint him?

He braced himself, but a spark seared his arm when their hands connected. Hosea let go as soon as he could. "I, um, I'm Hosea King. Welcome to Cheese Please." Hosea tried not to wince. He'd been far from welcoming. To make up for it, he curved his lips up into a semblance of a smile.

Her face creased into worried lines. Was she concerned about working for him?

"It's almost eight," Emily said so softly Hosea could barely hear her over the blare of "Rudolph, the Red-Nosed Reindeer."

He bobbed his head, strode to the stand, opened the low half-door, and motioned for her to enter. She skidded along.

"Maybe you should take off your shoes," he suggested after they both went in.

Her eyes widened. "What about the health inspector? We had strict rules at the restaurant so we wouldn't break any laws."

"Nobody can see your feet here."

Emily chewed on her lower lip, not looking convinced.

"Seems like going barefoot would be less of a hazard than slipping and falling."

"I guess." Reluctantly, she bent and untied her sneakers. Then she stole a glance at him and seemed to be reluctant to remove them.

He busied himself with getting out stacks of party-sized plastic trays and lids, but he studied her out of the corner of his eye. Had he embarrassed her by insisting she go barefoot? Amish women often went barefoot. Maybe it was the restaurant rules that bothered her.

She took off her sneakers, held them so he couldn't see them, and looked around.

"You can put them under the table." Hosea pointed to the low shelf below where he stored the huge boxes of plastic wrap, waxed butcher paper, and stacks of smaller plastic containers.

Emily bent and shoved her shoes underneath, but not before Hosea spied a few quarter-sized holes in the tread that had worn all the way through.

"Looks like you could use a new pair of shoes, especially in this weather." The minute he said it, Hosea regretted it. He hadn't meant to sound critical. He'd gone from being mean to being judgmental. From the moment he'd encountered her, she'd thrown him off-balance, but he couldn't blame her for his awkwardness or his unkindness.

Emily kept her head bowed and pushed her shoes farther back, out of view. She mumbled, "Not yet. Maybe after we pay off a few more bills."

Heat flushed up Hosea's face and across his cheeks. Now he'd embarrassed her. From the looks of her shoes, she definitely needed a job. That made him curious.

"Daed said you worked at a restaurant downtown." Wouldn't she make more money there than here? Maybe not. Some people didn't tip. "What made you decide to come to work at the market?"

"The restaurant went out of business."

"I see." He should have thought of that. Many restaurants hadn't weathered the loss of business the past few years. Perhaps she hadn't made much after all.

Gideon Hartzler strode by the stand, keys jangling, interrupting Hosea's musing.

"*Ach!* The market's opening, and I haven't even filled the cases yet." Hosea had never been this distracted in his life.

"What do you want me to do? Your *daed* showed me where everything goes in the cases. I can help you set up."

Hosea sent her a grateful glance and then wished he hadn't. His heart hitched—only a little—but enough to be disturbing. From now on, he'd have to avoid looking in her direction.

He cleared his throat. "Could you do this one?" He patted the smallest one on the end. "We'll have to hurry."

Emily rushed to the refrigerator in her stocking feet. At least he didn't have to worry about her falling, but everywhere she went, she left wet footprints. Dainty footprints. Footprints that reminded him of—

Hosea slammed down that door in his mind and busied himself with avoiding collisions, setting out cheeses, and forcing his attention away from Emily. She finished the first case and headed for the longer one he was working on as customers streamed to their end of the market. He gave her a wide berth as they passed each other. He didn't want to chance bumping into her.

A woman wrapped in a hooded wool coat approached the counter. "I'm here for my cheese tray."

He groaned internally. If only he'd fixed the trays instead of questioning Emily. "I'm sorry, Ms. Marshall. It'll be ready in ten minutes."

She huffed. "Freeman promised it would be ready when the market opened."

"We got a late start today, but I'll fix it quickly."

"I don't want a rushed job. I expect my order to be treated with the utmost care."

"I promise I'll do that."

Ms. Marshall stood tapping her foot as Hosea raced to the refrigerator, danced around Emily, and piled several kinds of cheeses into his arms. He dumped them on the cutting table and began hacking up cheese cubes, while Emily rapidly placed cheeses in the refrigerated cases.

"What can I do to help?" Emily's quiet question broke his concentration.

He lifted his head, surprised she'd finished so quickly. "Could you cube the pepper jack so I can cut a wedge of brie?"

When she nodded, Hosea headed for the case to get the large wheel of brie. He slid the door open and stopped. No brie. Emily must not have gotten it from the refrigerator. But when he checked, all the cheeses had been set out.

"Emily, have you seen the brie?"

She pointed her knife to the case beside the cash register. Hosea sighed. She'd put it in the wrong place. He should have watched her more closely. They didn't get as many orders for brie as for cheddar and Swiss, so it made no sense to keep it close to where customers ordered.

In fact, now that he studied the layout, he realized she'd laid it out perfectly, except that everything was in reverse order. He had no time to fix the layout now, but he'd have to show her the correct way to do it and explain why.

As he set the brie on the opposite side of the table from her, Emily arranged the last of the cheese cubes on the tray. "Do you want me to cut this too?" She motioned to the Havarti.

"*Jah, danke.*" Hosea bent his head and concentrated on cutting an exact wedge. Both to make sure Ms. Marshall's tray looked perfect and to avoid looking at Emily.

Eleven minutes later, he handed Ms. Marshall's tray to her and discounted it ten percent to make up for the lateness. Then he turned to Emily, keeping his attention on her feet. Even they proved diverting.

"We, umm, need to rearrange the cheeses."

"Didn't I do it right?" her voice quavered. "I tried to memorize the order when your *daed* showed me."

The hurt in her words made Hosea feel as if he'd tromped on a tiny kitten's tail. "You got them all correct, except you need to flip them. If you start at the far end and follow your list, you'll have them in their proper places."

"Oh." Emily hung her head. "I'll fix them."

He almost offered to help her but stopped himself in time. "Great. I'll get started on the other cheese trays."

After she finished, he checked her work. Only two needed to be switched. "There, now it's perfect. Just so you know, we keep the cheeses people request most near the register. That saves a lot of steps."

"I see." Her face had lost its earlier smile.

Hosea suspected his attitude had caused that change. He didn't want to crush her lively, eager expression. He vowed to be kinder and treat her as nicely as he did all his customers.

One thing he could do to start was make sure she had safe shoes to work in. While she waited on a customer, he took a piece of a cardboard carton from the trash and bent down behind the table to trace the outline of her shoes. Then he slipped it into the drawer where he kept his paperwork.

After he washed his hands, he went to slice the cheese the *Englischer* ordered. He wasn't about to let Emily use the slicer. It was much too hazardous.

As he'd suspected, business was slower than usual, giving them a lot more time to get caught up on the cheese trays. Emily proved to be a steady, careful worker. From time to time, she lifted her head as if for approval. His gut twisted as she tilted her head to one side like a little bird begging for small crumbs. He tried to say something positive without looking directly at her.

But even with his head down, he had to force himself to focus on slicing cheese cubes or arranging trays. Otherwise, he'd keep staring at her pretty hands moving so gracefully. If he let them, her dainty fingers could be a terrible distraction.

And he'd break the one rule Daed always emphasized: Never,

ever let your mind or attention wander when cutting cheese. It leads to accidents.

Unfortunately, Emily working here had put Hosea on a collision course for multiple accidents—not only physical, but also of the heart.

Chapter 3

Emily left early on Thursday morning and braved icy roads to be sure she arrived before Hosea. Because the market stayed closed on Wednesdays, she'd done as many of today's chores as she could and took over caring for the sick little ones to give Mamm a day off. Emily also premade tonight's supper casserole so her sisters could stick it in the oven and have more time to help their mother.

Tired from her busy day yesterday, Emily wasn't looking forward to a long day of work. The market remained open from early morning into the evening hours. That was bad enough, but remembering Hosea's attitude toward her on Tuesday set her on edge. Nothing like sliding into a man's arms the first time you met and then messing up the whole cheese display. Today, Emily intended to erase her first bad impression.

Maybe he'd warm up once he saw how hard she worked. She arrived an hour before the market opened. After wiping the smudged glass on all the refrigerated display cases, she put everything inside in the case in the correct places. She mopped the floor, scrubbed the cutting table, and picked up the stack of orders for the day. She'd completed two party trays by the time Hosea showed up.

His eyes widened when he walked in. A gleam of appreciation glowed in them before he blocked it and lowered his head. It seemed like it upset him to look at her. Maybe it bothered him that his *daed* had hired an employee when Hosea now owned the business. Had he planned to hire someone else?

Fists clenched at his sides, Hosea crinkled the plastic bag he held in one hand. "Good morning. You're here early." His words came out as stiff as his back.

Emily wished he'd unbend a little, relax, and smile sometimes. But the tenseness in his face and the set of his jaw made that unlikely. With a soft sigh, she went back to work.

But he stopped beside her. "I see you have on the same sneakers."

She wasn't about to admit they were her only pair. She had black shoes she wore to church, but they'd never do for standing all day and evening. He seemed to be waiting for an answer, so she said, "*Jah*, I do."

He cleared his throat. "I thought you might be more comfortable in different ones."

Two sides warred inside her. The proud side wanted to throw back her head, glare into his eyes, and say, "I happen to like these shoes." But her conscience warned her against *hochmut*, so she opted for humility. "I'm sure I would."

He thrust the plastic bag at her abruptly. "Here. These should be the right size."

What? She opened the bag and gazed down at black sneakers. "I can't accept—"

"Take them," he said gruffly. "They're not new."

"Even used ones cost money. I'll pay you back." Although it would put a dent in the money she could turn over to Mamm.

"These didn't cost me anything. They are"—he swallowed hard—"they, umm, were . . . my wife's."

Emily didn't like being thought of as a charity case, but she couldn't reject his offer without being rude. Staring down at the floor, she forced out, "Please thank her for them."

"I-I can't. She—she's dead." His voice came out harsh, but waves of pain radiated from him, weighing down the air between them with the heaviness of his despair.

Her head jerked up. "I'm sorry. I didn't know." She almost cried at the raw agony in his eyes before he looked away.

He bobbed his head once as if to acknowledge her words, then turned his back. Before walking around the table to hang his coat and hat on a hook, he choked out, "I, um, don't want you to get hurt."

"*Danke.*" For caring. "And *danke* for the shoes."

Emily bent and slipped off her worn sneakers. Then she stuck her feet into the ones Hosea had given her. They were a bit tight, but if she laced them loosely, they only pinched slightly on the sides of her toes. The canvas would give after she wore them for a while, and she'd wet and stretch them tonight after she got home.

Since Hosea had been kind enough to bring them for her, she wasn't about to complain. And they'd be better than leaky sneakers.

She'd been so engrossed with the shoes it took a while for the meaning behind Hosea's words to sink in. *He's a widower.* At least now she wouldn't feel so guilty for her automatic reaction to his touch when he'd steadied her arms. She'd closed her mind to those thoughts as soon as she'd noticed he had a beard.

Now some of them flooded back, but Emily still tamped them down. She'd been hurt by her recent breakup with her boyfriend, but even more off-putting—Hosea disliked her. No point in getting interested in someone who'd rejected her before he even knew her. Although it still hurt, it was better to have the rejection happen right up front rather than after three years together.

Moisture blurred Hosea's eyes as he hung his coat on a peg next to Emily's black cloak and bonnet. His wife's used to hang in the same spot. And now he'd have to see that every day as well as her sneakers on someone else's feet.

Nobody would ever know what it cost him to measure those sneakers and put them in the plastic bag last night. He'd agonized over bringing them. Twice, he'd almost returned them to the closet.

But a quiet nudge from God and a dream of Alana confirmed he'd made the right choice. As he slept last night, Alana reassured him she'd be happy that someone else was using them. That was so like her. She also would have insisted he give away her clothes to someone in need instead of hanging on to them.

But clearing out her things would leave a huge gap in the closet and in his life. And it would mean accepting that she was really, truly gone and would never come back.

"Hark, the Herald Angels Sing" rang out from overhead, startling him from his reverie. He needed to get ready for the day. He squeezed his eyes shut and rubbed them with the backs of his fists. Not that he'd been crying. His eyes were just a little blurry.

He took a deep breath and prepared himself to talk to Emily civilly today. He'd prayed about it last night, asking God to guide his words and guard his feelings. Gathering his courage and God's grace, Hosea stepped around to the opposite side of the table from her.

"You don't have to come in so early." As soon as he said it, he realized how she might take it. "I mean, you don't need to be here until seven thirty." He wasn't sure that made things better.

Emily hung her head. "I wanted to make up for the things I did wrong on Tuesday. You don't have to pay me extra or anything if that's what you're worried about."

That hadn't entered his mind. "*Neh*, I'm happy to pay for whatever hours you worked. And you didn't do anything wrong."

The worry in her voice made him ashamed of his behavior on her first day. She must have gotten that impression from his grumpiness. He forced himself to compliment the things she'd done right. Then he added, "You've done quite well for your first time here."

The smile that blossomed on her face took his breath away.

To distract himself, he reached for the orders. "You've finished a lot already."

She had two completed and was working on a third. Although he appreciated it, niggling doubts crept in. What if she'd mixed them up or gotten something wrong? It was only her second day. But he didn't want to question her or hurt her feelings.

After sending up a quick prayer to be diplomatic, he reached for the receipts. "I'll tape these to each order and then refrigerate them." That way, he could make sure she hadn't made any mistakes.

"*Ach*, I'm sorry. I should have done that."

He hastened to reassure her. "It's fine. You've done the hardest part."

A sliver of a smile peeked out, and Hosea had an urge to make it bloom into sunshine again. But that might be too dangerous.

Instead, he picked up the order forms and stacked the trays to carry to the refrigerator. Once there, he matched them with the correct receipts. To his relief, she'd gotten them all right.

"Good job," he said when he returned. This time, he kept

his eyes averted. Watching for her smiles could become addicting.

The overhead speaker blared a lively rendition of "We Wish You a Merry Christmas" as Gideon strode by to open the doors. Hosea kept one eye out for customers while he helped Emily prepare more party trays.

He stopped midcut. "I just remembered. I forgot to put out sample trays on Tuesday."

"I can do that. What cheeses do you want on them?"

"We always set out one of the cheddars because they're the most popular. And for our gourmet customers, maybe a little of the Robiola Bosina. It's expensive, but some of them will like it. People like fancy cheeses for holiday platters."

A woman headed for the counter, and Hosea hurried over, calling over his shoulder above the loud racket of "Grandma Got Run Over by a Reindeer," which had just started, "Please add a few water crackers to the plates and set out some toothpicks. Sample trays are on the lower shelf near the refrigerator."

While Hosea tended to several customers, Emily scurried about fixing eye-catching sampler plates. When she returned, she'd even added a touch of the parsley and a few of the peppermints they used to decorate the party trays. The displays looked festive.

"*Danke*," he said as she arranged everything on the higher counter beside him. "It looks nice." He quickly turned his attention back to another woman, who had ordered several sliced cheeses.

As Hosea opened the case, the sparkling glass caught his eye. He'd been emotionally drained the other day, so he'd gone straight home without doing all his usual cleaning and straightening. Not only were the cases pristine, but the cheeses and their price tags also had been lined up neatly. Emily must have done all this. She was quite a treasure. He'd have to thank her for this too. If he wasn't careful, he might end up appreciating her a little too much.

Emily's heart warmed at the appreciative look in Hosea's eyes as she set the sample trays on the counter. His gaze hadn't been directed at her, only at the display, but that was a start. Maybe in time, he'd come to appreciate her and direct a smile her way. A genuine smile, one in which he met her eyes instead of staring at the floor and mumbling his thanks.

Still, one step at a time. Over the years, Emily had learned how to cajole shy or ornery foster children into blossoming and becoming loving members of their family. Maybe she could use the same techniques with her boss. Not that Hosea was a child, but he reacted with the same avoidance and prickliness the children who came to her house displayed. And when he'd given her the sneakers, he'd revealed the same hidden anguish.

She resolved to soften that outer protective shell so she could get to know his real inner personality. It took patience and persistence and a thick skin. You had to let their brusqueness roll off you and not get offended. Emily always reminded herself she had no idea the pain each child had been through. That went for adults too.

For now, she'd accept Hosea the way he was. Already he'd shown some signs of softening. Several times today, he'd complimented or thanked her. That was a great start, even if he avoided looking directly at her. And bringing the sneakers showed he had a caring and generous heart. Knowing that, she could wait until he dropped his wariness and learned to trust her.

Chapter 4

As the sun warmed the icy roads and melted the last of the snow, business at the market grew brisk. Emily did her best to be helpful by working on party trays between filling orders and ringing up customers. So far, she'd made no mistakes. Or at least, Hosea hadn't pointed any out. And he'd thanked her for cleaning and organizing the cases.

He'd even flashed her a sympathetic glance when she'd encountered a dissatisfied *Englischer*, who complained about everything. Emily had gone out of her way to satisfy the grumpy lady, and to Emily's surprise, the woman thanked her when she left.

Hosea leaned over and whispered, "You did a *wunderbar* job with her. She's not easy."

"*Danke.*" Emily turned away to hide her grin. *Jah!* She'd done it. If she'd been at home, she would have given a fist pump like some of their foster kids did when they succeeded. Hosea had given her the first spontaneous compliment. Emily's spirits soared.

By midafternoon, the sample trays needed to be refilled. She cut more cheddar cheese cubes, arranged them on the almost empty tray, and set it back on the counter. As she turned away, a small, grubby hand reached over the counter and grabbed a fistful, knocking over the toothpick container.

Startled, Emily spun around. A scrawny *Englisch* boy of about nine, wearing tattered clothing, ducked behind the nearest post. He glanced around to see if anyone noticed, and she pretended not to be paying attention, but she kept an eye on him as he shared more than half the handful with a small girl in a tattered dress and sweater. With their strong resemblance, they must be brother and sister. Neither of the children were dressed for this cold snap.

Once they'd finished the cheese, the boy pointed to the post as if indicating his sister should stay hidden. Then he sidled over to the open containers at Nick's candy stand and glanced around. His hand snaked out, and he snitched a fistful of caramels and stuffed them in his pocket. He moved on to the next jar.

Emily rushed from the stand. She didn't want him to get in trouble.

As she came up behind him, his sister squealed, "Jax, look out."

He jerked his hand back and whirled around. When he saw Emily looming over him, he leaned to the right but darted to the left. Used to dealing with many foster children's antics, she'd anticipated his ploy and moved in the correct direction to head him off. Before he could escape, she set a hand on his shoulder and held him in place.

His sister launched herself at Emily, yelling, "Let him alone." Her small fists pummeled Emily from behind, but mostly got tangled in the fabric of Emily's skirt. "Let go."

Emily tried to reassure the little girl. "I'm not hurting him."

When the boy glanced past Emily's swishing skirt at his sister, the worry in his eyes increased. "No, don't. Get back there," he ordered, motioning to the post with his chin. "You gonna get in trouble. She gonna snatch you too."

"I'm not trying to snatch either of you." Emily squatted in front of the boy so they were at eye level. "But you do need to pay—"

Trying to look innocent, he blustered, "That there cheese is free. Says so right on the sign."

"You're right. It is, but the candy isn't, Jax."

The boy lifted his chin and shot Emily a defiant glare. "That ain't my name."

"Is too." His sister opened her mouth to say more but stopped dead at his *don't-you-dare-snitch* glare. "He's . . . he's, um . . ."

"David," he supplied. "I'm David." He gave his sister a warning look. "Rose, get on back over there."

A confused look on her face, his sister swiveled her head around. "Ain't nobody else here."

Jax squeezed his eyes shut for a second. Then he stared directly at his sister and flicked a hand in the direction of the post. "*Rose.*" He drew out the name a little to emphasize it. "'Member?"

Light dawned in her eyes, followed by a flicker of fear. She clapped a hand to her mouth. With a brief nod, she scurried behind the post and peered out.

"I'm not going to hurt him," Emily promised her. "We just need to pay for the candy."

"I ain't got no candy."

Emily's steady gaze showed she was waiting for the truth. When he lowered his eyes and refused to respond, she asked gently, "How many caramels do you have in your pocket?"

He hung his head and shuffled his feet.

"Pull them out and let's check." She kept her voice soft, but firm.

Reluctantly, he dug into his pocket and held out the handful without meeting her eyes.

"Is that all of them?"

When he nodded, she reached into her own pocket and counted out some change. "Take that over to the counter and pay for the candy."

"Huh?" He studied her suspiciously.

"Give the money to Nick"—she gestured toward the man in the rainbow-striped apron working behind the counter—"and show him the candy you're buying."

Jax blinked. "You giving me money?"

Emily smiled at him. "*Jah.* I mean yes. Yes, I am."

Eyeing her over his shoulder, Jax headed to the counter and paid. He returned with a spring in his step. "Thank you," he said shyly. "You're nice." Then he hurried over to his sister and shared the caramels.

Emily should get back to work, but something about the children called to her. She and Mamm had cared for many neglected and abandoned children over the years, and these two matched that familiar profile.

"Chew slow," Jax told his sister through a mouthful of sticky candy. "Last longer."

These scrawny and unkempt children tugged at her heart. The way they were devouring those candies, she suspected they hadn't eaten in a while. If they'd come with an adult, they'd gotten separated. She could at least request an announcement. And someone should stay with them until an adult came to claim them.

Emily knelt in front of them. "We should find your mom."

Immediately, the little girl backed away and flattened herself against the pillar, but the boy drew himself up straight. "We don't need no help. Ma's coming back soon."

His sister yelped. Eyes round with fear, she stared at her brother.

He squeezed her hand and whispered, "It's all right. She isn't really." He must have thought he'd spoken too quietly for Emily to overhear, but she had.

"Ma said to meet by the candy." His shuffling feet and the shiftiness in his eyes warned Emily he was lying.

When she studied him with the penetrating gaze she used to convince young children to confess, he thrust out his chin. "You ain't got to worry none 'bout us."

But Emily did. The girl's reaction to the word *Mom* affirmed what Emily suspected. Not only neglect, but possibly abuse.

She needed to call Children's Services. Their usual social worker, Millie, would know what to do. But Emily didn't want to alarm the children.

The aroma from the barbecued chicken wafted all around them. Fixing her eyes on the girl, Emily made a show of sniffing the air. "Umm, that chicken smells good, doesn't it? I'd like some. Are you hungry?"

The little girl nodded. She stared pleadingly at Emily until her brother grabbed her arm and tugged her back.

"Viol—" he whispered fiercely, then stopped abruptly, and corrected himself. "Rose, don't take nothing from strangers."

"She gave us candy. She's nice."

"I'm Emily." She thrust out her hand. "Are you Violet?"

Tangled blond curls bobbed up and down as Violet stared at Emily with adoration.

"No, you ain't." Her brother elbowed in front of her. "Her name's Rose. Rose, um, Miller."

"Oh, that's right. You did tell me that." Emily stood, brushed off her skirt, and held out her hand.

Violet rushed over and clung to it while Jax-David glared at his sister's mutiny.

Emily smiled at him. "And you said you're David, right?"

Some of the bluster leaked out of him. "Yeah." But he didn't look her in the eyes when he answered.

Another telltale sign.

Figuring he wouldn't deign to hold her hand even if she weren't a stranger, Emily beckoned for him to follow them.

He planted his feet. "Where you going?"

"Over there." She waved to the cheese stand, where Hosea stood with a long line of customers.

Ach! So much for making a good impression today. Without saying a word or asking permission to leave, she'd run off and left him to handle all the work. And now she was bringing two bedraggled children into his stand. Emily felt terrible, but she had no choice.

She smiled down at Violet. "Would you like to see inside the stand where we keep the cheese?"

"Yeth," Violet said around the thumb she'd thrust into her mouth.

Out of the corner of her eye, Emily caught a blaze of curiosity in Jax-David's eyes. He sidled up next to his sister and gently removed her thumb. "Yer too big for that."

"How old are you?" Emily asked.

Violet stared longingly at her wet thumb, but lowered it. "Six."

"You are big."

Her brother scowled as Violet beamed.

"And your brother is very grown up." Emily hoped the comment might soften Jax.

He did relax enough to let his lips curve into a semi-smile, then thought better of it, and replaced it with a scowl.

"How old are you?" Emily asked him.

He pinched his mouth tight.

"He's almost—"

Jax growled deep in his throat, and his sister snapped her mouth shut. Emily would get no more information from Violet unless she got her alone.

"You know," Emily said casually, testing for a reaction, as they accompanied her to the stand, "I can help you find your mom. We could have them make an announcement to let her know you're waiting here or . . ."

Violet pulled her hand from Emily's and cowered behind her brother. The terror on the small girl's face tore at Emily's heart, and she regretted frightening them.

Jax's eyes filled with panic. He glanced around wildly as if searching for an escape. Before he could dart off, Emily clamped a hand on his shoulder. If their mother truly was here, both of them dreaded seeing her. But judging by their slush-soaked shoes and ravenous hunger, they were runaways.

Jax twisted in her grip, trying to break free. Then a crafty look flickered in his eyes. "We don't need no help ta find her. We's supposed ta wait here." He reached for his sister's hand. "I know where she is." His voice rang with certainty, but his words were edged with desperation. "Let me go. I ken take Vi—Rose right to her."

"It's all right," Emily said, trying to soothe him. "Why don't we get you something to eat while you wait?"

Violet's face relaxed, and Jax stopped wriggling. He shot Emily a suspicious glance as if he suspected a trap.

"Would you like some more cheese while I go get the chicken?" She'd pay Hosea back for whatever they ate.

Their eyes lit up, but Jax dragged his heels as if uncertain whether or not to trust her. But hunger overcame his reluctance.

Hosea had his back to them as Emily opened the half-door into the stand. Both children stared around them, eyes huge, too fascinated to protest when she carried the one chair and a low stepladder to an out-of-the-way corner and waved for them to sit.

"Can yous eat all them cheeses?" Violet's hushed words revealed her awe.

Although Freeman had told Emily to help herself to a bit of cheese for her meals, so far, she hadn't taken advantage of it. She smiled at Violet. "I don't eat it. I only sell it."

Jax shook his head. "Ain't a good idea ta eat that much cheese, Vi. Make yer belly sick."

"You're right," Emily agreed. "But you can have some of it. I'll be right back with a snack."

She hurried to the refrigerator and took out the block of cheddar she'd used to fill the sample trays. Carrying that and a box of crackers along with an empty sample tray, she returned to the cutting table. After slicing and arranging cheese cubes on the tray, she added four crackers for each of them. That should ward of hunger pangs and keep them busy until she returned.

"Here." Emily handed the plate to Jax. "I know you'll share these with your sister while I get the chicken."

Jax had stuffed his mouth too full to answer, but he passed the plate to his sister.

"I won't be long," Emily promised. "Hosea will watch out for you." At least she hoped he would. "Stay right here until I get back."

Guilt nagged at her when she noticed the long lines waiting for Hosea. She hadn't been a good employee this afternoon, but surely once Hosea understood the children's situation, like any Amishman, he'd be glad to help. Youngsters' needs took first priority in an emergency.

Hosea wiped his brow with the back of his wrist. He'd been racing back and forth trying to fill orders as quickly as possible, but the line seemed to grow every time he turned around. If only Daed were here. And where in the world was Emily?

The last he'd seen of her, she'd been bent down talking to two children. He'd turned away rapidly. He couldn't handle any more strain.

He leaned far over the counter to hand change to a young

woman in a wheelchair. As he stood up, a breathless "Hosea?" made him jump and bang his elbow. Emily's voice so close to his ear unnerved him.

"I'm so sorry," she said. "I didn't mean to startle you."

He yanked his gaze from her contrite brown eyes before he got lost in them. Thank goodness, he had a lot of people waiting, so he had no time to focus on her.

Her voice low, she rushed out words. "I need to make an emergency phone call, but I'll be right back. I'll explain then. And I'll get back to helping you. I won't take a supper break to make up for all this time."

Hosea might not need her then. He needed her now. But if she had an emergency, he couldn't ask her to stay and help. With a quick chin tilt, he gave her permission to leave.

"One more thing." Emily trained pleading eyes on him. "Could you keep an eye on those two? I think they've run away from home, so we need to keep them here until I can get help." She gestured toward the back corner of the stand where two children sat gobbling down cheese cubes.

Hosea's chest clenched tighter than a fist. *Please, God, don't make me go through this. Especially not today.* "I-I can't."

But Emily didn't hear him, she'd already flounced away.

Hosea stared after her in shock. First, his new employee took off suddenly, leaving him stuck with all the customers. Then she returned with two children in tow and left them here while she disappeared to make phone calls. Not only that, she expected him to keep an eye on the two runaways to make sure they didn't escape.

He had enough grounds to fire her. And this time, he'd pick his own worker. If Daed had selected this girl to encourage Hosea to marry again, he'd made a poor choice. What employee ignored her duties and saddled someone else with extra responsibilities? What kind of a wife and mother would she be?

But that wasn't what upset him the most. He couldn't bear

to look in the children's direction. The minute he'd caught sight of that young boy, it had ripped Hosea's heart out of his chest.

Although the bedraggled boy wasn't Amish, looking at him sent a stabbing reminder through Hosea of the wife and son he'd lost four years ago. He couldn't bear to relive that experience. And today of all days. Every year, he struggled to make it through this day, to hold himself together, to wall off the pain. It took every ounce of his inner strength. Today would have been Daniel's birthday.

Emily didn't realize what she'd done. She'd twisted a knife in the raw wound in Hosea's soul.

Chapter 5

Emily found a quiet corner and pulled her cell phone from her pocket. Grateful Millie had insisted Emily and her *mamm* needed phones for emergencies with the foster children, Emily speed-dialed Millie.

As soon as the social worker picked up, Emily explained the situation and relayed what little information she had. "Boy, maybe eight or nine, called himself David, but his sister called him Jax. Girl age six. Real name seems to be Violet. Brother calls her Rose."

"Any chance you got a last name?"

"*Neh*. Sorry. The boy claimed their last name is Miller, but he hesitated before saying it, so it's likely fake."

"Not much to go on, but give me their descriptions. I'll check for missing person reports." Once Millie had jotted all the information down, she thanked Emily. "Can you keep an eye on them while I check this out?"

"Of course." Emily hoped to find out more about the children—and to feed them.

"I appreciate it." Millie sighed. "Most likely Children's Services will take them out to your house anyway."

As soon as Emily hung up, she bought chicken barbecue, fries, and applesauce at Hartzler's. Then she hurried back to the cheese stand, unsure how Hosea would feel about having two children underfoot the rest of the evening.

Jax cast a wary eye on the food bags, but Violet tore into hers. Then he gobbled his. They ate like they were starving. And when she handed them water bottles from her lunch, they gulped them down. How long had they gone hungry and thirsty?

Now that she had them settled, she needed to make things right with Hosea. "I'm so sorry for leaving you with all the work." She handed him the third bag of chicken barbecue. "I got this is for you. I can take over so you can have a break."

Hosea's face darkened like a thundercloud about to burst into storm, and Emily braced for a tempest.

Ever since Emily had pointed to the children, raging pain had swirled inside Hosea, until it reached the point of unbearable. The bag Emily offered as a peace offering and her soft, gentle words pierced him. Why did she always throw him off? Make him want to run a finger down her cheek, to—?

Stop it! Concentrate on something else.

Hosea gritted his teeth and forced himself to deal with the other problem he faced. "Could you take the children elsewhere?" He regretted the harshness of his tone, but keeping his eyes averted hadn't stopped the longing to touch her. And it couldn't assuage the agony flooding through him at the thought of the boy.

"But—but they need help. The social worker is trying to find their parents. Where can I take them?" Emily sounded desperate.

"I don't know. Anywhere but here." Hosea squeezed his

eyes shut to stop them burning. Nine years ago today, he'd been the happiest man in the world. He'd held his son in his arms for the first time. His wife, exhausted and wan, had beamed up at him.

Hosea had prayed to be the man God wanted him to be, so he could model godly living for his precious boy. A boy snatched too soon from this world. He reminded himself over and over it had been God's will, but it didn't stop waves of grief from washing over him whenever he thought of all he'd lost.

And now, this boy the same age as Daniel was rubbing salt into Hosea's open wounds. To add to his distress, the girl appeared to be about five—the age Daniel had been when Hosea lost him.

"Hosea, what's wrong?" Emily's voice held a note of alarm.

"Nothing," he mumbled. But that wasn't true. He shouldn't have lied to her. Maybe if she understood his reasons, she'd take the children somewhere else and leave him alone.

Emily couldn't accept that. Not when Hosea's face had crumpled in distress. "Something's the matter. Are you upset about me not working?"

"*Jah*, but it's not that. It's—" He stopped dead and seemed to be searching for words. "Never mind. You can go home now if you want and take the children with you."

"You're firing me?" She deserved it, but what would she tell Mamm? With so many places closing, jobs were hard to find.

"Not right now."

What did that mean? He'd fire her tomorrow? "I'll take the children with me." She glanced over her shoulder to be sure Jax and Violet weren't listening. Then she lowered her voice. "I can leave them with Mamm and come back for the rest of the evening if you want."

"Up to you."

He didn't sound too enthusiastic, but Emily couldn't let him face all the customers alone. She gathered the children and rushed them to the buggy. Jax balked at first, but when he saw the horse, he was thrilled. Violet was frightened by the bumping in the buggy, so she was relieved to climb out at Emily's house.

Emily drew Mamm aside and rushed through an explanation. "I need to get back to work, but I'll call Millie to let her know the children are with you." Then she hurried back to the market.

The call with Millie proved to be disappointing. No missing person reports had been filed, but a school secretary had requested a welfare check for two children, Jax and Violet Wilson, who'd missed several days of school with no call-in.

Then Millie recounted the worst details: "The police spotted a possible meth lab at the trailer and have gotten a search warrant. The parents have priors for drugs as well as child neglect and abuse."

Emily sucked in a breath. *Poor kids.* They'd probably be staying with her and Mamm for a while.

Rush hour traffic delayed Emily's return, so she sprinted to the stand and took the next customer in line. Hosea's grateful glance and his half-eaten meal revealed he'd been busy the whole time she was gone.

He leaned toward her. "A lot of customers want to order holiday trays." He handed her the receipt book beside his chicken bag. "If you could take those orders, we'll get through things faster."

She nodded, and Hosea made the announcement over "Silver Bells." Quite a few people stepped out of line and headed for Emily. She wrote so many orders, her hand cramped, but soon the crowd thinned.

During a lull, Hosea turned in her direction. As usual, he avoided looking directly at her. "Look, Emily, I'm sorry for how I acted earlier. I didn't mean to be rude or unkind, it's just that"—he swallowed hard—"today would have been my son's ninth birthday."

Would have been? His son must have died. Maybe with his wife?

Emily's heart went out to him. "I'm sorry. That has to be hard." She started to reach out, but her conscience arrested her hand before she touched his arm. He might not take it in the way she intended—as a simple gesture of support.

Really, Emily? That's all you want to do? Just comfort him?

She'd been trying to ignore her attraction since he'd taken her arms to prevent her from falling and also when he'd given her the sneakers, but she hadn't been successful. Sympathizing with him only made it harder. She almost missed Hosea's next words.

"Seeing a boy the same age as Daniel . . ." He winced and shut his eyes for a moment. "And the girl . . . is about Daniel's age when he . . ."

"Oh, Hosea, I wish I'd known."

"I never should have snapped at you. And I do care about the children. I-I hope they're all right."

Twisting her hands in her apron to keep from touching his arm, Emily made excuses. Wouldn't she reach out if her best friend had shared a terrible loss? But Hosea wasn't her friend, and from the way he'd been treating her ever since they met, he never would be. Something about her bothered him, and she had no idea what.

Chapter 6

During the next week, the children's parents were arrested on multiple charges, so Jax and Violet stayed with Emily's family. Both children attended the Amish school with Emily's younger sisters and several other foster children. Violet adjusted quickly and loved Amish life. She even begged to dress in Amish clothes. But Jax caused trouble.

Some days, Emily felt as if she spent more time at school than at work or home. One Tuesday, she got up early to meet with the teacher at seven before hurrying to be at work before eight. Jax had been pinching and poking the boy who sat beside him, calling people names, and refusing to do his lessons. Emily had dealt with troublesome foster children before, but eventually she'd found ways to help them adjust. Jax ranked as her most difficult challenge.

When Emily entered the stand, Hosea looked directly at her for the first time since she'd started working there. "Are you all right?"

Emily blinked to hold back tears. She was reluctant to mention the boy who'd caused Hosea so much grief. "Just some things to figure out with one of the foster kids." She brushed past him to hang up her cloak and bonnet—and to compose herself.

Lord, please show me what to do. She'd tried listening to Jax's complaints, sympathizing with him, giving him extra attention, talking to him, scolding him, grounding him . . . Nothing worked.

She shook it off. She needed to work while she was here, not worry over her other problems.

When she came out front, Hosea's face creased in concern. "If you need to take time off, you can go. Dad will be here around noon. I can manage until then."

His father had been ill, but he planned to return part-time. Once Freeman came back full-time, would she still be needed?

Hosea must have read the uneasiness in her eyes. "Don't worry. We still need you."

"*Gut.* But I'll stay today. We have a lot of party trays to fix."

"*Jah*, we do. But if you need to go . . ."

Emily appreciated his understanding. "*Danke.* I think I've worked things out with the school." Teacher Mandy intended to move Jax to a desk at the front of the room near her and not close enough to bother anyone. He'd also lose his recess for the rest of the week.

But right before noon, as the lunch crowd rush began, Emily's phone rang. "It's my *mamm.*"

Hosea's brief nod let her know she could take the call. She stepped away from the counter and answered.

"Emily, Teacher Mandy insisted someone has to pick up Jax immediately. I know you're at work, but Millie's coming soon to bring a new placement, a ten-month-old boy, and Marco is in bed with the flu."

For a moment, Emily panicked. Leave at their busiest time? Hosea had said she could go, but he needed her. Still, Jax and his teacher needed her more.

She headed back to the counter. "Hosea, I need to pick up one of the foster children who's gotten in trouble in school. Mamm's caring for one with the flu, so I . . ."

"If you need to, you could bring them back here."

He'd actually let her do that? Emily hesitated. "That would be great, but it's Jax, the boy who, um—" She gestured toward the corner where Jax and Violet had sat.

His flat *oh* showed he didn't like the idea. He stared down at the floor and swallowed hard. "It's okay."

Emily sensed his reluctance. She didn't want to hurt him. She'd take Jax home to Mamm.

When she got to school, Teacher Mandy pulled Emily aside. "I've tried to give Jax extra chances because he's not used to our ways. But instead of writing his sentences at recess, he burst out of the building and kicked and punched Josiah, calling him a tattletale."

"*Ach*, I'm so sorry. Is Josiah all right?"

"He will be. But I don't want Jax to come back for at least three days."

"I understand." Emily's mind raced. Tomorrow she'd have off from the market. So that was no problem. But what about Thursday and Friday?

The teacher leaned close and confided, "Just so you know, Violet told me Jax is threatening to run away from here. She doesn't want to leave."

Ach, Emily would need to keep a close eye on him. Maybe taking him to the market with her would be best. That way she could ensure he wouldn't take off. Hosea had said she could, but Emily disliked making him face his loss.

Jax scuffed his feet when Emily collected him from the chair in the back of the classroom. Perhaps having him up front had proved to be too disruptive.

He muttered to himself in the buggy. "Ain't no fair. That Josiah—"

Emily interrupted. "You will not blame someone else for your misbehavior."

He tried again, but she cut him off. Jax crossed his arms and lapsed into sullen silence. Once they reached the market, he clumped along beside her, sulking.

As she neared the counter, Freeman greeted her with a huge smile. "Emily, good to see you. Hosea went to get me some chicken corn soup. How are things going with my son?"

The twinkle in Freeman's eye indicated he'd chosen her as more than an employee. *Ah-ha*, that might explain Hosea's reluctance to talk to her. Emily's cheeks heated.

She kept her reply neutral. "Hosea's easy to work for."

The way Freeman's face fell, Emily had guessed right about his intentions. She opened the half-door and motioned for Jax to go in first.

Freeman's eyebrows rose. "Who's this?"

"One of our foster children, Jax Wilson. Jax, this is Freeman King."

Freeman stuck out his hand for a shake. "Nice to meet you, son."

"I ain't yer son. I ain't nobody's son. I don't have no dad." Bitterness dripped from his words. "They done took him away."

Hosea arrived back at the stand in time to hear Jax's outburst. Freeman's eyebrows rose, and Hosea winced. Emily led Jax to the stepstool in the corner, leaving the chair for Freeman.

When she returned to the counter, Freeman said, "That boy's hurting bad."

She nodded. In a low voice, she explained that both his parents were in jail, and the teacher had sent Jax home for punching and kicking someone on the playground.

Freeman nodded. "I can see he's filled with anger."

"When I acted too wild as a boy, Daed always gave me hard chores." Hosea smiled at his father. "He said it helped get rid of extra energy."

"It always worked." Freeman laughed.

"Only because I didn't want to get stuck with doing those jobs again."

"I might have to try that," Emily said. "I'm at my wit's end." But a thought struck her. Making Jax do difficult jobs might drive him to leave. "Maybe that wouldn't work. The teacher said Jax is planning to run away."

Hosea's brow creased in concern. "Then it might be better to give him something to look forward to."

Emily brightened. "That's a great idea."

A light flush spread across his cheekbones, and Freeman turned to hide a secretive smile that only Emily caught.

Freeman lifted his cup of soup in a salute. "Why don't I go sit with the boy and see if I can help him any?" Then he stopped. "You know, Hosea, I always thought you were a good *daed*. Maybe you could—"

"We have customers." Emily cut Freeman off. She couldn't bear Hosea's anguished expression.

Freeman took the hint and hurried back to sit with Jax.

"I'll take care of the line," Emily whispered. "It's not long. Why don't you take a break?" She hoped he wouldn't think she was trying to boss him in his own business, but he didn't look in any shape to face people.

"I'll be right back," he said in a strangled voice, and spun around.

Emily managed the sales and filled out order forms. Luckily, they had a steady stream of customers, not big crowds. In the back corner, Freeman and Jax seemed to be chatting easily. Hosea had gone in the opposite direction. Would his *daed*'s suggestion about assisting with Jax cause more strain between Hosea and her?

Hosea struggled to calm his roiling emotions. He wished Daed would stop pushing. Daed acted like replacing loved ones you'd lost with a new wife and children would heal devastating grief. But it didn't work that way. You couldn't replace people like you did a pair of worn-out shoes.

Shoes reminded him of Emily. Every day as she wore those shoes, they became more a part of her rather than of his wife. It had gotten less agonizing to see them on someone else's feet. Would spending time around a young boy ease his sorrow over Daniel or increase it?

As Emily had confided about Jax's problems, Hosea longed to help her. He disliked seeing her distressed. But why had Daed suggested Hosea as a father figure for the boy? Didn't Daed understand how much it would hurt to assist with someone else's son when Hosea couldn't raise his own?

He'd had only five short years with Daniel. And now God had brought a needy boy right to Hosea. Nine years ago, he'd asked the Lord to help him be a godly example to his son. Why couldn't he do the same for a fatherless boy?

Because whenever he spent time with Jax, Hosea would have to face his grief over and over again. A still, small voice inside reminded him of Christ, who'd sacrificed so much more. Now God was asking Hosea to endure some pain to care for a hurting boy. Could Hosea stop focusing on his own heartbreak to mentor an abandoned child?

Hosea bowed his head and murmured a quick prayer, *Lord, if you want me to do this, I need Your help.*

Second Corinthians 12:9 came to mind: "*My grace is sufficient for thee: for my strength is made perfect in weakness,*" followed by Philippians 4:13, "*I can do all things through Christ which strengtheneth me.*"

All Hosea had to offer was weakness. But the Lord had promised His strength. This would be the hardest thing Hosea had ever done. But with God's grace, he'd do whatever he could to get Jax back on the right track.

Hosea wanted to spend time alone coming to grips with his decision, but Emily was probably swamped with customers.

When he went out front, she seemed to be handling things well. And Daed beckoned him over.

"I'll take over the orders for Emily," Daed said. "Maybe you could chat with Jax here. Do you know he's never been fishing?"

"A little chilly for that." When the light died in Jax's eyes, Hosea regretted saying it. He tried to make up for his mistake. "You'll have to stick around until spring and go fishing with us."

That earned him a half-smile.

Hosea pushed down the rising ache inside and tried to engage Jax in conversation. "Do you like to ice-skate?"

The boy thrust out his lower lip. "Ain't got no skates."

"I'm sure we can find you a pair."

"Really?" Jax brightened. "But what about Violet?"

Hosea gulped. What had he gotten himself into? But with Jax looking so eager, Hosea couldn't disappoint him. "Violet can come too."

"Oh, goody!"

Emily passed by to get more party trays. "That's the most enthusiasm I've seen except for him eating candy the first day." She beamed at both of them.

Warmth spread through Hosea's chest, filling him with unexpected happiness. He wanted to elicit more of her beautiful smiles.

Hosea turned back to Jax. "I'm not sure how long it'll take for the pond to freeze, but with the weather this cold, it should be soon. They're predicting snow this weekend. Maybe we could go sledding."

"Ya mean it?"

Hosea nodded. "And Violet too."

That promise spread even more sunshine across Jax's face. Hosea sensed now might be a good time to work off some of the boy's anger and excess energy.

"I could use some help, and you look like you have pretty strong muscles. Think you could help me move some boxes?"

"Yep." Jax hopped off the stepstool and flexed his biceps.

Hosea hid his smile. "We have to go outside in the cold to bring them in from the refrigerated storage units."

"I ain't scared of cold." Jax's face darkened. "Me and Violet slept outside in the doghouse when Dad and Ma was high and bad people was in the trailer. We done it even in the snow."

Doghouse? What had these two little ones endured? Hosea tamped down his anger. He reached out and set a hand on Jax's shoulder.

The boy jumped and twisted away.

"Sorry," Hosea told him. "I shouldn't have startled you like that." The poor kid probably expected abuse when someone touched him.

"It's okay." Jax stared longingly at Hosea's hand.

"You don't mind?"

"Naw."

Hosea replaced his arm over Jax's shoulders.

As they walked along, Jax blinked rapidly, then swiped at his eyes with the back of his fist. He sniffled a few times. "I got me a cold. It makes my eyes drip."

"Mine too," Hosea admitted. He swallowed the lump in his throat. For the past four years, he'd dreamed day and night of all the things he was missing with Daniel. And now he was doing them with a stranger. A stranger who desperately needed love and care and guidance. A stranger who was already wriggling his way into Hosea's heart.

Chapter 7

From the grin stretching across his face, Jax enjoyed helping Hosea cart in boxes. Emily's heart swelled as the two of them worked together. After they'd brought in the last batch, Jax fell onto the stepstool, panting.

"That there's hard work."

"You did a great job, buddy." Hosea shot him an impressed smile.

A smile that flipped Emily's heart upside down. *What if—?* She cut off her imagination. No way would Hosea be interested in her.

Just then he glanced her way with a bemused smile. She returned it with a wide one, expressing all her gratitude and admiration for what he was doing with Jax. Hosea's eyes widened, then flicked down to the young boy.

Emily regretted being so open with her feelings. She'd scared Hosea off.

While they'd been gone, Emily had cleaned the cases and straightened the price tags and cheeses while Freeman waited on the last few customers.

"Why don't you take Jax home, Emily?" Freeman asked. "Hosea and I can handle the rest of the cleaning and closing up."

Grateful, Emily collected Jax, who acted reluctant to leave.

As they headed off, Hosea called after them, "Thanks for all the help, Jax. And *danke*, Emily. See you both on Thursday."

Although it was only a friendly gesture, Emily's pulse accelerated when Hosea said her name. She forced herself to call out a casual goodbye.

The whole way home, Jax babbled on about how he'd lifted heavy cartons and all the plans he and Hosea had made. Emily marveled at the change in Jax's attitude. Maybe these few days off school and spending time with Hosea would work wonders.

By the time Thursday rolled around, Jax waited impatiently for Emily to hitch up the horse.

Her eyes sad, Violet called out a goodbye. "Wish you was goin' to school with me. I miss you."

"Goin' to market's way better than goin' to school." Jax slid the door open and climbed into the buggy.

Uh-oh. Emily hoped rewarding Jax for getting in trouble at school wouldn't result in more misbehavior.

Later that morning, she confided her worry to Hosea.

He stroked his beard. "Hmm . . . That could be a problem. I'll talk to him about it."

"Oh, Hosea, I don't know what I'd do without you." As soon as the words gushed from her mouth, Emily cringed inside. He might interpret that differently than she'd intended. Although if he took it that way, he also might be right.

The tips of Hosea's ears reddened, and he looked away. "I'm only doing what God's nudging me to do."

His *daed* had been right. Hosea must have been a good father. Jax needed a strong male influence, and Hosea had turned out to be a *wunderbar* mentor. If he found a way to convince Jax to behave in school, she'd—she'd—

The only thing that came to mind was *kiss him*, but that'd be totally inappropriate. After the way he'd recoiled from her overly enthusiastic praise, she had no idea how to thank him.

A rush of feelings overwhelmed Hosea, and he avoided looking at Emily after she'd stunned him with her compliments. And her smile had turned his whole world upside down. Instead, he concentrated on teaching Jax how to fill cheese trays and wait on customers.

Jax surprised everyone by eagerly doing every job he was asked to do. He shone when waiting on customers. Outgoing and friendly, he charmed the older ladies, who proclaimed him cute.

"You're really good with people," Hosea said after one sale, and Jax stared up at him hungrily, as eager for attention as a drought-stricken field soaking up rainwater. After that, Hosea tried to find ways to reinforce all of the boy's positive actions.

Jax dogged Hosea's steps so closely that sometimes Hosea almost tripped over him. The young boy's parched heart wasn't the only one being filled. Jax's constant company eased some of Hosea's loneliness. Nobody could ever replace Daniel, but Jax made Hosea realize how much he'd walled himself off from others.

When Hosea took a break for meals, Jax grabbed the lunchbox Emily had packed for him and wriggled onto the chair beside Hosea, who sat on the stepstool. Now might be a good time to talk about school.

After they'd each taken a few bites in silence, Hosea remarked casually, "You learn new jobs here so fast, I bet you do well in school."

Jax's face pinched up at the word *school*. "I ain't any good at school stuff."

"Why not? Anyone who works as hard as you should find schoolwork easy."

"Ya think?" Jax kicked his feet back and forth, banging the rung of the chair.

"I don't just think. I know. You learn fast and work hard. That's all you need to do a good job in school too." Hosea flashed Jax a teasing grin. "And listening to the teacher, of course."

Though he scrunched up his nose, Jax giggled. "She don't like me none."

Hosea raised his eyebrows. "That's surprising. You're so good with people. Look at how much the customers like you."

Jax crossed his arms. "Teacher Mandy's mean. I gotta stay inside at recess. Ain't fair."

Hosea gave Jax a pointed look. "You do everything she asks?"

He hung his head. "Naw."

"Maybe if you did what she says, you'd get to play outside at recess. What if you treated her like you do the customers? Who knows? You might end up being her favorite scholar."

Jax's face wrinkled in doubt, then he shook his head.

"Might be worth a try." After planting that seed, Hosea changed the subject. He prayed God would help it sprout.

Chapter 8

Snow flurries on Saturday morning grew heavier as the day went on. From the way it covered the ground by midmorning, Hosea was sure they'd have several inches by late afternoon.

Violet had accompanied Jax and Emily that morning, and she sat on one of the folding chairs Hosea had brought, watching in admiration as her brother worked. Inside the stand, it had gotten crowded, and so had Hosea's heart. His life was now filled with people he cared about more and more each day.

After they checked the snowfall in midafternoon, Hosea smiled at Jax. "Looks like we can go sledding today."

The boy's eyes shone. He turned to Violet. "We don't got to use cardboard no more. Hosea has a sled. A real one."

She squealed and clapped her hands.

Hosea ached to see how much simple pleasures meant to these two little ones. Pushing aside his own sorrow, Hosea determined to bring more joy into their lives.

After the stand closed for the day, he made plans to pick up the children after supper. When he asked Emily for her address, his *daed* stood behind her, grinning. Hosea shook his head to discourage his father's wild imagination. Hosea had no intention of getting involved with Emily.

But he hadn't expected Violet to cling to Emily's hand and beg her to come along with them when he arrived to pick them up that evening. Nor had he planned for all her younger sisters and the rest of the foster children to stare at him with pleading eyes.

Taking a deep breath, Hosea issued an invitation to everyone. Emily's grateful *danke* sent his pulse into overdrive. He scarcely noticed Jax's pout.

Jax crossed his arms. "I don't want none of them to come. I thought just you, me, and Vi was going sledding."

Hosea reached down, making sure Jax saw his hands first, and set them on the boy's shoulders. "We'll still have our special time, but isn't it nice to share good times with friends?"

"I ain't got no friends."

"Well, having fun together is a good way to make them, don't you think?"

"I guess." Jax looked unconvinced.

Emily drew Hosea's attention again. "If you're all going," she said to the children gathering in the hallway, "we'll need more sleds. Maybe Sarah and Rowan can get our sleds from the garage, while Hannah, Naomi, and I help the little ones get into winter clothes."

Hosea stared in amazement as Emily's fingers flew—pulling on jackets and hats, tugging on snowpants and boots, buttoning coats, tying laces, wrapping scarves. A girl, who must be Emily's sister, dug through huge boxes in a nearby closet and handed Jax and Violet winter outerwear and boots. Soon eight bundled-up, roly-poly, red-cheeked children waited by the door. After donning her own coat, bonnet, and boots, Emily opened the door, and they all tumbled out into the snow, shrieking with excitement.

Emily clapped her mittened hands, but it made little noise.

Still, the children stopped what they were doing to listen. Hosea couldn't believe it. The Amish children, *jah*, that was expected. But all the foster children, except Jax, paid attention.

"While we wait for the sleds," Emily announced, "the first ones to grab shovels from the porch can clear the sidewalk. But take turns with others."

Was she clever or what? Hosea smiled to himself as children rushed to claim shovels. Four small shovels and two larger ones stood near him. He took a large one and started on the porch. Jax missed out on the other shovels, but Hosea promised to let Jax use his.

In short order, the whole walkway was clean. When the sleds arrived, Emily suggested they trudge up Miller's Hill nearby, and soon everyone was taking turns sliding down the hill.

Hosea moved next to her as she wiped noses, kissed bumps, dried tears, separated arguers, briskly rubbed icy fingers, and organized sledding partners. "You're so good at this."

Emily laughed. "I have a lot of experience. Mamm's been taking in foster children since I turned three."

These kids were so fortunate. And Emily would make a *wunderbar* mother. Hosea shied away from that thought.

He nodded to the top of the hill where Jax and another boy were pushing a sled holding Violet and her friend. "Looks like Jax and Violet are settling in well."

"Thanks to you." Gratitude—and something else—burned in Emily's eyes. "You've done wonders with Jax."

"Let's hope it works when he gets to school on Monday. I did talk to him about that."

"I can't thank you enough. I'm sure it will help. He's been cooperating much better at home."

Her soft, thankful sigh sparked a reaction deep within Hosea's soul. A reaction he had no power to fight. A reaction he shied away from examining.

To distract himself, he blurted out, "Why don't you take a turn on the sleds, Emily?"

A few foster children nearby giggled. Then they chanted, "Do it, Emily, do it!" A few grabbed her hands and pulled her to the nearest sled.

Emily called over her shoulder, "If I have to do it, so do you, Hosea."

Jax started another cheer, "Do it, Hosea, do it!"

Laughing, Hosea followed Emily to the sleds. Once they were seated next to each other, the boys gathered around his sled, and the girls around Emily's.

"Let's see which one's faster," Rowan challenged. "One, two, three . . . Go!"

Hands shoved Hosea, rocking the sled forward until it tipped over the edge of the slope. His stomach whooshed downhill as he bounced over ruts and rocks.

Beside him, Emily shouted, "Whooo!" as she swooped past him.

He steered his sled around a large hillock, but Emily hadn't seen it. She flipped off and tumbled downhill.

"Emily," he yelled, holding out a hand to help her as he glided past. But he overbalanced and toppled sideways, landing in a heap next to her.

She scrambled to her knees, but when she tried to stand, her foot hit an icy patch and slid out from under her. Hosea reached out and caught her before she face-planted in the snow.

He chuckled. "This is familiar." But when he glanced up, his laughter died. Their faces were so close, he could see each snow-coated eyelash framing her lovely, golden-flecked brown eyes. Eyes that flashed a message of kindness and caring and something else . . .

Her soft, bow-shaped lips formed a startled *O*. An *O* he wanted to trace, to kiss . . .

Hoots and cheers above them on the hill broke their connection.

Hosea let go of Emily's arms, pushed himself to his feet, and offered her a hand. They collected the overturned sleds, and he held her mittened hand as they pulled the sleds back up the hill. "To keep you from slipping," he whispered.

She nodded, keeping her eyes averted.

They reached the summit amid cheers and teasing. Once the sleds had been turned over to the children again, Hosea led her to one side.

"That was fun." Despite the spill—or maybe because of it— he'd enjoyed himself.

"It was." Emily lifted starry eyes to his. Eyes that offered an invitation to fulfill his earlier wish.

Hosea's pulse kicked into overtime. Would she welcome a kiss? Only the group of children on the ridge kept him from answering her invitation.

Emily lowered her lids. Hosea had stared straight into her eyes. Had she imagined the interest in his eyes?

She'd never know because his face soon shuttered his feelings, and he stepped back. Although his hands had lifted as if to take her into his arms, they dropped to his sides. Or had all of this been wishful thinking on her part?

She didn't have time to find out. The children needed to get in bed so they could get up for church tomorrow. She called out, "Who wants hot chocolate?"

The children stampeded toward her, dragging their sleds.

"You do know how to get them to obey quickly," Hosea said admiringly.

Emily didn't turn to see if his expression matched his words. Better not to get her hopes up. And within seconds, she was engulfed by chaos. Children chattered about their scariest or fastest rides, and although she answered by rote, her mind remained on her own sled ride. What had started out as frightening had turned to exhilarating and romantic. And then fizzled into disappointment.

Emily had been through that once before in a relationship. She wasn't about to let herself get caught up in it again.

But when Hosea showed up at her house late Monday afternoon, her emotions didn't listen to reason. He smiled and met her eyes, and her heart thumped out a symphony against her ribs. Had he come to see her?

"I promised Jax I'd take him skating if he had a *gut* day at school," Hosea explained.

Emily should have known Hosea's only interest was in Jax. She tried not to let her disappointment show. She balanced a toddler on one hip while feeding a bottle to the infant cradled in her other arm, and her foster sister Iris went out to the kitchen to fetch Jax.

After Hosea received a *gut* report on the school day, he beamed at Jax. "Looks like it's time for skating." He went out to his buggy and returned with a box full of skates. "My cousins' kids have outgrown these, so let's find you a pair that fits."

Once again, the other children surrounded Hosea and Jax, begging to go along.

"I'm not sure we have enough skates for everyone." Hosea sounded disappointed.

Emily didn't want to see anyone miss out. "Rowan can take the others out to the barn to try on the skates we have hanging on pegs out there. If you're willing to take them, that is."

"Will you go with us?" Hosea asked her.

Emily longed to say *jah*, but she tilted her head toward the babies in her arms. "I need to take care of these two."

Mamm entered the room holding a screaming two-year-old. "You deserve to have some fun, Emily. All you do is work."

"But, Mamm, you have your hands full."

"I've had them fuller many a time. Give me Joseph and his bottle, and set Dimante on the couch. I'll read to her and Liam." She gestured with her chin to the bawling boy in her arms.

Rowan herded several children inside carrying skates and handed Emily a pair. Hosea's eyes lit up, filling Emily with hope. *Maybe...?*

But keeping track of eight children and helping the younger ones skate gave Emily and Hosea little time together. After a while, her sisters took over and nudged Emily onto the ice, encouraging her to have some fun. Four children, including Jax and Violet, sat on a bench sipping hot chocolate, so Hosea was skating alone.

As soon as he saw her, he glided over and took her hand. The wind whipped her face and flapped her bonnet strings as they moved in perfect rhythm. Emily's spirit soared, joyful and weightless. If only . . .

Hosea had never seen anyone as pretty and animated as Emily. Her rosy cheeks, her mouth curved in contentment, her eyes shining with delight sent sparks of happiness racing through him.

But Emily's true beauty came from her strong faith, her generous nature, and her caring personality. She shared her warmth and kindness and her ready smile. Being around her was beginning to heal the dry, brittle places he'd concealed from the world after losing his family.

"Emily?" The brisk breeze blew the word away before she heard it. Maybe it was better that way. She had so much to give; he had so little to offer in return.

He wished they could go on skating together in harmony all evening, but the children needed to get home to bed. Emily appeared as reluctant to leave as he was.

Jax begged to ride with Hosea on the way home. A few

other children rode with them, but Jax sat up front, chattering about all the fun he'd had. He'd even made it partway around the pond by himself. His movements had been wobbly and jerky, but Jax beamed with pride.

When they returned to the house and Hosea walked the children to the door, Jax slipped his hand into Hosea's. That trusting gesture, that sweet connection between them, shot straight to Hosea's icy heart, thawing it. For the first time in years, love flowed freely like a mountain stream fed by melting snow.

Maybe he had something to give Emily after all.

Chapter 9

As November slipped into December, Hosea's bond with Jax deepened, so when Emily told him at work one day that Violet and Jax might be moving in with an elderly aunt in Virginia, Hosea was devastated.

"Their aunt is a shriveled old prune." The words shot out of Emily's mouth, startling him.

He'd never heard her criticize anyone. She always looked for the best in people, even the grouchiest customers.

When his eyebrows shot up, she apologized. "I'm sorry. I know God wants us to love everyone, but she was so mean to Jax. She likes Violet, but in front of Jax, she said boys are unbearable and messy and dirty and naughty." Emily's eyes filled with tears.

Hosea longed to comfort her. "Jax is so engaging. Maybe she'll come to like him."

"I don't think so. When he heard what she said, he acted horrid. Maybe he's hoping she'll change her mind about taking them."

"*Ach*, no." Jax could be quite a troublemaker. And if he felt unloved . . .

Emily's eyes filled with sadness. "This is the hardest part of caring for foster children—coming to love them and then having them taken away. It's even worse when they're going to relatives who are only doing their duty or have no idea how to parent."

"Can't you find a way to keep them with you?"

"I wish I could. If I had a home of my own, I'd offer to adopt them. I think their aunt sees parenting them as her duty. She didn't even want them to come until after New Year's Day. Maybe she'd be relieved not to have that burden."

This aunt didn't even want Violet and Jax? Hosea's chest constricted. "Isn't there anyone who can adopt them so they can stay in the area? What about your *mamm*?"

Emily sighed heavily. "She's in the process of adopting Dimante and Joseph. She can't think about another adoption for quite a while."

"I see. I'll pray that God will find the perfect home for Jax and Violet." He didn't want to see Jax go to live with someone who disliked him. After all the positive changes Jax had made, it weighed on Hosea's spirit to think of the cheerful young boy going back to his anger and rebelliousness.

That evening Hosea had promised to take Jax and Violet for a ride to see the *Englischers'* Christmas lights. Just the three of them. Hosea hoped he might be able to persuade Emily to make it four rather than three.

The moment he stepped through the front door, though, Jax barreled across the room. He flung his arms around Hosea and hugged him tightly. "I don't wanna go away. I wanna stay with you. And Emily."

A fissure opened in Hosea's slowly healing heart. Until now, Hosea hadn't realized how attached he'd been getting to the young boy. How could he add losing Jax to the older, deeper wounds?

"I ain't gonna live with that stinky old witch."

"Jax," Hosea scolded.

"Well, she is. She smell real bad." Jax pinched his nose. "Like yucky perfume. And she don't like boys. She said so."

Emily had made that clear, so Hosea couldn't deny it. "Maybe she'll come to like you."

"She ain't gonna change."

Hosea brushed Jax's hair off his forehead and tried to give him hope. "Remember how you got Teacher Mandy to change her mind."

"That's different," Jax mumbled. "Teacher Mandy don't hate me. She just don't like some stuff I do. But that ugly Bertha? I didn't do nothin' to that meanie, and she already hate me."

It amazed Hosea that Jax had seen into the hidden motives behind people's actions. Hosea turned to the only solution he could offer. "Let's pray about it."

"That don't work. Emily taught me to pray, and I been prayin' and prayin', but God don't answer."

"What did you ask for?"

Gazing up trustingly at Hosea, Jax whispered, "A dad for Christmas. A dad to love me. A dad like you."

Jax's request knifed through Hosea. He desperately wanted to answer that prayer. But how could he?

"God don't listen," Jax wailed. "All I got is a stinky, mean aunt."

Hosea didn't have the heart to correct him.

Jax continued complaining during the ride, and although Emily had agreed to come along, she sat in the back with Violet, while Jax sat beside Hosea. So Hosea's much-anticipated time with the kids and Emily turned into a huge letdown.

As they headed back, Violet, oblivious to the tension around her, burbled on about next week's events at school. "I ain't never been in no Christmas program before. Teacher Mandy says I done real good saying my part."

"That's wonderful, Violet." Emily, too, seemed determined to inject some holiday cheer into the outing.

Violet beamed, then added, "But Jax don't listen to the teacher. He makes faces and don't say his piece right."

"Stop tattling, Violet." Jax's angry words zinged around the buggy.

"Jax," Hosea warned, "be nice to your sister."

Jax wrapped his arms around himself and huddled in the seat. In the rearview mirror, Violet's chin trembled as tears splashed onto her cheeks. Emily hugged her, and the sight of the two of them cuddled together accelerated the thumping in Hosea's chest.

An idea niggled at his brain. He couldn't be a single dad, but he and Emily had been spending a lot of time together recently. Sometimes when his eyes met hers, Hosea had sensed a flicker of interest. At least, he thought he had. Would she consider a marriage of convenience for the children's sake?

He still had to pray about it, but it might be a solution. Right now, he had another smaller problem to handle.

When they pulled up to the house, Hosea asked Jax to stay for a minute. When they were alone, Hosea studied Jax. "What's this about the Christmas program?"

Jax flicked a hand, dismissing it. "Who cares?"

"That's not a good attitude to have."

"Don't make no difference. I ain't staying here."

"I understand how you feel about that, but is that fair to everyone else?"

Jax sniffed, but then lowered his head under Hosea's steady gaze. "It ain't fair."

"I agree, and I know you're hurting now. But Emily is looking forward to seeing you in the program. Do you want to spoil it for her? Or for the other children and their families?"

Jax didn't answer. Hosea waited, giving Jax time to think.

After a while, Hosea continued, "Sometimes we have to do things we don't want to do. It's part of growing up and being a man."

"I ain't a man yet," Jax muttered.

"You've been brave and gotten through a lot of hard times in your life already. Seems like saying a few lines at a Christmas program would be easy after that."

"Ain't nobody there to see me."

"I'm sure Emily will bring the little ones."

"They's just babies."

Hosea smiled. "Emily's not."

"She ain't gonna watch me. She got too many other kids to look at."

Emily did have several sisters and foster children, but somehow, she managed to be there for all of them. Hosea found that amazing, but he doubted he could convince Jax she'd pay attention to him.

Jax looked up at Hosea with pleading puppy-dog eyes. "Will you come?"

How could Hosea possibly say no?

The day of the Christmas program, Hosea gave Emily time off to attend the morning presentation. "Tell Jax I'll see him tonight," Hosea called to her as she left.

She returned around noontime, her brow furrowed.

"Is everything all right?" Hosea asked.

Emily shook her head. "Jax refused to say his part. He's practiced it every day for the past two weeks so he knows it."

"Maybe he got stage fright?"

"*Neh*, he was clowning around with the boy next to him, and Jax spoke out of turn twice, but only to make jokes. When his turn came, he pinched his mouth shut, crossed his arms, and stayed silent."

"*Ach*, I can't believe he did that."

The discouragement in Emily's eyes made Hosea want to reach out to her—in more ways than one. "Maybe he'll do better tonight. After all, it's his first program."

Emily didn't look hopeful, but Hosea planned to arrive early and have a talk with Jax. When he arrived, though, the teacher had all the children gathered around her at the front of the room. Jax spotted Hosea, and his face lit up like holiday lights. Maybe that would be enough to remind Jax to say his part.

Ten minutes later, Emily slid in beside Hosea, and his pulse kicked into high gear as her sleeve brushed his arm.

She leaned over and whispered, "Mamm came this morning, and we brought all the children, but I helped her put them to bed before I came."

Outside of work, Hosea rarely saw Emily alone, so he enjoyed the pleasure of her company and conversation until the children lined up across the front of the room. He spotted the first problem right away.

All the children wore signs around their necks with their names and their parents' names. One by one, they introduced themselves and told who their parents were. As Violet took her turn, Jax scowled when she mentioned their mom and dad.

When it was his turn, Jax frowned and pinched his mouth into a straight line. Hosea shifted in his seat to get Jax's attention.

Looking into Hosea's eyes, Jax straightened and said with confidence, "I'm Jax Wilson." Then he hung his head and mumbled, "And I ain't got no parents."

Several people in the audience gasped. Beside Hosea, Emily sucked in a breath and blinked back tears. He reached for her hand, tucked under the folds of her apron, and gave it a quick squeeze. His pulse hammered out a staccato rhythm that accelerated when Emily lifted teary eyes and sent him a sweet, thankful gaze.

But the hope that filled him didn't erase the sharp sadness piercing him ever since Jax spoke. Jax had been through so much in his life already. Hosea couldn't let that hurting young boy go to an aunt who despised him.

Up front, the children had been taking turns saying their parts. Hosea had been so deep in thought he'd missed the first four. He concentrated on the program and on shooting encouraging looks Jax's way. Jax returned them with a halfhearted smile.

Jax did perk up when Violet recited her part. Emily beamed at her and gave her a thumbs-up. But as the next boy started his poem, Jax stiffened, and his face scrunched into grim lines. His lips thinned into a narrow slash during the next two recitations. Was he worried about his turn? Hosea wished he had a way to calm Jax's nerves.

The boy next to him held up a globe. "John 3:16. *For God so loved the world—*"

"That's a lie," Jax yelled. He burst into tears and blubbered, "If God loves me, how come I ain't got no dad and mom?"

Hosea shot out of his metal folding chair so fast it rocked back and forth, nearly tipping. He didn't care if he was disrupting the whole program. He had to get to Jax, who'd collapsed to the floor, crying.

"I love you, Jax." Hosea swept the bawling boy into his arms and hugged him close. "I'm here for you."

Emily knelt beside them and took Jax's hand in hers. "I am too, Jax. We both love you."

Suddenly realizing they were the center of all eyes, Hosea scooped Jax up and carried him to the back of the room. They passed sympathetic glances and people with their heads bowed and eyes closed, who must be praying for Jax. It warmed Hosea to see the community surrounding a brokenhearted little boy with God's love.

By the time they reached the back of the room, Jax's sobs had subsided into whimpers.

"I'm going to take him out to the buggy," Hosea whispered to Emily. "Maybe a ride will help calm him."

"Let me get his coat." She hurried to the cloakroom and returned carrying Hosea's too.

How had she known which one was his? He didn't have time to ask. He mouthed a quiet *danke*.

Emily smoothed the hair back from Jax's forehead, her eyes filled with caring and compassion. Then her love-filled eyes met Hosea's, and the growing attraction he'd been holding back flooded through him.

He wished he could share all his feelings, but now was not the time or place. Maybe he could talk to her when he brought Jax home later.

Her soft "I'll be praying" fell on Hosea like a gentle benediction. He smiled at her, hoping his eyes conveyed promises for their future.

Chapter 10

Emily returned to her seat, shaking with emotion. Her mind whirled with hopes and possibilities. Ever since she'd met Hosea, her dreams had held tantalizing images of spending a lifetime with him. As they'd skated and sledded and worked together, she'd woven a beautiful imaginary tapestry of their relationship blooming into courtship. Was it about to become a reality?

She clasped her hands tightly to stop their trembling and focused on the program. But her spirit soared into lovely fantasies of the almost-kiss transforming into the actual touch of his lips on hers.

At the front of the room, Violet studied her brother's empty chair with panic. She looked on the verge of bolting from the stage and running out after him.

Emily caught Violet's eyes, gave her a reassuring smile, and mouthed, *He's okay.*

Violet still appeared uneasy, but when Teacher Mandy directed them to their places for the skit, Violet hurried into place. She acted a bit flustered, but said her lines at the right time. Emily swelled with pride. Every one of her sisters and foster family—well, everyone except Jax—had done a great job.

After the program ended, she congratulated all of them and joined them at the refreshment table, but she couldn't wait to reconnect with Hosea—to check on Jax, first and foremost, and then to find out if she'd interpreted Hosea's meaning correctly.

Violet slipped a hand in Emily's and tugged her toward the cloakroom. "We gots to find Jax. He's gonna run away."

Emily set a hand on her shoulder. "He's fine. Hosea will take good care of him, but we should hurry home. It's getting late." She pushed the worry about Jax running away to the back of her mind for now. Once Hosea arrived, she'd discuss it with him.

She gathered everyone and headed to the house. Once everyone had gone to bed, she sat on the couch to wait for Hosea and Jax. Although Emily normally went to sleep soon after the children, the anticipation of talking to Hosea kept her wide awake. She couldn't wait to hear how his talk with Jax went. And to find out—her stomach flipped with both anxiety and excitement—whether or not she'd imagined his interest.

Once they'd reached the buggy, Hosea sat in the passenger seat and held Jax close as the little boy broke into a fresh spate of weeping, releasing years of pent-up anguish. Hosea understood that bone-deep grieving.

Jax had every reason to cry—he'd lost both his parents. They might be alive, but with all the charges they faced, they'd be in prison for at least a decade. Jax would be grown by then. He needed someone to care for him now. Someone who was not an uncaring relative.

Jax's crying turned into intermittent hiccupping sobs. Hosea rubbed Jax's back until his tears ended in sniffles.

"It's getting cold in here," Hosea said gently. "Will you be all right if I put you on the seat and drive around for a bit?"

When Jax nodded, Hosea got out and retrieved a heavy wool blanket from the back of the buggy and wrapped it around Jax. "Are you warm enough?"

"On my outside, but not my inside."

"What would make you warm inside?"

Jax stared down at the floor as Hosea got into the driver's seat. Finally, he mumbled, "Having a dad. Somebody who loves me."

"I love you, and Emily does too."

"You ain't gonna be around no more. Not after we goes to that mean, smelly aunt."

"I hope you won't have to do that."

Jax huddled down in the blanket, so his voice was muffled. "Me too."

Hosea clicked to his horse and pulled the buggy out onto the dark country road. He stayed on the shoulder to let cars pass. As they drove by houses lit with Christmas lights, he pointed them out as a distraction. But he ached to comfort Jax by offering him a love-filled future.

A field full of huge inflatable characters—Santa, reindeer, and even a giant green Grinch—caught Jax's attention. He giggled at the Grinch, but the sound held traces of underlying sorrow.

With the reins dangling from one hand, Hosea reached out with the other and squeezed Jax's shoulder gently. "You know, no matter what happens, there is someone who will always be with you and love you."

"Who?" Jax sat up eagerly and leaned toward Hosea. Then he deflated and slumped back. "Ya mean Violet? Yeah, she loves me. But I want a grown-up."

"*Jah*, Violet loves you, and she depends on you. But that's not who I'm thinking of." Hosea paused, then added, "I know this upset you at the program tonight, but God really does love you."

A mutinous expression settled over Jax's face. "Then why'd He give me a bad ma and dad? And why don't He answer my prayers?"

"We don't always know why God allows sad or bad things to happen. We just have to trust that everything is His will and remember He'll help us with everything."

Jax glared. "He didn't help me none when Dad and Ma hurt us. And He ain't doing nothing about ugly old Aunt Bertha."

"Why don't we pray about that and ask God to help you?"

"What God gonna do?"

"God wants the best for you and so do I. Let's ask Him what to do." Hosea pulled into a nearby graveled turnaround and stopped the horse. A huge Christmas star shone atop a nearby barn. "Look, doesn't that remind you of the star the wise men followed to find Baby Jesus?"

"That baby didn't have no home neither. He slept in a barn."

"*Jah*, He did. Yet Jesus grew up to do miracles and later gave His life to save us from our sins. Since He had the power do that, He can help us with problems if we ask. Do you want to pray about it now?"

"You go first," Jax said nervously.

Jax fixed his eyes on Hosea as he bowed his head. Hosea wasn't used to praying aloud, but he asked God to take care of Jax and show them both what to do. Before Hosea lifted his head, he tacked on a silent plea for guidance about Emily.

Mimicking Hosea, Jax lowered his head and closed his eyes. He stayed quiet for a few moments and then began tentatively, "God? I . . . um . . . I don't believe in You, and I ain't sure You can hear me, but here goes. I want a nice dad and mom. And for me and Violet to have a good family. One that loves us. Amen."

"You know, Jax, I spent several years being angry at God."

Jax's eyes widened. "You did? How come?"

Hosea choked back the grief that rose every time he thought

of his loss. "I had a wife and a little boy named Daniel." Just saying his son's name expanded the ache in Hosea's chest until it constricted his breathing.

His next words came out choked. "They died in an accident. I still miss them so much, but meeting you has helped me."

Jax stared at Hosea in disbelief. "I helped you?"

"You certainly did." *More than you'll ever know.* Hosea reached out and ruffled Jax's hair. "You've helped me not to be so lonely. Being with you filled an emptiness inside me. You've let me see what it would be like if my . . . my son had lived."

"But I ain't Amish." Jax stared down at his lap. "And I ain't even a good kid."

"I love you just the way you are. You've brought a lot of joy into my life. And I hope I can bring happiness into yours."

Jax's hand slipped out from under the blanket and slid into Hosea's. "You make me very happy." Tears rolled down Jax's cheeks. "I'm gonna miss you so much."

Hosea's eyes leaked a few tears too. "I still plan to spend time with you. No matter what." He didn't want to get Jax's hopes up and then let him down if Emily said *neh*, but Hosea would never lose his bond with this young boy. "And I'll be there if you need me. You'll always be part of my life."

"Promise?"

"*Jah*, I do." He'd been taught not to make vows, but as the Bible said, he intended to let his *yea* be a *yea*. This was one promise he had no intention of breaking.

When a buggy rattled into the driveway, Emily jumped up and hurried to the door. Finally, they were here. It seemed as if she'd waited days rather than hours.

She greeted them enthusiastically as they came up the walkway. Seeing Jax holding Hosea's hand filled her with admiration for this man who loved a young stranger as if he were his *sohn*.

"It's late, Jax," she said. "You should hurry up to bed."

Rather than turning to leave, Hosea stepped inside the house. "I know it's late and we both have to work tomorrow, but would you have time to talk for a short while?"

She stopped herself before she blurted out an overly excited response. "Of course," she said demurely.

When his gaze met hers, he didn't look away, and she was drawn into the depths of those mesmerizing, crystalline blue eyes.

"Emily?" His husky voice held tenderness and caring.

Her "*Jah?*" came out soft and breathy, expressing her anticipation. She shivered.

Concern flashed into his eyes, breaking the spell. "I'm sorry. I didn't mean to make you freeze." He stepped closer to her so he could shut the door behind him.

Emily hadn't even noticed they'd left the door standing open or that the wind had blown a light dusting of snow on the mat by the door. She should shake it off, but with Hosea standing so close, she never wanted to move. If only she could stay here basking in his warmth.

Her cheeks heated. What must he think of her? She hadn't even asked him in. "*Kumme* in, *kumme* in." She led him into the living room, but with those words, she also invited him into her heart and life.

Still stunned by Emily's response, Hosea followed her, dazed.

As he sat in the seat she indicated, he thanked God for the size and sturdiness of the chair, because nervousness knocked his knees together in a syncopated rhythm that would have set a lighter chair wobbling. When she settled across from him on the couch, his mouth went dry.

Lord, please give me courage to express what's in my heart.

She gave him an easy opening. "What happened with Jax?"

Hosea relaxed a bit as he recounted his conversation and prayers with Jax. But the admiration shining in her eyes made it difficult to focus on retelling everything in the correct order when his mind whirled with unanswered questions and future possibilities.

He ended with his promise to Jax. "I told him I'd always be there for him." He hesitated before adding the most important part of that conversation. "I also said he'd always be part of my life." The same words Hosea longed to tell Emily.

Emily gazed at him, her eyes shining with tears.

"I didn't just mean as a friend who visits Jax and Violet every few weeks. I meant as a *daed*, a real *daed*. Is there a way I can adopt them?"

"That would be so wonderful for both of them. If the aunt doesn't really want the responsibility and their parents sign them over as wards to the state, Millie can help with that. I'll check with her tomorrow."

"But I don't want to be a single *daed*. After their rough start in life, I want them to have a stable family life with two parents. A while back you said you'd like to adopt them, so I wondered . . ."

Emily leaned forward as if eager to hear his proposal, and his thoughts got so tangled, he couldn't find the right words.

". . . about a marriage of convenience."

Her shining eyes dimmed.

Before she could answer, he plunged on. "I mean, I'd planned to ask you to marry for Jax's and Violet's sake, but . . ."

He stopped abruptly when disappointment flashed across her face.

Ach, he was messing this all up. "I don't want a marriage of convenience." He cleared the choking tightness in his throat. "I've come to care for you and wondered if you'd be willing to court?"

The sparkle returned to her eyes. "Oh," she breathed out on a soft sigh. Then she, too, seemed at a loss for words.

Hosea hoped her eyes held her answer, but he waited anxiously for her words to confirm it.

Emily bowed her head, and her lips moved.

Hosea prayed along with her. *Please, Lord, if this is Your will, help her to say* jah.

When she looked up at him, Hosea had his answer even before *jah* crossed her sweet lips. He gripped the arms of the chair to keep himself in place, although he longed to kiss her.

"Oh, Hosea, I've been praying to find a way to adopt Jax and Violet."

"So that's why you said *jah*?" he teased.

"*Neh.*" Her eyes twinkled. "I care for you too."

"I'm so glad." His heart rejoiced in the special smile she sent his way.

Chapter 11

During the next few weeks, Hosea and Emily spent as much time together as they could. Most of their dates included Jax and Violet, but Hosea stayed long after the children went to bed to discuss plans for the future. And Emily came into work early so they had more private time together.

After Freeman came in one morning to find Hosea and Emily had become so engrossed in their conversation, they'd forgotten to set up the cases or make cheese trays, he smiled broadly and rushed around helping them get ready for customers.

Later, he cornered Hosea. "Well, son, I thought you were upset about me hiring Emily. You even mentioned possibly firing her after the first day. Still think we should look for a new employee?"

Hosea stared at him, horrified. "I never said that," he blustered before remembering he had. "Um, I guess did," he admitted sheepishly.

Back then, he'd wanted nothing to do with his *daed's*

choice. Now, he had his *daed* to thank for his most beautiful blessing.

His *daed* chuckled. "We don't arrange marriages, but if we did, I know who I'd pick for you."

"So do I. And you made a great choice."

"I had God's help with that."

Emily hurried past with an armload of cheeses. "What are you two grinning about?"

"Arranged marriages."

She stopped short. "Arranged marriages? Marriage of convenience? Seems like you two had a lot of plots going."

A smile stretched across Freeman's face. "Neither of us wanted to lose the best employee we've ever had."

"That's all I am?"

Freeman gestured toward the cases she'd already filled. "She asks that when she's the only one working? I'd say I made an excellent choice—in more ways than one." He grinned at both of them before hurrying to the refrigerator for more cheeses.

"And I'd say," Hosea whispered close to Emily's ear, "you're the best thing that ever happened in my life." His heart overflowed with thankfulness for his father's wisdom, for Emily's love, and for two children he'd be parenting with her.

Millie had talked to the children's parents, who'd agreed to sign Violet and Jax over to the state. That cleared the way for an adoption. With Millie's enthusiastic approval and help, Hosea and Emily had begun the process. They hadn't told Jax and Violet of their plans because Hosea wanted to wait for the perfect moment. And he had a good idea of when that would be.

On Christmas Eve, all the children, dressed in their warmest outerwear, waited outside for Hosea and Emily to take them Christmas caroling. All except Jax.

Emily called him several times before he bounded down the steps, his face wreathed in smiles. Quite a change from his usual gloomy expression. Usually, he only lit up whenever Hosea arrived.

"I hafta talk to Hosea before we go."

Emily nodded, and when Hosea's buggy pulled into the driveway, she beckoned for him to come inside. She stayed near the door as Jax tucked his hand into Hosea's.

After sending Emily a loving glance, Hosea turned his attention to Jax. "You're looking cheerful."

Jax shuffled his feet and stared at the floor. "That's 'cause I been praying."

Hosea looked as surprised as Emily felt, but Jax didn't notice.

"Tonight, I told God I ain't gonna fight no more. Aunt Bertha ain't as bad as Ma and Dad. She smelly and grumpy, but she don't do drugs or beat us."

Emily's heart contracted. Hosea had asked her not to tell Violet and Jax their plans yet, but she wanted to ease Jax's mind. Hosea's pained expression and pinched lips revealed he was struggling too.

They both had moisture in their eyes when Jax declared, "I told God I'm gonna do His will. Even if it's really, really hard."

Hosea sank to his knees and enveloped Jax in a hug. "I'm so proud of you."

Emily marveled at their father-son bond. She could hardly wait until all four of them could be together as a family.

Later, as they tromped across the snow to the neighbor's house, Hosea held Jax's hand and Emily held Violet's. For a brief time when nobody was looking, Hosea took Emily's mittened hand in his, and she thrilled to his touch. She could hardly believe her dreams had come true. Not only did Hosea love her, but they were moving forward with the adoption. As her soprano joined his baritone and the children's joyous noise rang out too, Emily's spirit trilled a song of joy and thanksgiving.

The next morning, Hosea went to Emily's house for Christmas dinner and handed out small gifts to each of the foster children and everyone in Emily's family, but later in the afternoon, he invited Emily, Jax, and Violet on a walk. As snow drifted gently around them, they crunched through the icy top layer of drifts.

Hosea smiled at the three people who meant so much to him. This time, he held Violet's hand, and Emily held Jax's. Hosea had been spending more time with Violet recently, getting to know his future *dochder*.

Now he helped Violet roll the smallest ball for a snowman's head while Jax rolled a middle-sized ball with Emily. Then they all rolled a huge ball for the base. Jax, with Emily's help, set the middle ball in place, and Hosea lifted Violet so she could place the head on top.

"Let's see if you can make a snow child and decorate both of these snow people." Hosea handed them chunks of coal, carrots, twigs, stones, and a few worn scarves. "Emily and I will be back soon."

Fear flickered in Jax's eyes. "You ain't gonna leave us here alone?"

"Of course not. I'd never leave you." A promise he meant with all his heart. "We'll be right over there." He pointed to a grove of pine trees.

As soon as Violet and Jax started rolling snowballs, Hosea led Emily to the private spot he'd selected. Seeing her tender look at the children before she left, he longed to hug her. To stop himself, he shoved his hands into his coat pockets, where he'd secreted three small boxes.

Although he wouldn't be giving her a sparkling diamond like the *Englischers*, he wanted her to have a keepsake to remember this Christmas. He pulled out the largest box and handed it to her.

"But you already gave me a gift at the house."

"This one is special, just between the two of us."

He swallowed hard as she slid a dainty finger under the edge of the striped paper, and his pulse pounded in nervousness and anticipation.

After she smoothed the paper, she lifted the box lid. Nestled in cotton, a pink glass heart with golden letters revealed the words he wanted to say, *All my love.*

"Emily," he whispered her name reverently. "I love you now and always. Will you marry me?"

"Oh, Hosea," she breathed as her eyes misted. "I love you too. And *jah*, I'll be your wife."

He wrapped his arms around her, and she rested her head on his chest. Inside, his heart drummed a melody of joy. He kissed Emily's forehead. "I'll love you forever."

"Hosea?" Jax's worried voice shattered their peaceful interlude.

"Coming," Hosea called. Then he kissed Emily one more time before taking her hand and heading out of the trees.

"Look!" Violet grinned her adorable gap-toothed grin. "We made a family."

Beside the snowman, she and Jax had made a short snow woman and two snow children.

"How perfect." Emily glanced up at him with a secretive smile.

"For sure and certain." Hosea took a deep breath and told the children his and Emily's news.

Violet's face glowed. "Can I be in your wedding?"

Emily's eyes twinkled. "You'll definitely be there."

Hosea handed Jax and Violet each a small wrapped box. Unlike Emily, they tore into their packages.

His face creased in puzzlement, Jax stared down at the small wooden heart with the words *Family Is Love.* "Hunh?" He glanced up at Hosea.

Violet chimed, "It's so pretty." Her wooden heart had a border of violets. She ran her fingers over the letters and sounded them out slowly. After she did, her eyes took on a sad, faraway look.

"Read the other message inside," Hosea urged.

Jax unfolded his slip of paper first and read aloud, "'Will you be a part of our family?'"

He stood there uncertainly. "What that mean?"

Hosea went down on one knee so he could look straight into their eyes. Emily knelt beside him.

"After Emily and I get married, we want to adopt both of you and make you a part of our family."

Suspicion edging his voice, Jax asked, "We ain't gonna go to Aunt Bertha?"

"That's right," Hosea told him.

Violet squealed and threw herself into their open arms, but Jax hung back.

"Where we gonna stay till you 'dopt us?"

"With me and Mamm," Emily assured him.

"Really, truly?"

"*Jah*, really, truly," Hosea answered. "You'll stay with Emily until we get married, then you'll move in with us."

Jax squinched his eyes shut, bowed his head, and clasped his hands together. His lips moved.

When he lifted his head, his expression had smoothed into wonder. "I 'pologized to God fer not believing He'd answer my prayer." Jax's excited eyes met Hosea's. " 'Member when we prayed? God said *YES!!*"

With a loud "yippeeee!" Jax jumped into the group hug.

Wrapping his arms around the three people who meant the most to him, Hosea met Emily's tearful eyes and joyful smile.

God had answered *all* their prayers with a resounding *JAH!*

Epilogue

Christmas program, three years later

Emily could hardly believe three years had passed since Jax's first Christmas program. He'd meant what he'd said about following God's will even when things grew difficult. The adoption process had taken longer than expected, and he'd been the one who'd kept them all hopeful when they ran into snags.

"God has a reason for this," he'd say in a wise, grown-up voice. A voice guaranteed to make them all smile and pray harder.

And God did have a reason. His timing had been perfect. So had His choice for her husband. She leaned against Hosea's shoulder, and he smiled at her. Then they both gazed down at their tiny daughter with full-to-bursting hearts. God had blessed them with so much joy.

At the front of the room, Jax and Violet, in their matching green Amish shirt and dress, beamed at their parents and baby sister. Recently, Jax had decided to wear Amish clothes like his parents, and he now had on black pants and suspenders like his *daed*.

A lump rose in Emily's throat at God's gift of three beautiful children and a loving husband. She thought she couldn't be happier . . . until Jax said his part.

Jax had volunteered to say a poem about God sending His only Son because He loved everyone. Emily thought back to Jax's first Christmas program a few years ago. So much had changed for all of them since then.

When Jax squeezed his eyes shut as if trying to remember the words, Emily clenched her hands together in her lap. The poem had three verses, and Jax had struggled to learn it, but he'd worked as hard on that as he had on mastering grammar. She whispered a quiet prayer that her son would recall all the words.

Finally, he started and recited it perfectly. She breathed a sigh of relief. But then Jax interrupted the next child who'd started to speak.

Jax held up a hand. "Wait, I got something else to say." He fixed his eyes on his *mamm* and *daed*. "I didn't used to believe God loved everyone. 'Specially not me. But he does. And Hosea, back before he became my *daed*, taught me how to pray."

Beside Emily, Hosea shifted in the creaky metal chair and cleared his throat the way he did when overcome by emotion. Emily pressed closer to him.

"I didn't believe Hosea, but back then, I prayed for a ma and dad and a good family." Jax paused and met people's eyes. "And even though God sometimes says *neh* or wait when we ask, this time he said *jah*."

Jax pointed into the audience straight at Emily and Hosea. "He gave me and Violet a new *mamm* and *daed* and a baby sister, and I love them all. Just like God loves me." Eyes filled with love and caring, Jax waved a hand, encompassing the whole room. "And just like He loves all of you."

Not a dry eye was left in the schoolroom following his speech.

After Teacher Mandy wiped her eyes and got the program back on track, Hosea leaned over and whispered in a quiet, but raspy, voice, "I hope someday God chooses Jax in the lot. He'd make a wonderful minister."

Although they shouldn't joke about such a serious subject, Emily choked back giggles. "He's never at a loss for words." And he liked to remind people to trust God.

After the program ended, Jax galloped across the room and flung himself at his family for a group hug. Hosea switched the baby to one arm and reached over to hold Emily's hand hidden in the folds of her dress. Then he whispered close to her ear, "I wanted to interrupt the program to say some of the same things Jax said because you and our children have made me the happiest man in the world."

Her heart overflowing, Emily fingered the heart in her pocket. The heart she carried everywhere with her. She ran her fingers over the raised gold words. Hosea had promised her all his love, and he still reminded her of that every day. Her own heart expanded and filled her with exquisite joy.

"And you've made me the happiest woman ever." Then she sent up a silent prayer thanking God for all his blessings and for the way he'd gathered their wonderful family together. Then she met her husband's sparkling eyes and mouthed, *All my love always and forever.*

Loving Luke

KELLY LONG

Dedicated to the Real Ann

Prologue

Luke King caught the brown bag that the guard threw at him and hurriedly stripped off the ugly prison garb he'd become used to wearing over the past two years. It felt both strange and right to slip on his own clothes—the black pants, white shirt, and black suspenders over his shoulders. He pulled his battered straw hat from the bottom of the bag and finally, his cracked leather boots.

"Hurry it up, Aim-ish. I ain't got all night!" The prison guard's voice was harsh, and Luke knew he'd better obey. It wasn't too late for his freedom to be revoked or to receive a cruel beating like the others he'd endured.

The guard led him through the prison as men called out to him. "Good luck, Luke!"

"Stay outta trouble, friend!"

Luke blinked back hot tears as familiar voices reached him from the cellblock. They were hard men, yet most of them had become his friends. He'd found a community in prison that seemed healthier than what he'd known on his *fater's* farm. But he pushed these thoughts away as he stepped outside the prison gates, and the cold night air came to him like something from a dream. He'd been confined the past two years with limited access to the moonlight. Though hard on the heels of the sensual delight of freedom came the keen reminder that he desperately needed to find work if he wanted to eat.

He noticed a bench across the street with a ragged-looking man slouched atop a newspaper. It was the newspaper that Luke wanted, and he quickly crossed the street.

"Hey buddy. Can you read?" Luke asked, turning halfway around as the smell of strong liquor made him cough.

"Whadda say?" the drunken man asked. "Can I read? 'Course I can! Who can't these days?"

Luke sat down on the bench. "Me." He eased the newspaper out from under the scraggly man and opened its pages. "Now, I want you to find me a job."

"Why should I?"

"Because I just got released tonight and I've been waiting for two years to have a proper fistfight with someone."

The bleary eyes of the man stared at him in the light of a streetlamp. "Yer Aim-ish, ain'tya? One of 'em peace lovers, right?"

Luke sighed. "Yes, I'm Amish. And I have nothing to give you nor any desire to beat you in a fight. I need a job. Can't you ever remember a time when you really needed help?"

Something wavered in the old man's eyes. "Had me a son once . . . Had black hair like you."

Luke waited.

The man coughed. "Let's see this here paper. Must be somethin' you can do. Mmm . . . truck driver?"

Luke shook his head.

"How 'bout a dishwasher . . . though that don't really seem ta suit you—Hey! Here's one . . ."

WANTED: Amish Mail-Order Groom. Age 27–37. Will be second husband as bride is a widow. Must never drink alcohol or use curse words. Bride desires a gentleman in nature and fact. Must be willing to wait on customers and be excellent with *kinner*. Blackberry Falls, PA.

"Damn! She expects a lot." Luke smiled and eased his straw hat back on his head. . . .

Chapter 1

Grace Fisher felt every one of her thirty-one years, especially when she was trying to manage her three *kinner* and the running of the general store for the *Amisch* community of Blackberry Falls. Lately, she was tired so often, she could barely keep up with all the chores. It wasn't as though she needed the money; a far-off *oncle* had only recently left her with a large inheritance. But she felt safer with the familiar routine of managing the store, despite all its small daily problems. And, after a life with Sam Fisher, her abusive late husband, taking over the work seemed to boost her feeling of inner strength. But now tears pricked the backs of her eyes and she swallowed hard. She felt as if her dead husband still lingered in the shop, as though all his hateful words clung to the walls. And despite Grace's growing confidence, she often jumped at shadows and in the last month she seemed to feel nauseous all the time.

She sighed now as five-year-old Amos, her youngest *sohn,*

pulled on a rack of heirloom plant seeds and the various packets came raining down around him, much to his delight.

"Eli?" she said softly. "Mind your *bruder* for a few more minutes, *sei se gut.*"

"*Jah*, Mamm," Ten-year-old Elijah stared at her solemnly through his glasses and her heart hurt as usual when she thought of all the violence he had seen in his life. He was quiet—almost too quiet at times, but always helpful despite his seriousness.

Grace snapped out of her thoughts just as a shelf of jam began to wobble and watched in horror as the heavy glass jars began to fall. Eli wasn't close enough to Amos, and though Grace moved as fast as she could, she knew she couldn't prevent the disaster. It seemed a miracle when a strong arm reached out and lifted Amos to safety.

She hurried around the smashed display and stretched her arms to her youngest child. It was only then that she acknowledged the tall, black-haired *Amischman* who stood with splatters of strawberry jam on his white shirt.

She clutched Amos tighter while he struggled to get down. "*Danki*," she said quickly, looking away from the stranger. "Thank you very much." She strove to manage the tremble in her voice.

"You take the *kind* away, and I'll clean this mess up for you." He sank down on one strong knee and began to pick the larger pieces of glass into a pile.

"Please, you'll cut yourself." She looked over at Eli, her eyes communicating with her *sohn.* Eli took Amos and went back behind the green curtain that separated the store from the living quarters of the family.

Grace was about to kneel on the floor herself, but the man shook his head and looked up at her. "*Nee, geh* get a broom, *sei se gut.*"

Grace obeyed; it had been ingrained in her ... to obey a

man. Her late husband had never wasted a slap when a bruise would serve to remind her of what he expected.

She returned with the broom and dustpan and stood waiting until he reached up to take them from her. A sudden shot of sunshine pierced the window opposite the spot where they were, and she saw that his eyes were gray—as gray as a picture she'd seen once of the Atlantic Ocean in winter. She cleared her throat—what *gut* was it to notice some stranger's eyes? *I have* kinner *to raise and a business to run . . . and I am finally free.* She didn't feel free, though, and she wondered if Sam Fisher would haunt her forever. . . .

"Can I put this glass in a bin somewhere?"

Grace snapped out of her dark thoughts and stared at the man. "Wh—at?"

"A bin and then I'll scrub up the jelly left on the floor."

She stood perfectly still and listened as the stranger spoke. The words he spoke in a husky voice were alien to her—she'd certainly never heard her husband offer once to help her in any way . . . nor had her *fater.*

"Ma'am?"

She jumped. "*Ach, jah.* Out back, there's a barrel. Here, let me show you."

Grace moved fast over the hardwood floor, then opened the side door. She was intent on keeping some distance between her and the *mon.* "Here's the waste barrel." She was almost in tears once more as she listened to the glass crash into the rusty bottom of the barrel. *That's me,* she thought. *I'm broken glass . . . no shape, only sharp edges that cut my throat when I want to scream. . . .*

She remembered not to brood, a promise she'd made two days ago, and here she was already breaking it.

"Ma'am?"

She looked up at him and bit her lip as her thoughts drifted once more. *Why did I write that* narrisch *ad, anyway? I'm not normal anymore.* . . .

She frowned at the scarlet spots on his shirt and gestured suddenly to the rain barrel. "You can wash if you'd like before you *geh*."

"I'll be glad to wash up—but, uh—I need to ask you something." She watched him reach into his front pocket to pull out a piece of wrinkled newspaper.

He looked her in the eye. "Did you write this ad for a mail-order groom?"

He handed her the ad and watched her hug the paper to her breast, but then he had to look away. He hadn't so much as touched the sleeve of a woman in two years or more, and the idea of touching her, even her plain sleeve, left him wondering if he still knew how to behave with a woman, let alone be the gentleman mentioned in the ad.

"You're here to be my . . . mail-order groom?" she asked.

"If you'll let me." He suddenly realized that he was holding his breath as he saw her studying him, apparently gauging his worth. Clearly, she found him lacking.

"You need a haircut," she finally murmured.

"*Jah*, that's true," he said in clear tones, thinking that she had a strange way of responding.

She nodded and pointed over to the deep barrel brimming with fresh water. "The rain barrel is over there. I'll *geh* inside and get a towel and leave it here on the steps." She slipped past him, and then she paused on the steps. "*Ach*, I'm Grace Fisher. . . ."

"And I'm Luke King."

He watched her step inside, then tested her name on his tongue. Grace . . . Unmerited Favor. The only grace he'd known since childhood. But now he ran a rueful hand through his unkempt hair and concentrated on the brisk December air and the pleasant warmth of the winter sun. He lowered his suspenders as he walked to the barrel, then stared down at his watery reflection. Bathing was always by shower in prison, and it had been a long time since he'd had this much water for his personal use. Of course, he wouldn't do more than take off his shirt, not in the cold and with the wide-eyed *mamm* and *kinner* inside.

Despite the chill, it was pure pleasure to slide the fabric over his head. He inhaled the sticky sweetness of the strawberry jam and was suddenly transported to a time when he was ten years old and his *mamm* was still alive.

"Bring the next batch in, Luke." He remembered her saying his name with tenderness as he fetched the pail of strawberries. He thought that his *mamm* was beautiful as she smiled at him. She was tall and graceful like a lily, her face a cheery pink. And, somehow, she seemed more alive when his *fater* was not at home. . . .

He pulled away from the bittersweet memory and picked up the bar of homemade white soap that sat nearby on a makeshift table. He plunged the soap into the rainwater and had started to wash his arms when the squeak of the screen caused him to stop for a moment. He watched her place a towel on the steps before quickly disappearing back into the *haus*.

He wondered about her. *A widow, with* kinner, *and a store to run. No wonder she needs a mail-order groom. She probably gives no thought to the marriage bed though, and I can't . . .* He swallowed hard, then worked up a lather with the soap, ruthlessly rubbing at his chest.

Grace felt skittish around all men and wished she knew how to defend herself from the harsh words or wounds they inevitably dealt her. She had chosen to send for a mail-order groom to help her raise the *kinner* and to have a gentle*mon*'s example in the *haus*. But here was a *mon* who looked like a pirate, with his moonlit gray eyes and black hair.

She wondered uneasily if he might display a nasty temper, though she believed she would have been able to sense that. Although he looked scruffy and needed a haircut, he was the only man to apply, and after he'd saved Amos, she was willing to give him a trial.

Now she reached above her head to straighten an already neat shelf of towels that she'd ironed yesterday. She knew it was ridiculous, this ironing of towels. But her husband had commanded it, making extra senseless work for her. *And I knew better than to disobey . . . ach . . . that man, that monster . . .* She yanked the towels down, careless of where they fell, then pressed her hands over her eyes, longing to sob aloud. . . .

But the store bell rang, and Grace stepped behind the counter, trying to ignore the fact that there was a stranger, a mail-order groom, bathing from her rain barrel.

Ann Bly, her dear friend, entered the store with her usual directness and wasted no time in going to the window and discovering the fact of the stranger's existence. "Just exactly who is that?" she asked in a hissed whisper, and Grace shrugged.

"A stranger, stopping for a bit."

"A strange *mon*. You let him in here? Have you seen his back?" Ann asked sharply.

"His back?" Grace repeated. "You shouldn't be looking at a man's back when he's bathing." Still, a strange prick of curiosity ran through her consciousness as she wondered what Ann saw.

"Mmm-hmmm," Ann muttered. "That man's been beaten and badly too. Where did he *kumme* from?"

"I don't know. He saved Amos from a near accident, so I let him use the rain barrel. He'll likely be gone in a bit."

"Why don't I believe you?" Ann asked with a frown.

Grace bent her head, then looked into Ann's sherry-brown eyes. "Actually, he's *kumme* to be my mail-order groom."

"I see. Hmmm . . . tell me, Grace. How long has it been since Sam Fisher laid hands on you?"

Grace had no difficulty remembering. "Two months and ten days. He struck me about an hour before he died." Her thoughts veered to the moment she'd been told that Sam had had a heart attack. Her emotions had run from relief to guilt and fear. She blinked now as Ann went on.

"I won't say it served Sam right, but it served him—"

"Ann, *sei se gut* . . ."

"All right." Ann gestured with her chin. "Is Herr Bare Back truly here in response to your ad? Or is he here because he heard somehow about your money?"

Grace sighed at her friend's words, then glanced out the window in time to see the *mon* shake the water from his dark hair.

"I still say that writing that ad for a mail-order groom was just plain *narrisch*," Ann said. "You don't need a man to run this place. Why, look at the way I teach the *kinner*—I've never been plagued by a—"

"What about Wander?" Grace suggested softly. She watched her friend's face flush. Wander Smucker had long pursued Ann, but she would have nothing to do with him because he was ten years younger than she.

"Wander Smucker . . . Well, he's Wander and that's all, and I sure don't need him," Ann muttered, then lifted the plate she carried. "I brought you some butter pats with roses on top. You deserve to have a little more beauty at your table."

Grace smiled at her friend.

"There's a knife beneath that counter, right?" Ann asked.

"*Jah*, I know," Grace said. "But it's a knife for packaging and cutting string, not self-defense." Grace watched Ann's pretty brows knit. "Are you're sure you don't want to stay and defend me?"

"I cannot help but worry, especially after . . . well. I'd best get over to the school."

Grace reached out and gave her friend's hand a squeeze. "*Danki*, Ann, for caring about me."

"You know I do. Be safe." Ann smiled and turned, then hurried out of the store.

When Ann had gone, Grace considered the fried chicken, mashed potatoes, and fresh asparagus she had made for the *kinner*. She herself had no appetite these days. She could hear the light clinking of pottery plates as her daughter, Rachel, unwillingly laid the table. Grace's friend Abigail had made the pottery, pretty bowls and plates of light blue and sunshine yellow. The dishes had been the first luxury Grace had allowed herself to purchase after she'd inherited her *oncle*'s estate, but even now she wondered if they were too frivolous.

Grace was used to a scarcity of beauty. She had become conditioned to believe she deserved her harsh existence. Behind the green curtain, she'd known a life of bruises and swollen eyes and feeling that she was less than nothing. *Why didn't I leave? Why didn't I pack up and go? I was so dumb, so foolish . . . But maybe it was better than to go it alone.* Grace thought of the times she'd had to stuff down her emotions like wrestling a snake into a sack.

But for now, she decided to feed the mail-order groom. . . .

Chapter 2

Luke approached the back steps, where Grace stood with a napkin-covered plate in her hands. He sensed that she was unsure of the situation, and he moved slowly toward her, having no desire to frighten her.

She lifted the cloth napkin, and the delicious smells of fried chicken and fresh gravy assailed his senses. "*Sei se gut,*" she said softly. "Please have some dinner before you—er—we *geh* to the bishop to marry."

Geh to marry? So soon? He realized in that moment that he wanted to be her mail-order groom—to have a purpose, though he knew he should find that purpose in *Gott* and within himself. Perhaps he should try to talk with Grace about the wedding, give her a way out if she wanted. But even as he accepted the plate from her small, work-worn hands, the basic draw of hunger outweighed the need for more discussion about this marriage.

He longed to wolf down the chicken and the rest of the food. Prison had been cruelly lacking in tasty meals, and he found that he was almost sick for want of what she offered.

She gave him a knife and a fork and indicated the back steps. "Please, sit down and eat."

After he watched her enter the *haus*, he walked slowly to the steps, keeping a tight rein on his emotions. She trusted him on some basic level, or she wouldn't have fed him. And he had *nee* desire to betray that feeling of trust in her.

She went back in through the screen door, and he needed no further invitation. He sat down on the steps and lifted some mashed potatoes to his mouth as he considered the woman inside who'd served him with such kindness. She was clothed in plain garb, her dress a washed-out gray beneath her apron. Her mousy brown hair showed in fine wisps escaping from her *kapp* to frame her somber face. And her eyes were as green as new grass, shining beyond the worry lines that marked her pale skin.

He ate fast and dropped the fork on the empty plate, then decided to take the dish back inside. He eased the screen door open, not wanting to startle her. The store was empty though, the only sounds coming from beyond the long green curtain that apparently hid the family from customers. He walked to the partition, unsure of what to do. Then he finally knocked on the wall beside the curtain. All sounds from beyond stopped abruptly.

He cleared his throat, "Uh, ma'am, I hate to disturb you. Just wanted to give your plate back and tell you how good everything was. . . ."

He heard footsteps and stood back respectfully. Grace Fisher pulled aside the curtain. "*Danki*—if you'd like I've got some gingerbread too."

He gave a grateful nod. "*Jah.*"

He saw her look up at him and wondered what was going on in her mind. She was about to turn from him when a child's voice called fretfully. "Mamma, you said I could have gingerbread if I ate my chicken. I want my treat, *sei se gut.*"

She sighed briefly. "I'll be back."

Luke nodded. "Uh . . . I'll *geh* outside."

He watched her flush a delicate pink.

"*Ach, nee.* I'll be right with you."

"Mamma!"

"Are you related to the King men who've recently moved to the area?" she asked above the children's clamor.

"King men? Maybe . . ." At Grace's question, his heart missed a beat. Could it be that his *fater* or *bruders* had moved to Blackberry Falls while he'd been in prison? It had been several years since he'd heard from any of them.

"Mammaaaa!"

"*Sei se gut, kumme* in, and sit at the table while I get the gingerbread." She turned her back on him and he rather sheepishly moved into the kitchen and took a cautious seat at the side of the oaken table where three children sat.

The youngest child, the one he'd lifted to safety, had stopped his crying and stared at Luke as if he were some sort of strange, unwanted bug at a private picnic. Luke cleared his throat, then looked across from him to encounter a pair of round glasses on the nose of a thin *buwe.* The third *kinner* was a girl—she regarded him, clearly furious, as if he were a predator who might attack them at any moment.

Prison had taught Luke to be hyper-vigilant, but he'd also learned empathy there. And the raw emotion the *kinner* presented now made his heart ache for some reason. He was glad when Grace returned to the table with the delicious-looking dessert. She handed him a platter of the fragrant gingerbread and passed the cream. She filled a bowl for herself and the *kinner*, and they were silent as they ate.

Luke swallowed the sweet and spicy gingerbread and recalled Christmases when his *mamm* had baked special treats for the family. He had to struggle not to close his eyes at the bittersweet memory. Instead, he looked at the *kinner*. "What may I call each of you?"

He heard the woman sigh. "Forgive me for not introducing you sooner. These are my children. Amos, you should remember. And this is Elijah and Rachel."

Luke nodded and tried smiling at the group, but he got no answering welcome.

"Are you the one who's *kumme* to be our *fater*?" Rachel fired the shot across the table, her tone as sharp as the fork she pointed at him like a dagger.

"Rachel. That will be all," Grace said softly.

Rachel pushed back her chair and it screeched against the hardwood floor. "Why does it have to be all? Why do we need another man here? Why did you write that *narrisch* ad? Why?"

Luke saw tears begin to slip down the girl's thin cheeks, and he was unsure whether to leave the table or not. Rachel slipped out of her chair to disappear up the exposed staircase.

"I'm sorry," he said. "Maybe it's better if I eat outside."

"*Nee*," Elijah said, peering at Luke through his round spectacles. "Rachel's been upset since . . ." He peeked at his *mamm* and went on. "Since our *fater* died."

Luke suddenly realized that becoming a mail-order groom might not be as easy as he'd thought. . . .

Chapter 3

Ann Bly hurried along the path through the pine forest and soon came in sight of the small school*haus*. It was a cheery building, decorated for Christmas by the scholars with pine boughs and holly. Ann had convinced Bishop Kore that although their people avoided the lavish ornaments of the season, such adornments celebrated the beauty of *Gott*'s Creation.

Now she set out materials in expectation of the twelve *kinner* who would emerge from the green woods within the next half hour. They would be working on a special presentation for the Christmas program. Though she wondered if Grace's *kinner* would be too busy getting to know her mail-order groom to attend this afternoon. She always excused their absences. She hadn't the heart to chastise because she knew they were still struggling with the death of their *fater*.

Don't start down the Sam Fisher path.... I've thought enough of that brute.... She started to hum instead, pushing down the worry she felt for Grace and her *kinner*—not to mention the thought of her friend marrying some stranger who might turn out to be as bad as Sam.

Still, Ann reflected, as she set out materials for papier-mâché, perhaps *Gott* was in this idea of Grace marrying—it was certainly true that two other women from Blackberry Falls had had great success with their mail-order husbands.

Ann sighed as she stirred the flour and water into a paste, then glanced up and caught her breath at the sight of Wander Smucker standing in her classroom.

"You scared me half to death," she snapped.

Wander shrugged his broad shoulders, then pulled a bouquet of holly and ivy from behind his back. The red berries and green leaves looked bright and cheerful at this time of year.

"*Danki*," she said finally, looking up at him. Any girl in her right mind would surely have snapped Wander up by now. His blue eyes and russet hair were more than attractive, and his big frame radiated strength. But he was ten years younger than Ann and his interest in her just didn't seem right.

Now she frowned at him, hoping to make him *geh* away, but he stood firm and gave her a smile. "A busy morning with the *kinner*?"

Ann's frown deepened. "*Jah*, and shouldn't you be at the leather shop by now?"

"I came to look at the sunshine on your red hair, where it peeks from beneath your *kapp*."

Ann felt her face suffuse with color. "Don't say such things, Wander! Why not find some young woman to build a life with—why not—"

He laughed softly. "*Jah*, and you are that woman, Ann."

She drew a deep breath, ready to do battle, when he crossed the room and placed a lean finger against her lips.

"Shhh, my sweet. The *kinner* are coming, so don't rustle your feathers. I'll *geh*." He slid his hand from her lips, put his felt hat on, then turned to walk out of the school.

Ann could only breathe a sigh of relief, though the fact that he always called her "sweet" in some way or another made her heart pound. And she was not about to examine the reason. . . .

Wander left the classroom and walked slowly the half mile to his leather shop, a faint smile on his lips. He automatically tipped his hat to those *maedels* he passed, but barely noted their frank glances. *Nee,* he knew he was stuck on Ann Bly, and he didn't want it to be any other way.

He understood that Ann believed there was no chance for them as a couple, but he also knew the proverb "much water wears away stone." And Wander believed that the needed water would *kumme* from *Derr Herr* Himself.

"Hiya, Wander!"

His apprentice waved from the back of the leather-scented room.

"How are things going, Jon?"

"Right as rain. I've made the sheath to fit Herr Lulu's knife perfectly."

"Great!" Wander had to smile at the sound of Porkchop Lulu's name. A good nickname was a sign of acceptance and love from the community of Blackberry Falls.

Wander's own name had been given to him as a babe though, and he liked how folks reacted with a thoughtful expression when they were introduced to him.

He picked up an intricate leather bookmark that he'd been working on with diligence. He believed that his craftsmanship as well as the leather's quality made for the shop's success.

He'd been thinking lately of a new design for one of the *Englisch* saddles that his shop had been commissioned to make. He saw the intricate embossed leather scrolls in his mind, these and the roses that would trail along both sides of the saddle—beautiful, but not nearly as beautiful as Ann's face highlighted by the sunshine.

*   *   *

It was a bit after three o'clock when Grace smoothed the folds of her best dress, a simple gray one, and made sure that her *kapp* felt straight. She had no mirror in the *haus*—it seemed too fancy for her, and in the past she'd had no desire to look at the bruises Sam inflicted on her. But now she decided that she'd spent enough time concentrating on her appearance and left her room to check on the *kinner*'s preparations for the wedding.

She had reached Rachel's loft when the sudden gust of wind outside took her to the window. The temperature had been dropping all afternoon, and now snowflakes had begun to fall. These storms brewed quickly in Blackberry Falls in the winter. A bit superstitious, Grace hoped that the weather was not a bad sign for her coming wedding. But then she hastily dismissed the thought and said a quick prayer to *Gott*.

She knocked on Rachel's door and waited. The door was finally opened, and Rachel appeared dressed in blue. Grace was relieved to find her *dochder* seeming calmer than she had at dinner, though the *maedel*'s eyes reflected both anger and sadness. Grace prayed under her breath that she might find the words to soothe Rachel's mind. *But what is there to say? And surely the* kind *has reason to be angry. . . . Why didn't I ever leave Sam?* Grace heard the words inside herself, scratching like tree branches in the cold wind. *How can I help Rachel when I don't know the answers myself? It is the duty of the* Amisch *wife to abide by her husband, but Sam was so awful. . . .*

"Rachel, may I *kumme* in for a moment?"

Her *dochder* widened the door with visible reluctance and Grace stepped inside.

"Rachel, I know you are hurt deep inside," Grace began cautiously. "But *Gott* can—"

"Mamm, please don't speak to me of *Gott*. I don't believe in Him anymore. I cannot believe that He loves me or any of us."

"Rachel, stop." Grace swallowed hard. "*Jah*, you are angry at *Gott*. And He knows and will struggle with you as you find your way forward with Him."

Rachel shook her head as tears filled her eyes. "Those are easy words for you, Mamm. Empty words. And you hire another man in place of Fater? Fater has only been gone a few months. And you, you were the one who made him so angry all the time. He loved us."

Grace knew a terrible fear inside as she considered Rachel's words. *The child is so far from the truth and can only see the love she had for her* daed. *Sam left more than bruises. He scarred Rachel's heart and mind though he never touched her. She needs a doctor to help her, a doctor of the mind . . . or maybe Aenti Fern.*

Grace resolved to talk to the mountain healer about her *dochder* and Eli as well. Then she wondered about Luke and whether he would have the patience to deal with her fears and especially with the scars Sam had left on her troubled family.

"I don't want to talk, Mamm. I must finish dressing for your wedding."

Though her *dochder*'s words were provoking, Grace longed to wipe her face and hold her close, as she had done when Rachel was a *boppli*. But there was no magic touch that might help Rachel now, and Grace bowed her head and asked *Derr Herr* to find comfort for her *kinner* and to give them all the strength to get through the wedding.

Wander went to the woodstove at the back of his shop and poured himself a cup of the hot cider brewing there. He took a sip, then swiped an arm across his mouth. He took another sip and nearly choked when he noticed the two women at the front counter. His *mamm* and younger sister, Holly, were obviously brimming with some excitement and, as always, he felt faintly nauseous at the prospect.

The last time they'd looked so merry, he'd found the kitchen at home completely overrun by a litter of piglets. After he'd spent a good hour gathering them into a basket, his sister had laughed about the curly tailed invasion, and his *mamm* had briskly written it off as an experiment in animal husbandry.

Now he circled the counter to give them each a genuine hug but still sighed when he stepped back. "Okay, ladies. Let me have it—pigs, homemade hair remover, the skunk trap, the unfortunate brewing of bootleg whiskey—do I have to go on?"

"*Ach*, Wander, those things were just meant for fun." Holly gave him a sassy smile and stretched on tiptoe to kiss his cheek.

He sighed again but gave her a tender smile. Despite her foolery, Holly could probably ask him for the moon, and he would try to fetch it for her. She was seventeen to his twenty-five, but he still thought of her as his *boppli* sister.

"Ach, Wander. It seems that our activities are a trial for you." His *mamm* pouted.

"Mamm, you know that you make my life exciting, but *sei se gut*, please, no experiments today."

"We knew you'd say this, didn't we, Holly? So, I have no choice but to tell you that we've sent for Granny Mead."

Wander groaned aloud. Granny Mead believed that she could solve any problem with a vile brew of her concocting. He, himself, had had to drink the stuff on more than one occasion when he'd been ill. And, in truth, he'd always gotten well—mainly because he couldn't stand the thought of another draft of the stuff.

"Mamm, you know that Aenti Fern is the healer of Blackberry Falls. How will she feel?"

"*Ach*, the two of them love to exchange recipes and chat—they're thick as a murder of crows."

Wander shook his head and closed his eyes. "*Jah*, that's what I'm afraid of. . . ."

* * *

Ann Bly sighed as she hung the final *kinner*'s project on the clothesline behind the school. Papier-mâché was, as an art form, both fun and easily teachable. Except, Ann considered, when a particular student got sick while running the paper through the congealed flour and water. Like John Miller, she thought grimly, a vomiter if ever there was one. Still, things could be more challenging, like when Wander Smucker chose to enter her schoolhouse with a walking stick insect or wooly worm caterpillar and proceeded to tell outrageous stories about the bugs. The students would *geh* wild, and it would take her quite some time to restore order.

Now she frowned at the thought of the man. It was true that he was kind and laughed a *gut* deal, but that only emphasized his youth as far as she was concerned. She picked up a mass of soaked *Budget* newspaper strips and frowned as the flour and water splashed onto her apron, immediately soaking through to her dress. She dropped the papers, then sucked in her breath as she realized that Wander stood in the open doorway of the school*haus*.

Ann shook her hands, careless of the droplets that splattered everywhere. "Why are you here, Wander Smucker? You know I must tidy up here so I can go home to change my clothes for the wedding celebration."

"*Ach*, it seems that I am in time to help." He gave her a less than innocent grin and started toward her down the center aisle, between the desks.

She felt her throat tighten in frustration to appear such a mess in front of him. "I do not need help."

"Uh-huh." He stopped in front of her and raised a lean finger to stroke her cheek.

Ann instinctively pushed against his clean shirtfront, but Wander seemed unconcerned with the messy handprints she left on him. "*Geh* away!"

"Why? Because we're having a bit of fun? *Nee*, I forgot you're too *auld* for fun! But I have an antidote for that."

He spun her around smartly and, despite her protests, marched her to the pump.

"I am so mad I could spit. . . ." She set her teeth on edge and gritted out the words.

He laughed, a rich, jovial sound that begged for others to join in with him, but she wasn't laughing. He pulled her to the pump just outside and then dropped down on one strong knee to take her damp hands in his own much larger ones. The pump was already primed, and he started to wash water through her sticky fingers.

Ann stared down at his bent head, where snowflakes had landed in the rich russet of his hair. "This isn't necessary, Wander."

He looked up at her with his bright blue eyes. "Not necessary, true. But your hands are so small, so gifted in all the work you do with the *kinner*, and your sewing . . . and on and on. *Sei se gut*, let me take care of you for a moment."

Ann shook her head and snatched her hands away from his. "You could have any *maedel* you wanted in Blackberry Falls. I've tried to tell you this. You cannot choose someone like me. I sit with the *auld*, unmarried women in church meeting."

"And I stand behind you often, with the unmarried men."

"The young unmarried men—young. Now please let me be." She shook her wet hands and then quickly ran away from him, finding refuge in the warm school*haus*.

One hour. One more hour and then he'd be a man with a *frau* and *kinner*. Luke wandered along the path that led past the Blackberry Falls, and he stopped for a moment to appreciate the cascading rush of white water that poured down into a deep pool. He walked a bit closer and saw that the snow was starting to accumulate on what must be blackberry bushes lining the stream. What a lovely spot this must be in summer, and with luck, he would be here next summer to enjoy the sweet but sour flavor of the berries. He realized again as he walked on that he was free. It was a striking sensation, and he pushed aside the thoughts of his past and the time spent in prison. He hoped in time that he would feel he could tell Grace everything that had happened, but he wanted a chance to prove himself first. And he also had to meet with his *bruders* and discover the lives they'd found in the small *Amisch* community.

Grace had sent him to meet with the local bishop and arrange for the wedding ceremony, which was to take place at four this afternoon. During his conversation with Bishop Kore, the man had confirmed that the King men Grace had mentioned were, indeed, the brothers he had not seen in years. Fortunately, his father was not living in Blackberry Falls.

Bishop Kore was an odd duck, but Luke had seen plenty of oddity in men during prison and had not been alarmed by the *auld mon*'s speech.

"Where is Grace?" the bishop had demanded when Luke arrived at his cabin. "I expected you both for the marriage today."

"Grace sent me ahead to make the arrangements. She is preparing and I was glad for a walk to clear my head."

"*Ach*, walking is *gut* for the horseradish!" the bishop had replied unexpectedly.

Smiling, Luke had responded in kind. "Snail shells and cakes with wings, can you tell me if it's true that my *bruders* live here in Blackberry Falls?"

Luke wanted to laugh when he saw the bishop's expression. The *aulder mon* peered up at him and stroked his long white beard. "You be strange, *buwe*, but I won't let that bother me."

"*Gut!*"

The bishop cleared his throat. " 'Tis true that Matthew King married our Tabitha. And Caleb King, our most recent mail-order groom, lives at the pottery—Abigail is his wife. Are those your *bruders'* names?"

After exclaiming over the miracle that had led him to the same community as his brothers, Luke once again focused on the woman who had brought him to Blackberry Falls. He wanted to ask the bishop about Grace and the children. But he couldn't form a single question.

"You're wondering why Grace put that ad in the paper."

"*Ja.* Why does she need a husband so badly? And why do she and her *kinner* seem so frightened?"

"Is that truly your question? I could give you answers, but you wouldn't accept them—not, I think, with your own life's questions."

Luke exhaled sharply, feeling frustrated. "Perhaps you're right, Bishop Kore. Clearly I don't understand enough about the situation. . . ."

"I'd say that you know more than most, *sohn.* Now, follow the way to the pottery."

Luke continued on the path now, but a dark refrain beat round his head . . . *More than most . . . More than most . . . I know more than most. . . .*

He walked *slowly* to the cabin that Bishop Kore had indicted as being Caleb's. He could hardly believe that he hadn't seen his youngest *bruder* in so long. Not since his *fater* had thrown him off the family farm. But by the Hand of *Derr Herr,* here he was, walking in the community where both of them lived. *Still, they don't know my past—prison, or all the mistakes I've made, or the pain of Grace's kinner. . . .* He hung his head for a moment, almost giving in to fear. But then knew a foreign sense of forgiveness. . . .

He drew a deep breath and moved to the front door, only to discover that the carved wood panel stood open and welcoming. He knocked hesitantly and heard *nee* reply. He was about to turn back when a pretty *frau* came forward gaily. Her dress was on backward and her *kapp* was askew, but she was smiling in spite of it all.

"Hello! *Gut* day!" She spoke with a lilt in her tone, and Luke wondered if this was his new sister-in-law.

A tall man with blond hair and a handsome face came from the back room, hastily tucking his white shirt into his black pants. He stopped dead though when Luke lifted his head a bit higher.

"Luke? Luke King? Praise *Gott*!"

Luke felt the raw emotion of being recognized. How *gut* it was to be bear-hugged and looked over with genuine goodwill and affection. The *bruders'* hug broke off finally, then Abigail was swept into a new three-way embrace. "*Ach*, this is *Derr Herr*'s doing," she laughed.

Caleb grinned at her and pulled her in front of him, gently pressing his hand against her belly. "As well as this, my love?"

"*Jah*, surely." She smiled at Luke. "Now I'm going to leave you alone for a few minutes. I know you are getting married today, Luke. Word spreads fast in a small community like Blackberry Falls. Would you like to borrow anything from Caleb? I'll leave you alone to discuss—while I, uh—straighten my apron." She cast what Luke could recognize as a knowing glance at her husband.

Then Luke watched Caleb smile at her and wondered, as Abigail left the room, what it was like to have the kind of happy marriage his *bruder* seemed to have. But Caleb soon broke into his thoughts.

"Luke, I don't know where you went when Fater forced you to leave the farm, but we missed you so much! Here, sit down. What time's the wedding? I'll make some of Abigail's tea—it'll settle you."

Luke sat down at the small carved kitchen table and watched his *bruder* move quickly and efficiently through the kitchen. Caleb soon set a teacup and hot kettle before him.

Luke took a sip of the fragrant brew and found it to be delicious. "I did want to ask you, since Abigail brought it up . . . Can I borrow a few things to wear?"

Caleb grew quiet. "Sure . . . anything you want. But isn't it amazing that we three—Matthew, you will see shortly—have made it to Blackberry Falls and away from Fater."

Luke nodded. *Fater . . . our fater . . . cruel, miserable, violent Fater. I had to stand up to him when he began beating my bruders. . . .*

"You know we have to *geh* back there someday . . . to Daed's farm." Caleb frowned. "I want to see him and ask him why he treated us the way he did."

"It's not worth the trip." Luke swallowed. "He disowned his own *sohn* when I tried to protect you and Matthew from his hard hands. But then, if you're looking for a reckoning, you could try."

"*Kumme* on." Caleb smiled suddenly. "We can think of the hard things later. Today is your wedding, and I've got plenty to share with you in the cedar chest."

"Well, little *bruder*, I sure could use a new pair of pants and a dip in your bathtub."

Luke smiled as Caleb led him from the room, tasting the peace of brotherly love.

Later, Luke was grateful for the warm coat his *bruder* had pressed upon him. The mountain breeze was chilly and the snow was still falling. The clean, crisp air was scented of pine, a beautifully fragrant reminder that *Gott*'s love endures forever.

Luke found that the closer he got to Grace's store, the more his heart pounded, the way a kid's might at Christmas. He was getting married, and the thought was both tantalizing and terrifying. But he'd learned to not make decisions out of fear. His thoughts pulled him back to his time in prison. . . .

A clean-shaven *auld* missionary named Mr. G. volunteered to teach Bible Study on Wednesday in the prison's chapel, and Luke had decided to give him a listen, though he often felt despair and far from *Gott*. That *nacht*, Mr. G. spoke about the many places in the Bible that counseled believers not to fear. Still, Luke wondered if he could be truly fearless of a *Gott* who surely saw his deeds and might judge accordingly.

Mr. G. had posed a question to the small group. "Raise your hand if you knew fear or dread in the moments before you committed the act that has led you here tonight."

Luke watched a number of hands *geh* up, and he reluctantly did the same. He remembered the fear he'd felt at his father's anger, the anxiety that he would never make anything of his life, the dread that his future would be no better than his past. In truth, his heart had been catapulted to the back of his throat as he forced his way through that open window. . . .

Mr. G. had broken into his thoughts. "I tell you all that a decision made in fear will always be the wrong choice. Always. Do you agree, Luke?"

Luke looked at the *auld Englischer* and thought carefully. After a moment, he cleared his throat. "*Jah*, I acted that *nacht* in deep fear."

It was true. He'd almost thrown up as he heard the police sirens screaming and he had wanted to disappear. *Ach*, if only he could have gone back, never forced his way into that house . . . He'd shuddered helplessly with the knowledge that he was a failure. . . .

She was dressed and ready for the wedding with more than a half hour before it was time to go. The children were in their rooms, no doubt trying to adjust to the idea of having a new man in their lives.

A lull in the store allowed Grace to tidy some shelves to try to distract herself. But then she found herself struggling to hang on to a small paper bag of potatoes, overcome by vertigo. She felt the room swim before her eyes and heard the muffled sound of a woman's cry, and then Grace was falling.

She felt her body tense up, aware that a man's hands caught her—steady and strong. She struggled with sudden frantic energy. *I must get away from him. . . . He'll kill me this time. . . .* But, despite her thrashing, she was held close with tender strength. One muscular arm was wrapped firmly around her middle, holding her steady.

She gulped and kept her eyes closed; it was a way to shut herself off from him. Still, she shuddered when she felt him press his mouth close to her ear.

"How far along are you?" Luke whispered.

Chapter 4

Grace stared up at him, trying to fathom what he was asking. It can't be. . . . Her mind raced back to the last day of her husband's life. He had brutally claimed her body, as he so often did, and left her sobbing while he whistled and dressed without a care in the world.

Now Grace turned her face into Luke's shirt. "Let me up, *sei se gut*," Grace whispered. "I'm better now."

Grace felt him carefully steady her on her feet. She accepted the cup of water he brought and drank slowly. Grace was grateful that the children were still in their rooms and dropped weakly onto a more comfortable counter stool.

"I've turned the sign to 'Closed,'" Luke said as he came toward her with a handful of salted crackers from the store's barrel.

"We're never closed," she mumbled as she accepted one of the crackers.

She watched him smile, a flash of white teeth in a generous mouth.

"Not even for your own wedding?"

"Well, staying open is . . . well." She broke off, amazed that she contradicted him.

After a moment, she looked at him. "How did you know to ask me that question?"

He immediately understood. . . . "You mean about your *boppli*? I was with my *mamm* a lot when she was carrying and then at my *bruders'* births. I—well—I delivered my *bruder* Caleb myself."

Grace drew a sharp breath, wanting to ask more questions, but did not want him to feel that she was intruding. Finally, she couldn't silence the words that came to her lips as she tried to imagine someone so young in such a stressful situation.

"But where was your *fater* or some womenfolk?"

She watched a grim look *kumme* over his handsome features.

"My *fater* . . . He believed creating *bopplis* was his right but gave little thought to the rest. . . ."

"But it is *Derr Herr* who, as you say, creates a *boppli*." She bit her lip and put her hand over her belly. "Even if such a life is rooted in . . . well, violence." She felt tears prick her eyes as she remembered Sam's cruelty. Then she blew out a tired breath and nodded slowly. "*Jah*, you're right. I must be expecting again. My husband also had no care for the consequences of his actions."

Luke studied Grace's pale face and suddenly had the desire to wring the neck of the man who had brought such a stricken look to her green eyes. He swallowed hard. "Why did you send for a mail-order groom if your life was, forgive me, made troublesome by another man?"

"By my husband, you mean. *Jah*, he was a hard man, hard to me. He died two months ago of a heart attack."

Luke nodded. "I see." But he didn't really, nor could he explain why some men, or even women, could behave in a way such as his own *fater* had—brutal, and punishing.

A sudden image flashed behind his eyes. His father ordering him off the farm. The desperation he'd felt when he couldn't find a job because he didn't know how to read. The years of menial labor, and then the ultimate mistake—breaking into another man's home, the deafening alarm and flashing lights, the starkness of a prison cell.

Luke felt his heart pounding in his throat and realized that Grace had been speaking.

"So that's why," he heard her finish softly, but he could hardly ask her to repeat all that she'd shared.

"Surely," he muttered, looking her straight in the eye. He'd been schooled by the harshness of prison to "let his yes be yes and his no be no." There was nothing worse than being known as a snitch behind those iron bars. Yet still he lied to Grace. *I might as well tell her I wasn't paying attention. . . .* But looking into her gentle, searching eyes, he didn't have the heart to speak the truth to her, especially given the weight of the lie he carried in not revealing his past. Luke cleared his throat. "And . . . and the *kinner*?"

He watched her frown, then speak with obvious determination.

"Well, I know that Bishop Kore expects both of us as well as the *kinner* to adjust with the support of the community. And then, after the wedding, as the ad implies, I hope you will court me as a gentle*mon*. And we . . ."

She can't get it out, he thought, feeling his face flush. *No touching . . . nothing.* He noticed that she looked distraught and immediately stopped his thoughts. "I will do whatever seems best to you."

"*Gut. Danki.*" She smiled briefly. "Well, it's almost time for the wedding service, and then there will be a gathering at Tabitha King's father's home with just the family.

"Perhaps tomorrow we might *geh* over the lists of stock items that are here in the store. I guess I want some kind of normalcy to *kumme* but I also know that relationships and normalcy take time to build. Unless . . ."

"Unless what?"

She heard the note of concern in his voice and wondered if she should simply end this outlandish arrangement she'd orchestrated. She could release Luke from his mail-order groom role. And surely, it would be understandable if Luke did not wish to proceed. Why would he want the responsibility of a ready-made family of four and then trying to navigate a new relationship with her and soon, a new *boppli*? She sighed and smiled up at him. "You don't have to do this, Luke," she whispered.

She saw his eyes darken with warmth.

"I want to do this. I want to be your mail-order groom."

She nodded and took his hand when he offered.

"Call the *kinner*," he said gently. "It's time for us to be married."

Luke felt his heart begin to pound as Bishop Kore stood before the small group assembled for the unorthodox wedding ceremony.

"We are gathered here this afternoon because Luke King answered an ad for a mail-order groom. But I believe *Gott* also had a hand in bringing about this marriage."

Luke saw young Eli raise a thin arm as he might do at the school*haus*, trying to get the bishop's attention.

"*Jah*, Eli. What is it?"

"Why aren't you talking the way you usually do?"

"Well, walleyes and sinkers, lace veils and turmeric, if I start talking like this, what do you think that bird will do?" He pointed a knobby finger at Luke. "He'll start talking strange too, and we cannot have that. Now, settle in for the wedding. Seems like we've got more than enough attendants, so let's begin."

Luke listened to the High German that Bishop Kore recited from memory. For a minute he felt his world tilt beneath his feet and then he realized the great blessing that *Gott* had given him. A chance for a family and children and a beautiful *frau*. A chance at a bright future that he'd thought forever beyond his reach.

But something whispered at the edge of his consciousness, something sibilant and challenging. *What happens when she finds out that I was in prison . . . that I couldn't make anything of myself . . . that I can't even read?* He started when he heard the distinct sound of silence and looked up to see the bishop, apparently waiting for him.

Luke cleared his throat and waited himself.

"Do I have to repeat myself again, *buwe?*"

"Uh . . . *nee.* Shall I kiss Grace Fisher . . . er, King?"

"That's up to your wife. I wanted to know if you had it in your heart to welcome any *boppli* who may *kumme* along as well as the three *kinner* here?"

Luke gave the *auld* coot a piercing look only to hear the bishop sigh.

"*Jah,* of course. *Jah,*" Luke said.

"Uh-huh." Bishop Kore frowned. "You might have said so rather than join a midnight flight of heron to the south pole."

Luke couldn't keep from smiling as he answered the strange comment with an equally nonsensical response.

"*Jah,* cinnamon sticks and sage. You're daffy and right."

"See?" The bishop's frown deepened further. "I told ya, didn't I? Strange fella. Are you sure you want to marry this *mon?* He's got an odd way about him."

"*Ach, jah,*" Grace said softly.

Luke turned on impulse to look down at the neat *kapp* on Grace's head. She was everything he could wish for. So much more than a fantasy dreamed of in prison. He bent his back and lifted her chin with gentle hands. The fresh smell of mint made him think of his youth when he'd run from his *fater* to hide in a grassy meadow on the mountain behind the farm. He'd lie down flat, waiting for his *fater* to stop shouting his name, and then he'd become drowsy in the sunshine with the blue promise of spring and the sweet scent of mountain mint.

Now he could do nothing more than stare down at her pink mouth, her white-as-milk skin. For a moment in time, the watchers fell away. He'd imagined a kiss with a willing woman at least once a day while he was in prison. But now, looking down into Grace's eyes, he could do nothing more than place a chaste kiss on her forehead and then step away.

Grace had secretly been dreading the idea of a party after the wedding ceremony; she'd much rather have gone back to the store with just her family. But to her surprise, she was happy to be surrounded by the relatively small group gathered in the beautiful carved wooden home of Herr Stolfus, Tabitha King's *fater*. Grace saw each of the King *bruders* and their *fraus*— including herself—and it occurred to her that her family was going to grow now that she'd married Luke. The thought was a comfort; she was already close to Abigail King, the local potter of Blackberry Falls. And there was Wander's family too, and also Ann.

Everyone had brought white tablecloths, which looked elegant on the two long tables that had been set up. Candles flickered warmly all around the room, which was already decorated for Christmas with fresh greens and bright red ribbons. The guests took their places at the tables while the bishop remained standing to pray.

Grace was grateful for the support of Luke's strong arm as she sank to her seat at the *eck* and smiled shyly at the other guests.

"Let us pray a blessing on Grace and Luke King before we eat." Bishop Kore's voice rang out with the seriousness that governed his speech during Sunday meeting. At such times, he always refrained from the foolishness that he customarily indulged in. "I want you all to know that the marriage we bless today is one of hope and promise and new beginnings, not only for Grace and Luke but also for the rest of us. Let us welcome Luke among us and take to heart his commitment to build a new life with Grace. So too may we each look forward to building our best life with one another and with *Gott*."

Chapter 5

Ann glanced back at Wander after seeing the chaste kiss Luke gave Grace after the blessing, asking herself if she would ever accept such a kiss from Wander. But she felt like an old lady already, although Wander could change that, couldn't he? Maybe she should give in, see how it felt, let herself be free for a moment, however brief. *Don't I deserve happiness? A good man? Love?*

Who am I kidding? I am impatient, past my prime, and Wander is crazy. A silly man who just isn't thinking straight. He doesn't know what he needs. He needs a pretty, young girl who would give him lots of kinner *and would make his life cheery and pleasant. She would be a good cook, a good daughter-in-law.*

What am I thinking? The eck *isn't even finished yet. I should be concentrating on what I'm doing.*

Out of the corner of her eye, she saw Wander approaching. She asked, "What are you doing here?"

"I was invited," Wander replied.

"Grace probably just invited you to get us together."

"That is a great idea!" he said, grinning at her as he guided her to a seat beside him at the table.

The day after Grace and Luke's wedding, Wander leaned a hip against the wood of the small bridge that spanned the rush of water from Blackberry Falls. He listened to the cadence of the water hitting the stones and sighed within himself as he remembered eating the wedding dinner beside Ann Bly. She was so much more than a fascination to him, and he was sure that her heart was warmer toward him than she would have the community believe.

His thoughts were interrupted by the sound of a woman singing, her voice as clear as the sweet notes of the stream. He turned, not expecting to hear so pure a voice, and saw Ann coming straight toward him, leading the horse she usually rode to school. He smiled. Her head was down so she obviously hadn't seen him yet, and he joined in her singing. For a few seconds they sang in harmony, but then Ann stopped abruptly.

She groaned aloud when she saw him and marched across the bridge, her mare following docilely. "Why are you here?"

He gave her what he knew to be a mischievous smile and she rolled her pretty eyes. He had to laugh and saw that this only irritated her more.

"*Kumme*, sweetheart. How about a kiss to start the day?"

"I wouldn't kiss you if you did naked cartwheels in the cornfield!"

"*Ach*, don't tempt me with your imaginings, Ann. I might take you up on the suggestion. . . ."

She spluttered and looked as mad as the proverbial wet hen.

But her eyes gave him pause and he thought that, beneath her anger, something smoldered. He stepped forward and looked down at her.

"Ann, please . . ."

"Please what? Kiss you? Court you? I am ten years older than you. . . ."

"*Jah*," he said dryly. "I know how to count. But consider this, many *Amisch* men marry a *frau* younger than they. Even one who is more than ten years younger."

"That's different," she sniffed, then stepped around him. "I have school to teach, and you should find some useful work to do at this hour of the morning. *Gut* day."

On the other side of the bridge, she mounted up and hurried away from him, the sound of the horse's hooves drowning out his low voice.

"Definitely smoldering . . ."

Luke had begun the morning by making himself useful, chopping a huge pile of wood for the giant stove that warmed Grace's *haus*. Now he mounted the stairs in front of the store and hesitated. Should he knock? He still felt like a stranger in this *haus*, but he was Grace's husband now, even though he'd spent the night not in her bed but on a pallet on the hard floor.

Against his will, he recalled the sight of her curled in her bed, her light brown hair free, her green eyes open wide as she watched him lying there so near, yet so far from her; he wanted to care for her, hold her, and feel the new life burgeoning in her belly.

The door in front of him opened slowly and he saw Grace in the same gray dress she'd worn for their wedding. He smiled at her, noting the cautious look in her green eyes. She nodded at him and widened the door.

"The *kinner* are still asleep," she said in a half whisper. "And your face is sweaty from all that hard work chopping wood. Please let me bring you a towel." Then she motioned him inside and he took the towel she brought.

A hundred scents swam in the rich air of the storefront. He

hadn't noticed so much the day before, but then, he'd been eating dinner behind the green curtain and focused on the food and the woman who served him, as well as on the *kinner*.

He breathed deeply, smelling orange rind and cinnamon, fragrant teas, and the earthy scent of leather. His gaze swept the neat aisles of food, and he wondered if he would be called upon to read lists of stock items as they went over inventory. *A problem I am dreading.*

He smiled wryly to himself when his inability to read presented itself first off.

Grace asked him to look over the ledger book to examine the contents and costs of the store.

He sighed, then looked straight into her unusual green eyes. "Grace, I've got to tell you something that I had hoped could wait. . . ."

He watched her slide a hand to the slight roundness of her abdomen. "We all have our secrets . . . Please don't tell me if you'd rather not."

He was about to speak when the store door opened inward and his *bruders*, Matthew and Caleb, came cheerfully inside. He motioned for them to lower their boisterous voices and received broad smiles in return. Matthew had been at the wedding along with his wife, Tabitha, who had hosted the wedding dinner at her father's home afterward. The joy of their reunion poured into Luke's soul all over again.

The smiles on his *bruders'* faces seemed to match the zest of the store. They made no effort to contain their mutual happiness at seeing their big *bruder* at the dawn of the day. Luke watched them with genuine pleasure and saw Grace nodding to each as they swept their hats off with flourishes.

"Could I make a late breakfast for you three?" Grace asked after a moment. "It would be better if you have something on your stomach in this cold."

Luke gave her a gentle smile. "*Nee*, we will cook for you and the *kinner*. After all, I am now the third mail-order groom in Blackberry Falls." He was surprised and pleased when Grace's soft cheeks suffused with pink. It made him feel rare hope for his future. Could he find joy in serving her as her husband?

The delicious aroma of fresh-cooked bacon and its companion of scrambled eggs and blueberry French toast came to Grace like an enticement. Somehow, in just a few minutes, she felt herself drifting into a pleasant lassitude. The sounds from the cooking area faded softly from her mind as she sat on a bentwood rocker. It was only when sleep shimmered behind her eyes that she sat up abruptly. She felt so much better than she had done the day before, and she looked up to see Luke patiently holding one of her new plates filled with enticing fare. She sat up, then pulled herself to her feet. She saw Caleb and Matthew were already seated at the table and she looked up at Luke.

"May we have a quiet moment to thank *Derr Herr*?"

"Surely." He nodded. He walked behind her and carefully helped to seat her at the head of the table.

Then he placed her plate in front of her and joined his *bruders*.

The alluring smells also woke Eli, who appeared in the kitchen, barely managing to carry a half-awake Amos on his hip. They were followed by Rachel, whose steps were slow and dragging. Grace felt her *dochder*'s reluctance to deal with the coming day but thought it best to have everyone eat before facing any difficult emotions.

Grace concentrated on the delicious food the King *bruders* had made and marveled at the fact that she was being served a meal after years of brooding silences broken only by the occasional shattering of a dish and the abrupt departure of the *kinner*. For a moment, the familiar memory pulsed at her temples, and she nearly put her head in her hands as she usually had done when Sam was alive. But then her eyes met Luke's, and she thought she saw a flash of encouragement in the sea-gray depths. She wasn't used to being around a man who offered encouragement, much less hope. She started to eat, then let her gaze encompass the three *bruders*.

"This is excellent," she murmured.

Caleb grinned at her. "An *auld* friend told me never to tell my wife that I can cook, so I just surprise her once in a while."

Grace returned his smile cautiously. She realized that two and a half months after Sam's death, she was still tormented by thoughts of him. She took a forkful of eggs and felt her stomach turn. She clapped her hand to her mouth and rushed from the table to open the side door. Against her will, she fell to her knees and emptied her stomach. She sobbed afterward, then felt gentle hands on her shoulders. The unexpected touch frightened her, and she cowered instantly.

"Grace? Do you want my help?"

She recognized Luke's deep voice and shook her head.

"*Nee*, I'll be fine in a minute . . . I don't know what your *bruders* must think . . . let alone the *kinner*."

"Never mind," he soothed. "It's the *boppli*, isn't it?"

She nodded and moved to get to her feet. He helped her with gentle hands and led her to a bucket of fresh water, then waited until she'd washed her face.

"You're very kind to me. . . ."

"*Jah*, it seems easy to be kind to you."

"But are you kind when you grow angry or resentful?"

She felt her face flush with the weight of the question. *Perhaps I shouldn't have asked, but I deserve to know.*

"I would never hurt you," he muttered, his gaze seeming far away.

She nodded, knowing she must accept what he said before something happened to test his words.

She was about to *geh* to the kitchen side door when he asked a soft question.

"Grace, *sei se gut*, why did you write that ad for a mail-order groom?

He stared down at her once more; the expression in his eyes seemed far away, as if he were staring into a place where there was only a dark storm that brewed and ravaged his heart. Was he thinking of his own family, the *fater* who had no thought for his children once he sired them?

Luke stood at Grace's deep sink, pumping water over the breakfast dishes. Grace had gone to walk the *kinner* to school, and he was alone in the living area behind the store. His eyes traced the outline of the small window that faced the pump. It needed a wider sill and more light but the snow had stopped and a sudden blaze of sunshine cut through the gloom. Walking through that golden light was Grace, returning home to him.

Once she'd taken off her cloak and hung it up, an awkward silence filled the kitchen.

"Yesterday, you said my hair needed cutting," he said to break the quiet. "Perhaps this would be a good time for that." He hoped the small domestic chore would make her more comfortable with him.

He caught his breath as she addressed the length of his hair by running her hand down the dark strands and softly brushing her fingers across the nape of his neck.

He could barely speak when she began to talk to him in gentle tones. Her touch mesmerized him, yet he realized that she was still frightened on some level. The thought crashed through his own pleasure and caused him to sit up straight.

"Grace—you needn't do this. If you'd just let me have a pair of shears, I can rid myself of this mess."

"It's not a mess."

There, I bet she's just said what she must have told her dead husband a thousand times. It looks gut. *Nee, I don't mind . . . It's all right . . . I can hear the submission in her voice, and it makes me sick.*

"Please, Grace—I know I can only catch glimpses of what your—husband must have been like. I want you to know that I have no expectations in our life together for you to say things that you don't mean to me."

He could feel her tense up and now wished that he hadn't spoken. And yet his senses told him that Grace, the real Grace, had long been stuffed down and made not to talk. . . .

"All right." She moved to stand in front of him. "All right, Luke King. I mean what I say to you. You need a haircut, so lean back."

He knew that she had screwed up the courage to speak and he respected that bravery, guessed what it must have cost her. "Yes, ma'am."

He leaned against the back of the chair and stared upward, feeling lost in the green-grass summer of her eyes. . . .

"You need a new saddle," Wander offered casually at lunchtime when he intercepted Ann in the schoolyard. He'd noticed that the horse she was riding that morning had a worn and cheap saddle. He would use every gift he had to craft a new one of fine leather.

He had come to the schoolyard to shovel a path through the snow from the doorway to the outhouse, and to chop logs for the woodstove, so that the *kinner* and their teacher would be warm. But, in truth, Wander wasn't interested in the winter weather, only the pert red hair of the woman who seemed to carry a perpetual frown for him.

"When I need a new saddle," she muttered, "I will seek one out for dear Tea." Tea was the gentle mare who carried her across the mountains.

He grinned at her. "But not from my leather shop, I bet?"

"I will find the best leather for my needs," she sniffed.

"Well, all right, Miss Bly, I do have to ask you if you know that the library in Farwell is holding its winter exhibition of crafts for the holidays." He plunged on before she could turn him down. "I'd like you to *geh* with me."

Ann's frown deepened. "I'm sure you'll find someone else to accompany you."

Little Joe Miller piped up just then. "Let's 'company him, Miss Ann."

Other voices chimed in, and Wander knew that he had won the day. Ann loved the *kinner* of Blackberry Falls, and they would be proud to share the day with their beloved teacher.

"Well." Ann paused. "I was planning to *geh* through the craft fair at my own pace, to see each artisan who had entered. . . ."

Wander waited, then spoke in soft tones. "We'll *geh* at whatever pace you'd like." He knew his invitation had riled her up, but then again, she'd agreed to go with him. . . . Wander smiled and took up his shovel again with careful happiness.

Inside the school*haus* that afternoon, Ann moved one of the papier-mâché projects the class had done and sighed inwardly. Christmas was her favorite time of year, and the day's teaching had been fun. But now, as she stood alone in the school*haus*, the niggle at the back of her mind whirled into full tilt and she sat down on a wooden chair and wondered if she had lost her mind in agreeing to attend the fair with Wander.

Of course, it was quite appropriate for the teacher to attend. Though she'd be in the company of an unmarried man, she'd be chaperoned by most of the population of Farwell, the nearby *Englisch* town, and many inhabitants of Blackberry Falls as well.

But Wander would probably think they were courting, and she'd only have to calm his enthusiasm or she'd risk undoing all her hard work holding him at bay. She stroked the long needles of dark pine that decorated the windowsill and let her thoughts roam. *Why did I agree to* geh *with him? Is there anything I should admit to myself about the true feelings in my heart for the infuriating man?*

She might have gone on with her self-examination but as she bent to pick up a schoolbook from the desk, she had the odd yet distinct feeling that something had come loose in the back of her mouth. The sudden pain increased when she tentatively bit down and a filling fell out. She automatically wrapped the rather large piece of amalgam in her handkerchief and knew she'd have to get the molar refilled and quickly.

She put the book away on a shelf, then grabbed her school bag and went outside to ready her mare, Tea. She had just mounted up when the snow began again. She wasn't looking forward to making her way along the twisting mountain path to her home in the midst of a winter storm. But what choice did she have? she thought as she took up the reins. She had started down the mountain path that had been no trouble that morning, but now she found that Tea didn't feel like a stormy ride and was pulling back into the schoolyard. Ann was fighting the mare and her mouth was beginning to throb when she looked up to see a distinctive buggy turn in her direction.

Wander thrust his head out of one of the plastic side windows. "Stuck, are you? Well, what can we do for you?"

For some reason the mention of the word "we" made her even more irritable than the pain in her tooth. What *we*? she wondered, grimacing. Did the man really have a woman in that buggy? She suddenly didn't care if she had to walk the two-mile path home. . . .

"It's me." Wander grinned, ignoring the snowflakes on his face. "And Holly . . . my kid sister, right?"

Ann ignored the sudden relief she felt and scrambled down

from the mare while Wander jumped down from his buggy to unhook Tea and tie her to the back of the vehicle.

Ann tried to hurry and slid uneasily through the snow on the ground as she made for Holly's smiling face. But *Derr Herr* saw fit to humble Ann that day, and she wasn't all that surprised to fall facedown in the snow, naturally, at Wander's booted feet. . . .

Chapter 6

Grace could tell that Luke was troubled about something—although he seemed relaxed enough during the haircut. He'd even seemed drowsy beneath the touch of her hands. But now, when she wanted to *geh* over the stock book, he looked ready to bolt. Normally with Sam, she would be blaming herself for something she'd done or hadn't done correctly. But Luke seemed unconcerned about her writing as he backed away from the book as if it were an irritable rattlesnake.

"Is there something wrong?" She paused in the midst of sliding her finger down the list of stock items, stopping at cherry preserves.

He rubbed his lean-fingered hands across his face, then lifted his chin, his gray eyes bleak. "Grace—I can't read. I tried when I was in . . . when I was younger. But I just couldn't learn to do it. Even if I can't help you keep track of the inventory, at least I can be a stock *buwe* for you. I can lift and carry the heavy boxes and—"

"I'll teach you to read." She spoke the words with a confidence she truly felt. "It will be our secret, if you'd like, until you master the words."

She watched him think, sensing the wheels turning in his mind and then the slow smile that drew her eyes to his firm lips. She moved to close the stock ledger, but he stopped her by sliding his hand atop hers. "All right, *jah*, I will try."

She knew her cheeks flushed with warm color, and she felt a sense of purpose that had been gone from her life for a very long time.

As he sat in the kitchen bentwood rocker, he began to doze with a feeling of safety that prison had robbed from him. A prisoner always had to be careful, never knowing when someone might turn on him, though Luke had made no enemies that he knew of.

Still, it was a pleasure to rest, to know that Grace had listened to one secret and thought no less of him. He felt a sense of peace until he began to dream. . . .

His mother's cries seemed to morph into those of his young bruders as his fater's uncontrollable temper tore their family apart. The anger was turned his way as he struggled to make sense of the words swimming on the page before him. Letters danced across his mind—all shards and points that tapped his chest until he bled, gasping—

"Luke? Luke . . . it's me, Grace. I think you were having a bad dream. . . ."

He opened his eyes, frantically looking up at her.

"Do you want to talk about it?" she asked hesistantly.

"*Nee.*" He shook his head automatically though he wondered what it might be like to actually give voice to the horrors in his head. "*Nee, danki,*" he said again.

He sensed her reticence return as she backed away to lift a damp sheet from a wicker clothesbasket and hung it on a line rigged up at one end of the kitchen. Her threadbare dress clung to her hips and to the small bump of her belly when she turned in profile.

"Why do you stare so?" She asked the question without turning to look at him.

"I—you're . . . beautiful." He said the first thing that came to his mind, but seeing the surprise in her amazing green eyes, he realized that what he'd said was true. She *was* beautiful.

She looked over her shoulder at him and laughed lightly. He was tangled in the arms of her smile, not entirely sure what was funny.

Some confusion must have registered on his face though because she immediately sobered and spoke in soft tones. "I'm sorry. I didn't mean to offend you. It's just that no one has ever called me beautiful, and I guess I thought that you were still addled from your dream. . . ."

He watched her as if she were some sprite dancing in and out of the water. One moment she smiled, and it was like sunshine, and the next revealed the pain that was the counterpoint to her light. *What had that damn man done to her?*

"How long did you know Sam Fisher before you courted together?"

She blinked but answered steadily. "I knew him from childhood. We were *kinner* in school together. And then we began to court—I was fifteen."

"Fifteen. That's so young . . . Was—Did Sam always hit—"

"*Nee.* He fell on a deer drive and struck the back of his head on a rock. He had a bad concussion and never was the same."

Luke doubted that a concussion alone could make a *mon* beat his wife. Sam could have sought help in the nearby *Englisch* town of Farwell. Then something occurred to Luke; it rattled him. "Grace, you don't think that you're to blame for anything that happened between you and Sam?"

She squared her slender shoulders, as if to meet a foe, then looked him in the eye. "Of course I was to blame. If I had only done more around the *haus*, or cooked his favorites, or spent more time—"

Luke got to his feet. "*Nee*, Grace. I know that I have no right to talk about this with you—"

"Certainly you have a right. You should know what you've married into."

"Grace, you said it. We all have our secrets, but I know what it is to live with a man who cannot control his temper. My *fater* beat my *mamm* and my *bruders* too. When I finally stood up to him, he threw me off the farm, told me I was no *sohn* of his. For a long time, I thought I was at fault. But now I know fear is never *Gott*'s way and we never deserve to be afraid of those who should give us love."

Ann folded up the beautiful patchwork sleigh blanket that she and the *kinner* had been working on for the last several weeks. She had interested the *kinner* in the project not only because of the bright fabric patterns but also because the quilt would bring warmth and cheer to any who might dread the long winter days in Blackberry Falls. And Ann knew one woman in particular who would benefit from the joy of flying down a snowy hillside, bundled up on a sleigh. . . .

Ann bumped her hip against the door of the general store.

She struggled inside the door, careful that nothing ripped or tore the folded quilt in her arms; then she stopped dead.

Grace's mail-order groom was stocking a preserves shelf and he looked about as surprised as she felt. It was one thing to observe the man washing from the rain barrel or reciting his vows in front of Bishop Kore, and quite another to see him up close. He was handsome, true. His long, lean body rivaled Wander's. . . . She frowned fiercely, thinking she was mad to even consider what Wander looked like. . . .

She marched over to Luke and the words were out of her mouth before she could even think. "The *kinner* and I made a sleigh quilt, and I thought that I could watch the store while you took Grace for a fun outing."

He grinned at her.

"*Danki.* You are Ann Bly—I remember you from the wedding dinner. The *kinner* speak highly of you . . . so does Grace."

Ann sniffed. "Well, I am thankful for their praise. Now, what do you say to the sleigh outing?"

Chapter 7

Wander walked the quarter mile from his leather shop to the general store, reveling in the beauty of the afternoon. Sparrows flitted from one snowy branch to the next and seemed to sing of *Gott*'s pleasure in life. As he walked, Wander began to pray. *Dear Fater in heaven, I know that you touch me with Your love every day. You have given me my work with leather as a talent. Please let me remember to use my work for You. I realize that I haven't prayed much about Ann but I know that You are the true source of love, and I ask You to bless Ann even if it's Your will that she does not choose me. . . .* He paused and wondered if his prayers were too stiff and formal. He believed that he had a relationship with *Gott*—one that required hope and love and acknowledging that *Derr Herr* was always with him, in good times or hard times . . . and this faith made Wander's life worth pursuing.

He was so absorbed with his thoughts that he nearly missed Rachel and Eli as they came out of the woods near the school-*haus* onto the path. "Hiya, *kinner*. School out already?"

Eli stared up at him. "We finished a quilt today—a sleigh

quilt. But we're supposed to let the people who are feeling sad use it first."

"*Jah*, and we should be first in line," Rachel muttered.

Wander heard her. "Are you sad, Rachel?"

She glared up at him . . . her flashing eyes speaking the answer to his question.

"*Jah*, she's sad," Eli offered from behind his glasses. "She doesn't like Luke, or Mamm liking Luke—"

"How can she like him?" Rachel snapped. "She doesn't even know him . . . He's a stranger!"

"Maybe you don't want to like him, Rachel." Eli paused. "Anyway, he's not like Fater."

Rachel sobbed aloud, then turned to run back into the forest. "No one can be like Fater!" she cried before dashing away through the trees.

Wander sighed and wondered if he should *geh* after the *maedel*, but then decided that she probably needed some time alone and would not be especially appreciative of a *mon* trying to speak to her. He put his hand on Eli's shoulder and they walked on toward the store.

"A sleigh quilt?" Grace touched the fine fabrics that were stitched into such a gay pattern. "It's beautiful and something that I never would have thought to make." She met Luke's gray eyes from the back store counter and found that his handsome face looked almost boyish at the prospect of an outing. Ann stood in the aisle and waved them to the front door.

"I'll watch the store and see to Amos and the other *kinner*," Ann promised briskly. "Now, you two *geh* and find that old sleigh the *kinner* use each winter."

Grace wanted to protest. It was afternoon and the older *kinner* were due back from school and Amos would be getting up from his nap, and—

Luke touched her hand and she looked up at him with a sudden break in her thoughts.

"It seems to me that Ann Bly is more than capable of taking care of the *kinner* and watching the store," Luke said. "And I bet you haven't had a sleigh ride in a long time."

Grace smiled then. "*Nee,* not for a very long time. There's a fine sledding hill near the falls. I think we've had enough snow to get a good ride."

Luke handed her the gay quilt and offered his arm to her in a courtly manner. She felt years younger as she accepted both and wondered with fleeting thoughts if this was the real Luke. But she was determined not to brood as they pulled the old sleigh out of her shed and walked with light steps toward the falls.

When they got there, the hill looked like a faerie garden in the snow. Ice coated the trees nearby and snow softened all the contours of the countryside, while the sound of Blackberry Falls was a powerful rush in the distance. They walked to the top of the hill and Luke placed the two-person sleigh in the snow.

"Should I sit behind you? Are you ready?"

Luke positioned himself behind her on the sleigh, then placed the quilt over her lap and wrapped his arms around her.

"*Geh!*" she hollered, feeling the freedom in her throat. She felt him push off, his long legs stretched out beside hers in front of the sleigh. Grace gasped as the sleigh picked up speed, skimming over the snow faster and faster. She watched the world around them fly by as they sped down the hill, the wind rushing in her face. As the bottom of the slope approached, the angle changed and the sleigh turned abruptly, throwing her off-balance. She laughed as the snow rushed toward her and then everything went black.

* * *

Luke ran to her as soon as he saw her delicate frame fall into the snow. "Grace? Grace . . . are you all right? Is the *boppli* hurt? Please wake up."

Her lashes fluttered and he felt as if his heart would stop.

"Do not rush her, *sohn*. She needs time."

He glanced up, the snow momentarily blinding him as he tried to make out the woman speaking to him. He squinted and saw an *auld* woman with lively dark, raisin-colored eyes bent over a carved and knotty cane. Luke thought that this might be the local healer and he nodded and moved aside when the woman moved closer.

He watched for a moment, then spoke quietly. "She carries a *boppli*."

"Hmmmm, *jah*, a baby *maedel*. But that is not why she fainted."

"Why then? Was she hurt in the fall?" he asked, still wrangling with the idea that this healer knew that the *boppli* was a girl. "We weren't going that fast."

"She fainted because she felt joy, only for a moment, mind you, but joy just the same."

Luke frowned. "I don't understand."

"You should . . . how much joy have you had in the last two years?"

"I—I don't know what you are talking—"

"It's best to face the truth head-on. Grace Fisher has had only moments of happiness in the past years. Your sleigh ride was too much joy for her. She fainted but she's awakening now. And take faith in your new marriage—the *kinner* will come around—even Rachel."

"So, you're the local healer?" He bent to cradle Grace closer in his arms, then looked up, only to find that the *auld* woman was gone. . . .

* * *

Grace came awake by slow degrees; part of her wanting to keep her eyes closed to savor the moment and yet, part of her felt comforted, held, and as if someone knew her heart. She opened her eyes and found that Luke was staring down at her—intense and almost loving.

"Do you hate the *boppli* I carry?"

She saw his surprise at her question, but she had to know. How could a *mon* be happy to welcome the child of another husband?

"Why would you ask me that?" Luke looked at her and settled her more comfortably against him, wrapping the warm quilt about them both. *He feels as steady as an oak,* Grace thought in confusion.

"*Nee,*" Luke said softly. "How could I ever hate anyone or anything that is part of you? I want all your *kinner* to love me and I want to learn how to love them. I want to help you through this pregnancy, but most of all, I want to be a *gut* husband to you."

Grace caught her breath. "*Danki . . .* Luke." She pressed her hand against the small bump of her belly, and thoughtfully considered his words.

"You can help me know and love them, Grace. We will work together. Isn't that what a family does? You and I need to forget the pain and fear of the past and make our lives anew, I think."

Grace felt a lightness inside, more so than she'd ever known, and she sat up. "*Jah,* this is true."

"But I'll not have a bride whom I've never kissed." He leaned closer and she saw herself reflected in his eyes and she looked joyful.

"May I kiss you, Grace?" She nodded and felt his hands on her shoulders, shaking with desire. He pressed his lips against hers, gentle and slow. It was as if he meant to banish the memory of Sam's cruel kisses. She felt herself shyly kiss him back and she responded. It was like the blue of the sky and the sparkle of fresh-fallen snow to have him touching her. But then he pulled away, his dark lashes lowered, and he gasped as if running hard through a field. "I'm sorry, Grace . . . *Danki* for letting me touch you. I—it's been so long."

Grace was amazed at the tears that fell from his eyes. He half-laughed, swiping his arm across his face. "I—I love you, but I don't want you to be scared or for me to remind you of Sam—"

"*Ach, danki*, Luke." She bit her bottom lip, then looked down at the beautiful quilt wrapped around the two of them. Its bright colors stood out against the white snow, proclaiming to all that there was a new love in Blackberry Falls.

Ann calmly filled the orders of the women at the general store and actually found that she liked the work.

It was different from teaching, of course, but the store gave her the opportunity to advise people on products they should buy. Red potatoes versus white, a sweet onion for macaroni salad, a good blue cotton for a baby's summer dress. She was holding a jar of homemade peppers and touting its taste when Wander spoke loudly from the back of the store.

"I'll take seven jars!"

Ann's gumption lost steam and she suddenly felt embarrassed. She took refuge behind the nearby counter, refusing to meet his eyes as he made his way toward her.

"Why, Miss Ann! What a pleasure to see such a pleasant young *maedel* of a merchant." He leaned across the counter as if to kiss her and she longed to throw a bag of Brussels sprouts at his handsome head.

"It's a pleasure to serve you, Herr Smucker. Now, if only you'd wait your turn. . . ." She spoke with saccharin sweetness, but he responded cheerfully.

"I'm glad to wait my turn. I wanted to tell you that I

brought Eli home." He spoke in a whisper as if sharing some sweet secret with her.

Ann ground her pretty teeth. "And where's Rachel?"

He sighed. "Rachel—well, if I might speak to you in private?"

"What's wrong?" Ann felt her heart skip a beat. "She seemed much as usual in school."

"Nothing's wrong," he soothed. "Let's talk for a minute." He turned and faced the small gathering of women customers. "Ladies. Would one of you be willing to help Miss Ann out—could one of you mind the store while I speak to her? I'd be so appreciative. . . ."

Ann frowned at the numerous raised arms and gave the group a sour smile. Wander was simply proving what she already knew: no matter how much he said he cared, he would always be the charming, handsome young man she'd never be able match in looks, age, or personality. She was surprised at the vehemence of her thoughts, especially the part about feeling unattractive. It was something to work on. . . . She snapped her gaze back to the scene before her. An *auld* woman with a knotted cane was pushing through the other customers.

"I'll tend to matters here, young miss. I'm excellent at keeping accounts and serving others." The woman limped past Wander and hopped up on the wooden chair behind the counter. "*Geh* on, *sohn.*"

Ann wondered who the *auld* woman was and watched Wander exhale with a shrug of his broad shoulders, then turn toward her and motion for her to follow. Ann complied, but only because of Rachel.

She spread open the green curtain and Wander followed her through it.

Wander watched as Ann gave him a dark look once they were behind the curtain, in the living area of the building.

"Now, where is Rachel . . . and Eli for that matter?"

"Eli is outside. He wanted to look at the icicles that are forming under the eaves. They're sure pretty—"

"Wander? Where is Rachel?"

"She broke off from Eli and me, and she ran back into the forest by the school*haus*. She is fine. She needs to think over her attitude toward Luke and her *mamm*. But if you would watch Amos and Eli, I will go and fetch her."

He could tell she was upset, and he sensed he was doing nothing but adding to her anger. He turned to head for the side door but he heard her call after him. "Wander, who is that woman watching the store?"

He turned and felt himself smile ruefully. "That's Granny Mead, and once you meet her, your life will never be the same."

Luke had seen Grace safely back to the store and now walked the forest path toward the pottery. He had arranged to meet his *bruders* there this afternoon. The three of them had a lot of catching up to do. As he walked, he thought about the bright quilt that the *kinner* had made; in a million years he'd never thought that he'd be wrapping himself up in such a beautiful gift with an equally beautiful green-eyed *frau*. His troubles seemed far away for once, but then he heard the crying. . . .

Haunted by the riveting sound, he forced himself to move forward but almost immediately came to a stop.

Far up in the stiff branches of a fir tree, he spotted Grace's *dochder*, Rachel. And lower down on a sturdier branch was a black bear cub. He was surprised that the creature was not yet hibernating, but he had no time to ponder that mystery as the cub's *mamm* appeared from the encircling laurel. Just then, on the other side of the clearing, Luke spotted Wander walking right toward them. In vain, Luke motioned him away, knowing there was nothing so dangerous in this part of Pennsylvania as a mother bear with her cubs. But Wander had also seen Rachel up in the tree and now called out to her, apparently not realizing the danger from the mother bear.

Luke gave a high whistle that cut through the glen, hoping to stop Wander from advancing. Then he motioned to Rachel and spoke to her in level tones. "Stop screaming, Rachel. Stay where you are. Both of you."

He inched closer to the infuriated mother, then grabbed a thick limb from the ground. He found himself praying beneath his breath. He only meant to drive the bear off but at the first tap of the limb, the *mamm* whirled in fury and batted the branch away, catching his chest with her sharp claws. Luke was aware of a red-hot blaze of pain as the cub shimmied back down the tree. Wander ran toward him and Rachel began screaming louder than ever. But then the bear charged at Wander, and everything faded to black as Luke slid to the ground.

Chapter 8

In the hospital waiting room, Grace held Ann's hand tightly in her own. She didn't speak and neither did the others gathered. Caleb paced and Matthew brought everyone hot chocolate in Styrofoam cups as they waited to hear the extent of their brother's injuries. Frau Smucker and Holly prayed softly as they waited for news about Wander's condition. Bishop Kore was also there, bold in his prayers. They all joined him praying for the outcome of Luke's treatment and Wander's emergency surgery. The surgeon had not been overly optimistic.

"We'll try, of course," the *Englisch* man in light blue had said of Wander. "But he's lost so much blood. There's a good chance he'll lose that arm." The doctor had raised his mask and walked away before anyone could speak.

But now, as the last of the day faded into dusky evening, the second doctor came back into the patient waiting room.

"King family?" Everyone from Blackberry Falls held their collective breath.

Grace continued to hold Ann's hand and she could feel her own body shaking.

"All right," the surgeon said brusquely. "We've bandaged

Mr. King's chest and checked for concussion following his fall. He can be released this evening. Be sure he takes the full dose of antibiotics I've prescribed."

When he said nothing about the second patient, Ann began to move helplessly toward the man and Grace called out, "What about our friend Wander? How is he doing?"

"Mr. Smucker is a different story," he said coolly and Ann gasped. "It's not the end of the world, young lady, but we had to take a good deal of flesh from his shoulder. Still, it could have been far worse. What did he do for a living?"

Matthew and Caleb stepped into the line of sight of the doctor and the man took a hasty step backward. "He's a craftsman, working in fine leather. He needs the use of both arms to do that work," Matthew said.

The doctor swallowed. "Of course. I'm sure things will work out . . . You'll be able to see him soon, but be aware, he's suffered a severe trauma. Good evening."

Ann began to move toward the door as if to leave, but Grace stopped her. "Ann, where are you going? You must see him."

Ann turned to her with tears brimming in her eyes. "All I ever did in his life was push him away, and I made him think he was a burden." Ann swallowed. "I made fun of his love and rejected him. So why should I see him now?"

Ann sobbed and then a voice spoke with calm clarity. "Ann, dear Ann. He's told us how he feels about you. He was always sure he would win your love," Frau Smucker smiled through her tears. "Please see him . . . I will wait here with Holly until another one of us is allowed in. . . ."

Grace smiled at Wander's *mamm* for the gift she was giving and then led Ann to the ICU door.

Half an hour later Luke was wheeled out of the ICU to the cheers of the assembled group. After hugs from his brothers and kisses from all the women, he stood and turned to Grace.

"You saved Rachel," she said tremulously as she went to him and took him gently in her arms. "It truly was *Gott*'s will that brought you to Blackberry Falls to be my husband and *fater* to my *kinner*." She brushed her hand lightly over his cheek.

"I would do anything for them," he said, speaking softly so only she could hear. "And for you."

She felt him draw away then and was surprised when he turned to the bishop, smiling easily.

"Well, Wander is going to need some help, and since I wasn't able to help him escape that bear, I'd like to do all that I can for him now. I'm sure we all would."

"I think you'd be a fine friend to help, Luke," the bishop answered. "He may be angry for a while—especially at *Derr Herr*. And he may fear the future he faces now. You're the perfect man to help him with that, Luke. *Ach*, unless Ann has already taken on the task." Bishop Kore nodded and moved away.

Grace knew that *Gott* would reveal many ways that Wander could be helped, and she also knew that Wander's bravery had contributed to saving Rachel's life. She was about to ask her new husband about ways they could help in these early days when she realized that the *Amisch* Grapevine would soon spread the news of Wander's need—friends and neighbors would gather round him, offering all they could to speed his recovery.

For now, he would be convalescing in the hospital, and with Luke out of danger, Grace turned to Rachel, worried about her *dochder*. All night the *kind* had been unable to do anything but choke on tears and cling desperately to Grace. She had witnessed the whole horrific scene before the cub had gotten down and then ambled away with its *mamm*, leaving Wander and Luke bleeding badly on the snow of the forest floor. . . .

It was only now that Grace felt she could leave Rachel with

Frau Smucker and follow up on the promise she'd made earlier to a young hospital woman with a badge. When the social worker had seen the state Rachel was in, she'd suggested that Grace speak with her for a few minutes in a smaller family room.

Now, as Grace sat across from the young social worker at a utilitarian table, she had to struggle to pay attention. Eli and Amos were back home with Abigail—Luke's sister-in-law. But Luke was waiting for her in the main waiting room along with his brothers, Rachel, and the Smuckers.

"Mrs. King, I'm Ellen Stoudt, one of the social workers here. I know that you are deeply worried for your husband and your daughter. I think we here at the hospital can help you. Do you think that Rachel would be able to talk with me? With you present, of course. . . . What she saw was traumatizing—enough to consider that she may be in shock."

Grace clenched her hands, praying silently to *Gott* even as she spoke. "I'm not sure what you're saying."

The social worker nodded. "I think that Rachel might benefit from our mental health services."

Grace swallowed hard. "You think Rachel is . . . *narrisch*?" She choked at the strange concept, but then she recalled her own thoughts about Rachel needing help.

The *Englisch* woman slid her hand across the table and gripped Grace's fingers. "No—not crazy, but everyone needs help with their mind at one time or another, even if it's just talking about what troubles us. And I give you my word that you will be with Rachel any time we talk."

"I guess it's all right . . . I know that Rachel has much pain and anger bottled up inside. . . ." Grace swallowed hard, trying to grasp the kind of help this woman was offering. "I guess the bee builds its hive with the *Gott*-given urge to keep things both out and in. Maybe Rachel has built her own hive and doesn't know how to get out."

"That's a beautiful way to think about things, Mrs. King."

Grace looked at the *Englisch* woman and thanked her quietly. "I am grateful that *Gott* has given us hope and peace in so many different ways. Maybe you *can* help. . . ."

Ann crept to the nurses' station, where another hospital employee directed her to Wander's room. The hospital was a hub of unfamiliar lights and phones and the whir of computers. Piled charts were briskly consulted by the kind-faced nurses of the ICU. It was a place of ordered chaos and nothing like her neat, organized classroom.

Still, she understood the hospital staff's dedication, their drive to bring order out of chaos, just as she did when managing the *kinner*. She wished now that she had not always taken refuge in her work, or spent so much time putting Wander off. . . .

She blinked back hot tears and admitted to herself that she did care for him. . . . She was directed to one of the few rooms that didn't have its curtain drawn and she felt awed by the strange sounds and darkened lights. She saw Wander lying asleep, clothed in light blue, red lights blinking by his bed where he was connected to wires and tubes.

She stood there, quietly asking for the forgiveness of *Derr Herr*. . . .

"So, it only takes a bear practically ripping my arm off for you to *kumme* and see me?"

Ann jumped at the sound of his voice, then sniffed primly at his slow smile. "I would never have wanted you to be hurt, Wander. The doctor says your recovery will be slow, but I know you'll make it, and I will support you—"

"Ann, do you have to be so serious? I've lost the use of my arm, not my mouth. *Kumme* here and kiss me." He slurred his words and she leaned over to place a chaste kiss on his cheek but then pulled back.

"Ann. *Sei se gut. . . .*" His voice was low, and she knew he must be on strong pain medicine. She decided that it would do no harm to kiss him soundly on the lips, so she bent to him once more.

Ann was unprepared for his return kiss. He arched his back and groaned. She was sure it must be pain and not desire that made him catch his breath. She finally let his lips follow hers, slanting his head, until he controlled the movements of their kiss. Ann was shocked by her own desire, but the rational side of her knew that these movements so soon after surgery were probably not helping him.

She broke the kiss, feeling as if it were too warm in the room. Just then a dark-haired nurse came and insisted politely that Ann leave. Ann hastened to obey but not before Wander turned to her with a smile and a tender whisper. Years later, when they celebrated their Christmas anniversaries, she would remember his parting words, which still had the power to thrill her.

"Ann Bly, I love you . . . Now and always."

She got to the door of the ICU room and looked back once, and something in her spirit knew what he said was true. . . .

It was very late by the time Luke and his brothers, Grace, and Rachel returned to the general store. Back in the living area, Eli and Amos were sound asleep. After one last round of hugs and murmured gratitude that Luke, Rachel, and Wander had all survived the bear's attack, Matthew, Caleb, and Abigail set out for home.

Grace had gone up to prepare for bed, but Luke could hear the unmistakable sound of low sobbing as he paused on the steps. He knew it must be Rachel.

Grace had told him of her conversation with the hospital social worker, and both hoped that talking about the bear attack as well as her confused feelings for her *fater* would eventually bring Rachel peace. Still, he longed to bring comfort to the child tonight. He sensed that going to her would do no good, but perhaps he could pray for the young girl right there where he stood. He bowed his head and prayed silently for a moment for the *kind*'s well-being.

To his surprise, a door eased open. Luke was ready to bolt down the steps to make sure that Rachel didn't see him, but it was too late.

"What—what are you doing?" Rachel choked out, her voice full of tears.

"I—I was praying for you, Rachel."

"For me? Even though you could have died trying to help me? Even though I never wanted you to marry Mamm?"

"*Jah.* Even so. I want to protect your *mamm* and all of you."

"I . . . I believe you now."

Luke felt tears fill his eyes. Christmas was only days away, and this child had just given him the best present he could hope to receive. Her acceptance meant that their little family had every hope for a future together. Now he just had to bare his heart to Grace.

Chapter 9

The next morning, Luke stared blurrily up at Grace from his position on the pallet where he'd slept the night before. He felt both intense pain from the bandaged claw marks on his chest and a faint dizziness.

He realized that Grace was offering him something to drink. He reached out unsteadily, then heard the glass break and cursed out loud. At the anger and frustration in his voice, he saw her recoil, felt wetness falling on his lips and then tasted a tinge of salt. Tears. His *frau*'s tears.

"Grace," he muttered thickly. "Sorry. I'm sorry. I just feel so weak."

"I—understand." She backed away from the pallet and he groaned when she moved out of his range of vision.

She quickly returned though with the hospital medicine in a small cup as well as a measure of tea from Aenti Fern, the healer of Blackberry Falls.

Luke hated the noxious smell of the tea, and its terrible taste, but he swallowed it down for Grace's sake, along with the antibiotic that would fight the fever he'd developed.

He watched as Grace swept up the water and glass from his spilled drink. She said nothing but her face looked white.

"I cursed," he said.

"*Jah.*" Her green eyes flashed at him as she spoke with her tears still in her throat.

He had to look away for a moment but then nodded. "I-I did not act like the gentle*mon* you requested for your mail-order groom."

Grace expelled a sharp breath and tightened her fingers on the top of the broomstick. She didn't know what to say but she was surprised at the range of emotions that coursed through her veins . . . from anger to sadness to fright.

She moved closer to where he lay and stared down at him.

He regarded her with somber gray eyes. "I will try to break myself of cursing—even under my breath."

"Is it so much a part of you?"

"Sometimes," he admitted. "Did Sam curse?"

"*Jah.* Sam cursed the very name of *Gott* and he frightened me often."

As she spoke the truth, it brought fresh tears to her eyes.

"I'll try never to do it again, Grace. But I can honestly only truly promise for today. But I will pray to *Gott* every day about it. And I don't say that lightly. When I was in—well, the last place I lived, it was all around, cursing. It made every day dark and miserable. So, I will pray for the strength to ask *Gott* to help."

"*Danki* for that, Luke."

He reached for her hand and held her tenderly.

"Tell me," she asked. "Where did you live before *kumming* to Blackberry Falls? Where did you get those stripes on your back? What dark place are you running from?"

Luke knew the moment for complete honesty had come.

Grace had struggled to overcome her fear of men to trust in him. Now he must do the same with her.

"Prison," he whispered, looking down in shame. "I was so poor and hungry, so full of fear, I broke into another man's house against all the rules of the *Ordnung*. I hoped to find money; instead I landed in an even darker pit, even further from *Gott*."

"But you've paid the price of your wrongdoing, Luke," she protested. "You have a new life now, with the *kinner* and me. *Gott* has forgiven you."

"I believe He has, *jah*," Luke said. "But can you? Can you trust the man I am now?"

"For sure and for certain," she answered. "I saw the gentle-*mon* you are when you kissed me in the snow."

He nodded then realized he wanted to kiss her again. Suddenly, it became incredibly important that he should kiss her at that moment.

He raised a hand to brush at a stray strand of hair that had fallen from beneath her *kapp* and was about to draw her closer to him when a small, knowing voice spoke up from across the room.

"Are you planning on kissing my *mamm*?" Amos asked. Behind him stood Eli and Rachel with tentative smiles on their faces.

"If it's okay with all you *kinner, jah*," he said, "I'd like to kiss my *frau*."

One by one, each of the children nodded, and so he did.

This was their Christmas miracle, a family united at last in love.

Looking for more heartwarming Amish holiday romance? Don't miss *Amish Christmas Twins* by *New York Times* and *USA Today* bestselling author SHELLEY SHEPARD GRAY *USA Today* bestselling author Rachel J. Good *USA Today* bestselling author Loree Lough

In these heartwarming, faith-affirming stories, three Amish families face the joys, and challenges, of the holidays—with fruitful results. . . .

THE CHRISTMAS NOT-WISH
New York Times and *USA Today* bestselling author
Shelley Shepard Gray

When the foster parents they've cautiously grown to love discover they're expecting, orphaned Roy and Jemima Fisher, ages six and seven, are secretly devastated by the certainty they'll be given up. With Christmas around the corner, their only wish is for new foster parents as nice as Mr. and Mrs. Kurtz. Meanwhile, the Kurtzes have wishes of their own—and with faith, they all may be gifted with twice the blessings. . . .

NEW BEGINNINGS
USA Today bestselling author Rachel J. Good

Still grieving the loss of her husband and unborn baby in an accident several months ago, Elizabeth Yoder is oblivious to her neighbor Luke Bontrager's deepening affection for her. But while she bleakly faces Christmas alone, it's Luke who reminds her it's the season for giving. And when Elizabeth donates her handmade baby clothes to New Beginnings, a home for teen moms, she soon finds her gifts repaid beyond measure, with Luke's love—and new beginnings of their own. . . .

TWINS TIMES TWO
USA Today bestselling author Loree Lough

What happens when two secretive, stubborn people find themselves thrown together to help four rascally youngsters— twins times two!—create a Christmas surprise for their parents? Mischief and mayhem, and just maybe . . . love!